C

9/05

Victim Wanted:

Must Have References

Patricia A. Bremmer

Elusive Clue
Series

Victim Wanted:
Must Have References

Copyright © 2005

Patricia A. Bremmer

ISBN 0-9745884-4-X

For additional copies contact:

Windcall Enterprises
75345 Rd. 317
Venango, NE 69168
www.windcallenterprises.com

Acknowledgements

My thanks and acknowledgement to all that encouraged and helped me to create "Victim Wanted: Must Have References.

Martin Bremmer, **my husband, who took over my daily tasks so I could steal away to a private place to write.**

Jamie Swayzee, **for the hours and hours of grueling editing work.**

Detective Glen Karst, **used his expertise in his field to keep my crime scenes believable.**

Debbie Karst, **for her assistance in the development of the characters of Glen and Debbie.**

Trooper Sean Velte, **posing for cover art as the police officer.**

Eric Lang, **posing for cover art as both the dead body and the ghost.**

Jennifer Pelletier, **for allowing us to use her home as the scene of a crime.**

Dr. Paul Grow, **for his assistance with my medical research.**

Brandenn Bremmer, **allowing me to incorporate his music cd into my story.**

Jack Sommars, **a screenplay writer, for his suggestions and criticisms.**

Bridgette and Bailey, **my dogs.**

To my dear friend, Cindy Mielke,
who gently prods me to continue with
kind words of encouragement and
shared laughter.

Chapter 1

"Glen, what in the hell are you doing here? I thought you'd be out playing S.W.A.T. games," laughed Bill, slapping Glen across the back.

"Hell no, tonight's my night to relax and enjoy myself."

Glen slid his chair back to stand for proper introductions. Bill's voice boomed throughout the entire restaurant, making Glen's table the center of attention. But that was Bill; he was always the center of attention when he entered a room.

"How'd you rate two dates?"

"You remember my wife, Debbie. And this is Maggi Morgan."

Bill quickly planted himself in the extra chair at their table without an invitation. He studied both women intently, making them nervous.

Debbie was a beautiful blond with sparkling blue eyes and a figure to complete the package. Maggi was striking with her black wavy hair bouncing below her shoulders complimenting her piercing dark eyes.

In contrast to Glen's gentle manner, sandy brown hair and soft green eyes, Bill was bald, overweight and

1

overbearing. He was oozing with confidence that somehow made him likeable, despite his peculiarities.

It was obvious he had his eye set on Maggi. Everyone at the table was aware of his attraction. By now, everyone in the restaurant was aware.

Glen returned to his prime rib dinner, while Debbie and Maggi tried to ignore Bill's presence. The waiter returned to their table.

"Would you like a menu, sir?"

"Nah, just bring me whatever Glen's eating."

"So, Glen, where have you and Debbie been hiding Maggi all of my life?"

Oh brother, thought Maggi. This guy is so original.

"Maggi and I have been working together for years."

"Yeah? Doing what? I can tell by looking at her she's not on the force. She's too beautiful for police work."

"Actually"...began Glen, when Maggi cut him off.

"I kill people for a living and Glen helps me."

Debbie chuckled quietly to herself as she watched the look of shock and confusion surface on Bill's face.

Maggi loves the reaction when she explains to people that she's a killer.

Glen nearly choked, trying to swallow and laugh simultaneously. He picked up immediately on Maggi's lead.

"Maggi, I'm not sure telling Bill is such a good idea. He works homicide."

Maggi put her wrists up for him to handcuff. "If you must arrest me, I understand."

Debbie was chuckling loudly while Glen burst into a hearty laugh. The glamorous Maggi sat stone-faced, waiting for a reaction from Bill.

"Okay, I give. What's the joke?"

Bill was accustomed to being the jokester, not the butt of a joke. This new position was uncomfortable for him.

Maggi put her hands down and flirtingly looked at Bill with a smile on her face. She resumed eating. Debbie followed her lead, taking a bite of her roll. Bill turned to Glen.

"Maggi's a mystery writer. She kills people in her books. Together, we work through police protocol. We've been friends with Maggi for, oh, I don't know ... over ten years now isn't it, Debbie?"

Debbie nodded with a teasing sparkle in her eye. She enjoyed a good joke.

Debbie and Glen have seen Maggi through the success of her books and the failure of her marriage. They have been good friends to her. Maggi feels she can talk to them about anything.

The waiter returned with Bill's food. He pretended to be starved, devouring his food without a word. The truth was he was uncomfortable about the teasing.

Glen felt sorry for him. He kept the conversation flowing to avoid the obvious discomfort at the table.

Maggi had no sympathy for him; she felt he had it coming. Bitterness towards men still radiated from her every pore. She had no intention of pursuing a relationship. She was successful and happy with whom she had become. If she had to spend the rest of her days with her two dogs, Bailey and Bridgette, writing and traveling, she would be content. The anger she felt from her marriage helped fuel the emotion she needed in some of her characters to push them to the edge, to the point where they would commit murder. Much like an actress, she pulled emotions from her life to add realism to her characters.

Just as the waiter arrived with their dessert, Maggi's cell phone rang. She turned from the table while she spoke with her personal assistant, Teddi.

"I'd better run. I have an early flight tomorrow. I guess we're off to Germany in the morning. I'll be gone about three weeks. I'll call you two when I get back. It was nice meeting you, Bill."

Bill nodded. Glen rose as a polite gesture, but Bill remained seated. Debbie escorted her to the door and waited while the attendant went for her car. Maggi honked and waved as she pulled away into the night.

Early the next morning, Teddi arrived to pick up Maggi. Jean, Maggi's friend and neighbor, arrived at the same time to collect Bridgette and Bailey. She took excellent care of the dogs whenever Maggi had to travel. Jean was an animal lover who considered it more of a privilege than a chore to take care of the two beautiful Bernese Mountain Dogs. She never tired of playing with the two gentle giants; their thick luxurious coats were strikingly marked with black, rust and white. Maggi paid her handsomely for this favor. Jean did not want to take the money, but Maggi insisted. People who know Maggi wonder if she could ever be as close to another human being as she is to her dogs.

Teddi loaded the luggage into the trunk while Maggi smooched all over her dogs saying good-bye. This was the only time Teddi saw tears in Maggi's eyes.

On the way to the airport, Teddi read Maggi's itinerary to her.

"Stop, oh please, stop. I don't want to hear any more. I can't believe Warren wants me to be in so many places in such a short amount of time. It's not him that has to sleep in a strange bed every night." She paused ... "Well, maybe he does, but it's not for the same reason."

Teddi and Maggi laughed.

"I know it's pretty tough at times, but that goes along with all of the fame. I'm just grateful I can see the world right along with you."

The next three weeks in Germany were a blur. Motels, restaurants, shaking hands, signing books day in and day out filled the hours and days. One bookstore became the same as the next. The evenings ended with nice dinners, but total exhaustion. Many times the two women would order room service just to be able to relax in their pajamas.

"Two more days to go. Is there anywhere you'd like to go while we're here?" asked Teddi.

She hoped that Maggi would go sightseeing with her. She works very hard carrying her books, setting them up, selling them and talking to her fans about how wonderful Maggi is. It was easy for her to understand the pressure Maggi was under. However, she thought it would be nice if Maggi noticed how hard she worked as well.

Teddi lacked the confidence and independent nature that was part of who Maggi Morgan was. She was uneasy about sightseeing alone. When Maggi did not want to go out, it meant Teddi had to stay in.

The last day before their return to the United States, Peter, a friend of Maggi's, was in the bookstore. Maggi introduced him to Teddi. Peter was tall and muscular with pre-maturely gray hair. He offered to take the two women on a tour of the city topped off with dinner at an elegant restaurant.

Teddi held her breath. She longed to spend more time in the presence of this gorgeous man.

"Thanks, Peter, but I'm beat. It's been a long three weeks. We're heading home tomorrow afternoon. I could really use the time to sit back and relax."

Teddi sighed. She was not surprised.

"How about you, Teddi? Would you like to be my guest for the day? We can compare stories about how terrible Maggi is to work with," he chuckled.

Maggi tossed back her shiny hair in a flirtatious sort of way.

"Lies, lies, nothing but lies. Don't believe a word he has to say. I used to work for him at the newspaper office years ago. He's the one who's difficult to get along with."

Teddi smiled nervously. She wanted desperately to go with Peter, but Maggi was not giving her any signals to take him up on the offer.

Peter pressed, "Are we on or not?"

Maggi looked at Teddi.

"Oh, go on, Teddi, he won't bite. Have some fun for a change; learn to live a little."

Teddi agreed. She gave Peter their hotel and room number. He promised to pick her up as soon as the morning book signing was over.

He arrived promptly at one o'clock. He took her to lunch. She could barely eat in his presence. Maggi called on her cell phone to ask where her chocolates were packed. Before the meal was finished, Maggi called a second time to check their departure schedule for the following day.

Peter took the phone away from Teddi after the second call. He turned it off, putting it into his pocket.

"That might not be a good idea. She may need me."

"Today is your day. Remember, she said to have some fun, so let's go."

Magical was the best way to describe the day. Peter had transformed a mundane business trip into the most exciting, memorable day of Teddi's life. She was sad they were returning to the States in a matter of hours.

Peter kept her out until two o'clock. He walked her to her door where he kissed her goodnight. There was no discussion of seeing one another after this day was through.

Sleep was impossible. She relived every moment of the day with Peter. Teddi then realized she did not know his last name, nor he, hers.

The remainder of the stay and the journey home was filled with conversation about Peter. Teddi began to annoy Maggi with her many questions. Maggi felt telling Teddi about her brief affair with Peter would be hurtful; she kept that tidbit to herself.

Maggi was relieved to see her house just ahead. Bridgette and Bailey were bouncing on her front lawn. They always knew when she was approaching, no matter whose car she was in. The bond between human and animal was so tight that telepathy played a large role in the relationship.

Teddi unloaded Maggi's luggage.

"Do you need me for anything today?"

8

Not wanting to answer more questions about Peter, Maggi said, "I'm beat. Let's take the next couple of days off."

The next day Maggi kept her promise to Glen and Debbie. She invited them to dinner. Glen could not get away; he was involved with a case. Debbie joined her without him. Never having been to Germany, Debbie had many questions for Maggi. She was always amazed that with so many opportunities, Maggi did not take extra time to enjoy herself. She had a knack for taking the excitement out of her travels. If Glen and Debbie had the time and the finances, they would travel the world together, visiting every nook and cranny. Adventurous would be the word to describe the Karsts if they ever squeezed time away from their busy schedules.

Maybe that's it, thought Debbie. I have Glen. Maybe Maggi does not, or cannot, enjoy herself without a man to share it with. Is that why she seems to be a workaholic?

Poor Debbie is trapped between a close friend and a husband who do not know when to relax. Life is passing them by, but they are too busy to recognize it.

"Oh, I almost forgot. I brought something for you."

This was one part of Maggi's travels that Debbie liked the most. Maggi always came home with the most wonderful gifts. This time it was bottles of the most delightful German wine she could find, or rather had Teddi find.

The two friends stayed up late into the night. Conversation flowed with the wine and cheese. The sound of the doorbell startled them.

"Who could be at your door so late at night?"

"You mean early in the morning. It's two-thirty."

The dogs barked, running ahead to the door. Maggi always felt safe with he dogs, each topping the scale at over one hundred pounds. Of course, that was one hundred pounds of marshmallow. Neither of them had an aggressive nature, but the deep sound of their barks told anyone on the other side of the door that large dogs were housed inside.

Maggi peered through the peephole.

"Uh oh, are you in trouble now."

Debbie walked to the door to see what she meant. There was Glen, holding her cell phone in his hand. The look on his face told both of them he was worried about Debbie.

"Glen, what are you doing here?"

"I went home and you weren't there. I called your cell phone and it rang in the bedroom. I guess you forgot to take this with you again," he said angrily.

"Why didn't you just call on Maggi's phone?"

"I did, but there was no answer. I thought something had happened to both of you."

Debbie turned to Maggi, who was sporting a sheepish grin.

"I didn't want to be disturbed for a couple of days, so I turned off my ringer to let the voice mail pick it up in silence. Sorry, Glen."

"Really, Glen. Why do you think the worst every time you can't find me?"

"Debbie, if you had to see what I see on a daily basis, you'd worry too. Denver, late at night, is not the safest place to be. Have you totally forgotten the case I'm working on with the serial rapist? It's hard to separate the two worlds when the women being raped are no different than you and Maggi. Those victims are removed from their homes and their cars, blindfolded, driven to a secluded area, then beaten and raped. Two of the women were so badly injured they died. This guy is slick. We don't have one solid lead. Would you care to hear more or do you get my point. Certainly the amount of blood or how he abuses them would interest you ..." Glen answered, gruffly.

Debbie could tell Glen's reaction was one of love and concern. She felt badly that she put him through the stress. She stroked his face and rubbed his neck.

"I'm sorry, honey, I really am. I'll try to remember to keep that phone with me at all times."

"Yeah, Glen, I'm sorry too. I didn't mean to keep Debbie here so late; it was selfish of me to turn off my phone."

11

"Both you girls deserve a good spanking." Glen was trying to lighten the mood. He was embarrassed about his overreaction.

"How about a glass of bourbon?" asked Maggi.

"Sounds good to me." Good bourbon, such as Buffalo Trace, was one of Glen's vices. "Did you fill Debbie in with all the details of your trip abroad?"

"I sure did and I filled her with liters of German wine."

Debbie offered a glass to Glen, but he refused.

"Tell us more about this rapist. I'm not finding much in the paper."

"There's not a lot in the paper. We can't give too many details. One, because we don't have many leads. And two, because we can't show our cards yet. And no, you can't use the story for one of your books."

"Glen, you know me better than that. I can't write about women, children or animals being abused."

She appeared offended.

"Yeah right, Maggi. You have no problem killing women in your books."

"Oh, I know but I don't torture them or put them through any emotional distress. I just kill them and the body shows up, clean and simple."

"Boy, the world is a better place knowing you're not on the other side of the law. You could be one hard criminal to trap. You know too much and are far more clever than the average perp on the street."

"I'll take that as a compliment."

"Debbie, I need some sleep. Are you about ready to head home? If you are, I'll follow you in my car."

"It's been fun as always, Maggi, even if you did get me into trouble. Thanks for the wine. Give me a call when you feel you're finished secluding yourself from society."

Maggi waved good-bye as they drove away.

Glen put in long hours the next few days. He went in on his day off. It was fall. He and Debbie missed much of the summer. They recently managed to get away one weekend to go boating. There had been a time when they went every weekend. Glen wondered why things were so different now. Were his cases more difficult, were there more of them, or was he more dedicated to his work as the years progressed?

Sometimes Debbie feels as if she is losing him to the job. It is hard for her to share in his excitement about qualifying for the S.W.A.T. team. Every day when he leaves for work, she has to convince herself he will arrive home safe and sound. His new position adds more danger to his day.

Glen tries to reassure her that working on the S.W.A.T. team is actually safer than other police work. Training is more intense; you are with other well-honed police officers who work as a well-oiled team. Your back is always covered. You know what you are going into before you suit up. When on regular duty, if you get called into a

13

burglary in progress or a domestic dispute where weapons are involved, you stand a better chance of catching a bullet.

Debbie made lunch plans with Maggi. Glen made it a point to join them. He felt he had been neglecting Debbie too much lately. They met Teddi and Maggi at Stuart Anderson's.

Maggi was about to leave the area. She had a lodge in the mountains where she disappeared to write. She warned everyone, unless it was truly a death in the family, not to bother her. Teddi prepared to hold down the fort with her agent and publisher while she was away.

"What's this book about?" asked Glen.

"Oh, Detective Karst, you'll be one of the first to know. I'll email some chapters to you for your approval. Just be patient," she teased.

"Really, Maggi, don't you go crazy all locked up like that without anyone to talk to?" asked Debbie.

"Actually, it's talking to people that makes her crazy," laughed Teddi. "She does much better in solitary."

"She's right. People are far too distracting. When I feel like I've been caged up too long, it's time to take the two Berners for a romp in the snow. I'm not sure who has the better time, them or me."

"How long will you be gone this time?" asked Glen.

"As long as it takes," she answered.

"Can I at least talk you into taking your cell phone, in case you need help?" he asked.

"Nope, that's the whole point. I need to be out of contact with everyone. I'll email Teddi every few days to let her know I'm still alive. I go to the lodge office occasionally to use the Internet. I never watch television or open the newspaper. I live totally in the new world I create for myself. My characters are my friends. We live together and interact until the story is finished."

"I know, but I have to agree with Glen on this. That rapist is a pretty scary guy. I think this trip you should take extra precautions," begged Debbie.

Debbie wished Maggi would let Glen teach her to shoot and handle a gun. Debbie is accomplished, at the very least, with a gun and that sense of security is nice with Glen frequently away.

"I've got Bridgette and Bailey. That should stop him from coming after me. The dogs will bark up a storm. If that doesn't work, they'll knock him down licking him to death, giving me an opportunity to run for it."

Teddi looked at Glen and Debbie, raising her shoulders in a move of helplessness. She knew how strong-willed Maggi could be. She learned years ago to just agree with her while trying her damnedest to keep up with her.

Maggi looked at her watch. "If I'm going to get there before dark, I'd better take off. I still have to pick up the dogs. Wish me luck! I hope by the next time I see you, I'll have completed book nine!"

15

Teddi stayed behind to visit more with Glen and
Debbie. After a few minutes passed, Glen excused himself
to return to work.

Teddi was dying to tell Debbie about Peter. She
relived every detail in words. She would be mid-sentence
when she would disappear into her own world of thought.
Debbie knew this guy had made a huge impression on
her.

"Are you going to see him again?"

"I'm not sure. We never discussed it."

"Do you have a way to reach him?"

"No. Well possibly. Maggi knew him from before.
She used to work for him at some newspaper office."

"Is he still with the paper?"

"I don't know."

"You mean you spent twelve hours with Mr.
Wonderful and you don't know his last name or where he
works? How about where he lives?"

Teddi shrugged her shoulders.

"I can't believe you didn't ask him."

"There just didn't seem to be time. We walked and
talked about the area. He seemed infatuated with the
history. He made it all so interesting. I could've listened
to him all night. I guess I did. He was so romantic. I
think he liked me; he gazed into my eyes a lot. He always
had his arm around me or held my hand. He's one of
those touchy-feely kind of men; all the while being a
perfect gentleman. I didn't want to seem pushy by

16

pressing him for personal stuff. I thought he'd bring something up before the night was over. When we were at my door, I didn't have the nerve. Deep inside I hoped he'd show up at the airport to see us off. He asked about our flight schedule."

"Maybe he planned to be there, but something detained him."

"Yeah, maybe."

"Didn't he ask you anything about where you lived or how to reach you?"

"He asked a little about how I knew Maggi and if we worked together on a daily basis. I told him that she disappears to write. I thought maybe if he knew I'd be alone, he'd want to contact me."

"Did you tell him you'd be alone or with Maggi?"

"I'm not sure. I don't remember what I told him."

"You nut. Hey, I've gotta run. Let me know if he finds you."

Maggi and the dogs arrived at the cabin just as the sun was setting. The sky glowed the most beautiful shades of orange and pink. The dogs bounced at her feet while she leaned back against her car to take in as much of the sky as she could before she moved her things into the cabin. The dogs busied themselves with noses to the ground, totally unaware of the breathtaking sight above them.

After the car was unloaded, Maggi unpacked all of the food, both hers and the dogs. She gave each of them a

17

treat then plopped down on the bed to soak in the silence. Bridgette nudged her, gently waking her. She was surprised to see total darkness. She must have been more tired than she thought. She turned on the lamp to check her watch. It was ten in the evening. The dogs were hungry and needed to be let out. When she went to unlock the door, she realized she neglected to lock it. Glen would scold her if he knew how careless she was after his warning.

She unpacked a jacket then followed the dogs out of the door. Bailey sniffed around, exploring. Bridgette, as always, stayed at her side. Suddenly, Bailey sounded his warning bark. Maggi strained her eyes to see in the dark. It was hopeless. She had not taken time to search her bags and boxes for the flashlight she brought. Bailey continued his barking, soon joined by Bridgette. Maggi felt the hair stand up on the back of her neck. She backed up to the wall of the cabin. Having her body pressed into the prickly logs somehow made her feel safer.

She waited in silence for the dogs to cease barking. Finally, she called them in. It was obvious whatever caused them to bark was not going away. Bridgette came back immediately, but Bailey took a little more encouragement. Once she had her fingers slipped inside of their collars, she let them guide her back. She quickly closed the door behind her, locking all three locks. Next, she went to the windows to test the locks. This was probably unnecessary. The lodge management was

18

thorough with their security measures. She felt the need to double check for her own peace of mind. She was shocked to see that two of the windows were not locked.

She turned on all of the lights and closed the shutters. She was feeling uneasy. Maggi Morgan, the rock of courage, was having a weak moment. She fed the dogs before sitting down to eat. Both dogs left their dishes, dashing to the door barking. Maggi jumped. She told them to be quiet, but Bailey persisted. Maybe she should have taken Glen up on his advice to bring her cell phone just this one time.

It was time to close down the cabin for the night. She decided to wait until morning to finish unpacking. She set her dishes in the sink, re-checked all of the locks and prepared for bed. She sat up, trying to read. She realized after thirty minutes had gone by she was still on the same page and that she might as well give it up. She turned off the lights. The dogs jumped into bed with her. She let them stay, since being snuggled between two large dogs gave her comfort.

It was a long, sleepless night. Maggi dozed off just before dawn. With the shutters closed, the morning sun stayed away. It was nine o'clock before the dogs woke her. She quickly dressed and took them outdoors.

The normally quiet surroundings, her main reason for being there, were abuzz with people. One of the ladies from another cabin went for a walk under the stars last evening, but never returned. An officer searching the

19

grounds, asked, "Excuse me, ma'am, you didn't happen to see anyone last night, did you?"

"No, I didn't see anyone, but around ten my dogs heard something over there." Maggi pointed to the wooded area behind her cabin. "They didn't want to stop barking."

"Thank you," he said, as he walked in that direction.

Her eyes followed him until he totally disappeared into the brush.

She turned her attention to the man talking with the police officers. He appeared quite shaken. He must be her husband, she thought.

The sound of a voice coming from behind her cabin sent everyone scrambling.

"I found her, over here!"

Maggi and the dogs followed the group of people in the direction of the voice. There on the ground lay the body of a woman in her early forties. The two policemen were discussing their find and calling it in when the man rushed to his wife. He dropped to his knees to cradle her limp body in his arms. He sobbed. It all happened too quickly or the police would have stopped him from approaching the scene and disturbing the evidence. The best they could do now was to escort him away until they could take photos and secure the area.

Maggi knew that the dogs must have heard what went on last night. She wondered if she could have done something to prevent the death of that poor woman.

She was surprised how relaxed the police were about the crime scene in the beginning. She had worked with Glen enough to know they screwed up procedure. The first suspect would be the husband. Now his footprints will be at the scene, as well as soil on his shoes, to match the spot where his wife's body was found. Was he distraught or covering his tracks? Maggi's mind worked like a detective from having written numerous murder mystery novels.

She was dying to know all of the details. She had the urge to interrogate the husband herself. If this crime had happened in Denver with her this close to it, she would have begged Glen, making his life miserable until he would give her details.

Instead of writing that day she hung out at the lodge lobby. She wanted to watch people while listening to their conversations, to memorize every detail. There might be something she could use in one of her books.

The facts were not out. There was speculation that the husband did it. Others said they heard he did not arrive until this morning. He spoke to her on the phone last night before her walk and he was to join her here for breakfast. When she was not in the cabin, he noticed it looked as though there had been a struggle, so he called the police.

Maggi pretended to read the paper as she watched and listened. Maybe he planned to come up this morning, but sneaked in last night and killed her. He could have gone back down the mountain only to return this morning, the bereaved husband.

Piecing the story together, Maggi learned they come here every year. The management knows him well. He made it a point to stop in and visit with them when he arrived, to check their cabin number, before going to meet his wife. If they stayed in the same cabin the same weekend every year, why would he have to ask for the cabin number? Had he not talked to her on the phone the night before? Surely she would have told him if there was a change in housing arrangements.

Guilty, she thought. He has to be guilty. She looked at her watch. It was time to fix lunch and let the dogs out. Maggi was confident she was right. She will have Glen check it out for her when she returns. She would not allow herself to follow the story in the newspaper; it would be too distracting for her.

Maggi hiked the mile up the path to her cabin. The air was cool and crisp on her skin. Her cheeks ached ever so slightly from the chill. Fall was her favorite time of year. She wondered why she chose that time of the year to lock herself away indoors to write. Why not the dead of winter or the heat of the summer? Why ruin her favorite time of the year indoors? Scheduling, that is why. Deadlines have to be met.

Maggi realized this was the first time she was totally alone on the path at this time of day. Other guests use this path to return to the lodge restaurant at mealtime.

As she approached her cabin, she searched her pockets for the keys. She grabbed the doorknob to put the key in the lock, when the door opened. She called to the dogs and heard them shuffling around inside. She entered, slowly looking around. She would never have left without locking the door. She was always afraid someone would steal her dogs or accidentally turn them out.

Someone had been there while she was away.

Chapter 2

Maggi quickly snapped the leashes onto the dogs' collars to take them with her. They pulled her happily down the path to the lodge office. As she entered with the matched pair of dogs, all eyes were upon her.

"Good afternoon, Miss Morgan. Is there something I can help you with?" asked the clerk.

"I need to report a break-in, or at least, I'm pretty sure it was a break-in, at my cabin."

"Oh my, we've never had a burglary before. Please step into my office."

He was concerned after the death last night that the discussion of more criminal activity would send the remainder of their clients home.

Maggi with her two dogs moved the conversation into his office.

"Would you like a cup of coffee or tea perhaps?"

"No, thank you."

Joseph, the lodge manager, poured himself a cup of coffee. He straightened his black suit then sat at his desk across from Maggi. Concern filled his blue eyes as he looked at her over the top of his oval-shaped eyeglasses. He carefully picked a pen from his desk drawer then pulled a notepad onto the desk. Everything he did was with extreme precision. His perfectionism was apparent right down to his immaculately manicured white beard and fingernails.

"Please continue, Miss Morgan."

"I spent most of the morning in the lobby watching people for research for my books. When I realized lunchtime was near, I went back to my cabin to turn my dogs out and fix lunch. I always lock the door to make sure the dogs are safe when I'm gone. I was putting the key in the door when I noticed it was unlocked. Now, Joseph, I've been coming here for years and I've never had one bad episode. You and your staff have always been extremely gracious and thoughtful. But I am concerned."

"With due cause, Miss Morgan, with due cause. Was anything missing?"

"I'm not sure. I grabbed my dogs and came directly to you. Oh, and one other thing, when I arrived last night, two of the windows were unlocked. That's never happened before."

"May I go back to your cabin with you to look around?"

"Oh, sure. I'm sure no one is in there now."

"I'm aware of that, but I'd like to be with you while you check to be absolutely certain none of your things have been disturbed. You are somewhat of a celebrity, you know. I'm sure by now some of your fans are aware of your little hide-a-way for writing. Maybe a fan wanted a glimpse of you or your new book before it's released."

Maggi felt proud that he considered her a celebrity. After eight books, she still feels like she is "just Maggi who writes a few stories". She has not become accustomed to the added attention.

Joseph picked up the phone to call the front desk.

"Please bring my car around. I need to escort a guest back to her cabin. Thank you."

He stood to open the door for Maggi. He followed her and the two dogs outdoors where his car waited for them.

Maggi knew how pristine he was in appearance. His car was the same.

"I'm not sure you want these two in your clean car; they do shed."

"Nonsense, Miss Morgan. My staff will see to it that any hair left behind will be removed. Please feel free to load your two companions."

Maggi put the two in the backseat. She was feeling a little uneasy. She wondered if there had been a chance, with all of the morning's excitement that possibly she did leave the door unlocked. Now she found herself hoping that something would be missing, just to save her the embarrassment.

Joseph entered the cabin first. Maggi still had her belongings scattered around the rooms. Her plan to unpack in the morning never materialized. He walked from room to room. Other than Maggi's mess, nothing seemed out of place.

"I'll wait here while you search through your things." He stood near the door as tall and straight as if he were a soldier on sentry duty.

Maggi made a quick scan of the rooms, trying to tidy them as she went. She did not notice anything missing. Even if it was, it had no value. She did not bring jewelry or other belongings with her that meant anything, other than her computer and notes.

Joseph asked, "Did you receive your fresh towels this morning?"

Maggi checked the bathroom.

"No, there are no fresh towels. Why?"

"I have a theory. Let's go back to my office and clear this up."

Maggi locked the dogs in the cabin. During the drive back down the path, she kept trying to catch a glimpse of the backseat to see just how much hair the dogs had left behind. She was relieved none was visible.

While Maggi was seated in Joseph's office, he stepped out to speak to the staff. He was gone for nearly fifteen minutes. When he returned, he had answers for Maggi.

"I'm sorry, Miss Morgan, but it appears one of our new staff members went to take towels to you this morning. She knocked but there was no answer. You did not have a *Do Not Disturb* sign on the door so she

27

unlocked it to let herself in. When she attempted to step inside, your dogs met her at the door. They frightened her. She closed the door without locking it and left quickly. She is assigned to your cabin. She had the windows open to air out the rooms before your arrival. Chances are she left the two windows unlocked.

"Please accept my apologies. She is on probation for another two weeks. This was indeed a good lesson for her."

"Thank you, Joseph. I feel a bit edgy after last evening."

"I wish you luck on your writing. I'm very anxious to read your upcoming book. I'm quite the fan, you know."

Maggi shook hands with him then left to walk back to her cabin. Wow! Who would have guessed he was into murder mysteries, she thought.

The remainder of Maggi's stay was uneventful but very productive. In record time she finished book nine. She kept her word and sent emails to Teddi to let her know she was alive and well. Today she was going on a long hike with the dogs. She packed food for them and champagne, fruit and cheese for herself. She planned to stop at her favorite spot to celebrate.

Noon was approaching. She took a blanket out of her backpack to prepare the picnic spread. She lay back on the blanket in the warm sun. She felt sleepy after the food and champagne. She nearly dozed off when the dogs began to bark. She called them to her while looking in the direction that caught their attention. She heard the cracking sound of twigs on the path. Her tension eased when she heard the laughter of a woman's voice.

The closer it came to her, the more familiar that voice was. Finally, she called out, "Teddi, is that you?"

"Hi, Maggi. We've come to celebrate with you."

Maggi watched as Teddi and Peter stepped out from the trees.

"Peter! What in the world are you doing here?"

"He called yesterday to find out if you'd finished your new book. I told him that was quite the coincidence, because you just emailed saying it was done. He was in Denver on business and suggested we drive up to surprise you. I'm just lucky I remembered being with you at this spot for a celebration of one of your other books. I'll tell you, though, I was doubting my ability to find it again until the dogs barked."

"Pull up a spot on the blanket and help yourselves to what's left of the celebration. I'm afraid I've nearly polished off the whole bottle of champagne."

"Ah, but we've come prepared," teased Peter, his silver hair glistening in the sun. He pulled another bottle of champagne and two glasses from his backpack.

"Tell us all about this book," said Teddi, excitedly. A new book meant a new tour. She really liked to travel.

"Not much to tell. I killed a woman. Actually, one of my characters did it. I got the idea from a death that

29

happened here on my first night. Some lady was killed not far from my cabin. Did you read about it in the newspapers?"

"Yes, Glen called, checking to be sure you were alright, when the story went through his office. I assured him you were a good girl, emailing every few days. I had to admit though, waiting for the first email was a little nerve-wracking. But then again, if the world famous Maggi Morgan had been found dead, we would've heard about it right away."

"Tell me, did the husband do it?" Maggi asked.

Teddi answered, "Yeah, how did you know? He confessed a few days after they buried her."

"Yes!" said Maggi, punching her fist on her thigh. "My theory was he drove up the night before, did her in, then headed back down the mountain. He returned in the morning as planned, pretending to find his poor wife missing."

"Damn, Maggi, you should be a detective instead of a writer. Did you tell the police your suspicions?" asked Peter, impressed.

"No, they wouldn't take me seriously. Only Glen takes anything I say about police work seriously. Most of them have an ego that interferes when it shouldn't."

Maggi stood up to check on her dogs. "So what brings you to Denver?"

"I'm a freelance writer. I quit the paper years ago. I have a small house in California, but spend most of my time on the road in search of that one story that will make me famous, like you."

"Did you ever write your book?"

"Wow, you remember that? Sure, I wrote it. After a couple dozen rejections, I threw in the towel."

"You didn't try hard enough. Drop a copy off with Teddi and I'll see what I can do."

"No, thank you. I'd rather base my success on my own hard work, not riding on your shirttails," he answered, with a tone of resentment in his voice.

Both Teddi and Maggi picked up on his mood change. Maggi called the dogs in while Teddi gathered up their picnic celebration.

"I didn't want to tell you just yet, but you're booked for three talk shows over the next two weeks. Unfortunately, they're in Chicago, L.A. and New York," announced Teddi.

"What! I'm not even getting a break after all these weeks of writing?"

"Don't be such a whiner. It's part of your job," chimed in Peter, happy to see her angry about her success.

Peter and Teddi walked ahead of Maggi and the dogs back to the cabin. Peter knew she was watching as he ran his hand up and down Teddi's back, playing with her long, strawberry-blond hair. Maggi rarely saw her with her hair down. She always had it fastened on top of her head with a hair clip. Does Peter really have the hots for Teddi or is he using her in some way to get to me? She wondered.

While Maggi was unloading her car at home, the dogs bounced next door to play with Jean. She always greeted them with doggie cookies when they returned from a trip.

"I've got to be gone for a couple of weeks, looks like the kids will be staying with you again," she called from her yard, as she carried in luggage.

"Great. I'm looking forward to it," Jean called back.

Maggi's relationship with Jean had not always been solid. Jean used to be a handler for dog shows. She put pressure on Maggi to allow her to show the dogs. She felt Maggi owed it to her for finding the dogs for her in the first place. Maggi was not interested in putting her beloved pets through the pressure for a ribbon or trophy. They had a few heated discussions on the topic. Jean, with her short, blond hair and determined attitude, knew if she kept up the pressure, she would wear Maggi down. Jean was in her fifties, preparing to retire from the show ring. She wanted to go out in style, cleaning up the prizes with these two champion-bred dogs. The words flew between them when Maggi came home from the vet clinic, having spayed and neutered the pair, making them ineligible for the show ring.

Teddi witnessed the heated argument. Maggi can get pretty nasty when she is pushed too far. Jean was a winner; she had been for years with her career. She was a sore loser to Maggi. Teddi was fearful one of them would lose control and shoot the other over the pair of dogs but time healed their wounds. They made up and Jean returned to being primary caretaker of the dogs while Maggi was away. Teddi could always sense this underlying conflict between them. It reminded her of a divorced couple being civil enough to work out the custody and visitation of their kids.

Maggi maintained some conflict in her life at all times. Teddi wondered if she thrived on the chaos or if she nurtured conflict so she would always have that emotion to draw from for her books. Her longest lasting conflict had been with Daniel, her ex-husband.

They met in college. Daniel was tall, muscular, had wavy brown hair and glasses. Maggi was into glasses at that time. They dated for three years before they decided to get married. Their marriage started out a happy one. Soon after they graduated, Daniel landed a great job as an architect. He encouraged Maggi to be a stay-at-home mom. The only problem was the mom part. Both Maggi and Daniel dreamed of having five or six kids. They were ecstatic when they got the news that Maggi was pregnant.

They bought their first small house with a nice yard in preparation for the new baby. Their dreams of a large family were shattered when she hemorrhaged during childbirth forcing an emergency hysterectomy. Having the child ripped from her, as Maggi put it, caused them to dote on their baby girl.

Things were getting tougher at the office for Daniel. He lost many high-dollar accounts. He began drinking. Maggi could not count on him any longer. They began to argue. The more they argued, the more he drank. After one of their arguments he stormed out of the house, taking little Mary with him. He was drunk and driving too fast. He made the turn a little too quickly. He swerved, but it was too late, the semi-truck coming toward him from the opposite lane struck them. He lived through it, but Mary did not survive the crash.

That destroyed their marriage. Alcoholism caused him to lose his daughter, his job and his wife. Maggi threw him out of the house. That is when she went to work for the Rocky Mountain News to support herself. That is where she met Peter. She later divorced Daniel.

He accused her of having an affair with Peter while they were still married. He tried to push the blame for their break-up on anyone or anything other than his own actions just so he could live from day to day avoiding his guilt.

Daniel tried to drive Peter away. In a sense he did. When Maggi could not deal with the stress she broke it off with Peter and pursued a career as a freelance writer.

Maggi and Daniel have never made peace. She refused to be in the same room with him. He remained a drunk as she rose to fame and fortune with her books.

Her success enraged him. Glen had to step in a number of times to send him on his way when he would harass her, hanging around outside her new home, watching her. The past few years had been better without contact from Daniel.

Teddi paced back and forth in the green room at the studio waiting for Maggi to go onstage. Oprah was one of Teddi's favorite celebrities. She adjusted her hair, fidgeted with her taupe blouse then rearranged her hair again.

"Stop it! Just stop it. Sit down and try to relax. I'm the one going on soon, not you."

"I know, I know. I can't help being nervous. Do you think she'll stop backstage? Do you think I'll be able to actually meet her? Oh my God, I can't believe we're here!"

One of Oprah's producers appeared in the doorway. "Are you ready?"

Maggi stood up to follow her. Teddi glued herself to her heels, fluffing the back of Maggi's hair as she walked. Maggi turned around and slapped Teddi's hands.

Oprah began, "As a special treat for all of you, we were able to convince Maggi Morgan to pay us a visit. She's just returned from finishing her latest book. Welcome, Maggi."

Maggi approached the stage with total confidence. Nothing seemed to rock Maggi. She smiled and waved to the audience. She hugged Oprah then took a seat.

Oprah was dressed in a black and white pantsuit; Maggi in a red blazer with black slacks. She was striking with her black hair brushing her shoulders, glistening from the stage lights.

"Tell us about your new book, Maggi."

"I'd rather not say too much until my publisher gets a chance to review it. The idea came to me while secluding myself from society at a mountain lodge in Steamboat Springs, Colorado. A woman was killed very near my cabin. Actually, my dogs alerted me to something going on. I should've followed through but instead I called in the dogs. I spent a sleepless night wondering who, or what was outside my cabin."

"Why didn't you call for help?"

"I make sure they remove the phone while I'm there and I never take my cell phone along. I do my best writing when I lose all contact with the outside world. The temptation to watch the news, read papers or make phone calls is too great to overcome. Without the opportunity for distractions, all I can do is think about my book and write."

"It sounds like in this case, your distraction became your book."

"That's true. I had an entirely different plot in mind when I reached my hideout."

"You sound like a criminal, calling it your hideout," laughed Oprah.

"Sometimes I feel like a criminal. I sit around all the time plotting the best way to kill people and not get caught."

"That ain't nothin' new. We all do that."

The crowd laughed as applause rang out.

"Oh my," said Maggi to the audience. "Does Oprah have a murder scheme in place?"

It was obvious Maggi was a hit with the audience.

"My producers tell me this will be book number nine for you?"

"Yes, I can hardly believe it."

"How long have you been writing?"

"Just a little more than ten years. My first book took me three years to write. I had an incredible amount of research to do about crime scenes. I might think like a criminal; but I try to portray my story from both sides."

"How does one go about getting the police to teach you how to pull off the perfect crime? I'm curious."

"See ... I told you she's up to something," Maggi teased the audience.

"Oh stop," said Oprah, as she slapped Maggi on the knee.

"To answer your question, I just marched up to the front desk at the Denver Police Department and asked to speak to a detective. A short while later, this really nice man walked up to me and introduced himself as Detective Karst."

"Wait, isn't he the sleuth in your books?"

37

"You've done your homework."

More laughter from the crowd.

"I'll be the first to admit I don't normally read murder mysteries. But when your books began to cause such a stir, I had the urge to find out what was captivating the nation, so I read some of them."

"Notice she didn't say she liked them." Maggi worked the crowd.

"Let's talk about your Detective Karst. He decided to help you?"

"Yes, he's been wonderful to work with over the years. I've become close friends with him and his wife. He keeps me accurate and on the right side of the law. He says if I ever decided to join the other side, I have far too much knowledge and ability."

"How difficult is it to write a novel?"

"Very. I'm a perfectionist. I spend a good portion of the year doing research and writing notes. I plan every chapter completely before I sit down to write. I know everything that will happen to each character."

"Except for this last one," laughed Oprah.

"Yeah, I broke the mold on this one. I wrote it by the seat of my pants. I hope my publishers still accept it."

"How do you come up with characters?"

"I ride the bus."

"What do you mean you ride the bus?"

"I just get on the bus and ride around people-watching. I pull facial characteristics or clothing for

38

characters from the real world. Then I go home and open the phone book, close my eyes, and point to a name. That's how my characters get their names. Sometimes that name doesn't match the character, so then I try again."

"Oh come on. Be honest. Haven't you ever written in the name of character from your real life that pissed you off?"

Maggi smiled and rolled her eyes. The audience loved her interview with Oprah.

"Guilty. I have used the personality of a person that I don't like then killed that person off. It's really good therapy. There's nothing like having a really crappy day then going to the computer and killing someone. You know, it's like when a therapist says to write a letter to the person you're angry with, but not to mail it. It's the same thing, only I get paid to vent."

"When the show is over, can I give you a few names to add to your victim list?"

"Hey, why not."

Maggi turned to the audience. "If anyone has a person they'd like to see me rub out, just send your story to my email address on my back cover. If I think your person deserves to die, I'll kill him for you."

The audience stood, roaring with applause.

"I noticed she said she'd kill *him,* not *her,*" Oprah was quick to point out.

"Tell us Maggi, is there a man in your life?"

"Tell us Oprah, is there a man in yours?"

"Touché. It's time to go to a break now."

During the break, Maggi sent the producer backstage to escort Teddi up front. Teddi, shaking and white, returned with the producer.

"Oprah, I'd like you to meet my personal assistant, Teddi. She's one of your biggest fans."

Oprah shook hands with her. "Let's chat after the show."

Teddi thought she would faint. She was forever indebted to Maggi.

The commercial break ended.

"I had fun visiting with Maggi. How about you?"

There was a lengthy, loud applause.

Oprah's theme music began to play, signaling the end of the show.

"Everyone, quick! Look under your seats. You have a gift pack of not one, but all eight of Maggi's books. Enjoy!"

Oprah kept her promise. After the show, she joined Maggi and Teddi in the green room for refreshments.

"Girl, do you have any idea what you just did out there?" asked Oprah.

"Why? What do you mean? I thought we had fun."

"Oh, we had fun alright. But now you're going to be bombarded with millions of fans sending you death wishes for their not-so-loved ones."

"I wondered about that," commented Teddi.

"Oh, maybe a few will come in, but I doubt if we'll get bombarded with much more than the typical daily fan mail I get now."

Oprah laughed her strong laugh. "Okay, but don't you blame me when the mail trucks arrive!"

Maggi studied her face, realizing that she was serious. Teddi looked concerned. Had she really set herself up for something she couldn't handle?

Maggi and Teddi returned to their hotel room. There was a message from Maggi's agent. "Uh, oh. Do you think Warren saw the show?" asked Teddi.

"Let's hope not," replied Maggi.

Teddi returned the call, one of her tasks as Maggi's personal assistant.

"Warren, Teddi. What's up? Oh you did. They did? No, she's in the shower. Okay, I'll do that. Bye."

"What'd he say? How much trouble am I in?"

"He did watch the show. So did some of the big wigs at the publishing company. They thought this could be the greatest publicity stunt in the history of murder mysteries. They want to set up a staff for us to oversee opening mail and responding to the fans that want you to kill someone."

Maggi's cell phone rang. Teddi looked at it. "It's Glen."

Maggi grabbed the phone, confident now that her interview was a success.

41

"Hey, Glen, did you watch it? I made the name Detective Glen Karst famous," she laughed.

"Just what in the hell did you think you were doing?"

Maggi was stunned. Glen rarely lost his temper with her.

"What do you mean?"

"There's so many lunatics out on the streets. We have more homicides than we know what to do with then you go on national television, on Oprah no less, and glamorize killing people!"

"Oh, Glen, chill. It was just a fun interview. No one is going to take me seriously."

"Yeah, tell me that in about a week. Why did you publicize your email address?"

"It's on my books anyway, so what harm could that do?"

"Maggi, there's a smaller group of fans that read murder mysteries than the millions that watch Oprah. Your odds are lower that someone that reads books for entertainment will really want you to kill someone. You can bet, with the millions that were sitting in front of the screen, there will be creeps out there whose path you won't want to cross."

Butterflies and knots entered Maggi's stomach as Glen scolded her. She did not think before she spoke. She really did leave herself wide open to the unexpected.

She sighed. There was silence on the phone while she contemplated what she had done in innocence.

"Maggi, are you still there?"

"Yes, Glen. Now I'm nervous. What have I done?"

"Just watch your back. Be extra careful. Keep Teddi with you. Maybe I can find a few rookies that would like to make a few extra bucks to kind of hang out around your place until we see what happens."

"Thanks, Glen. I really appreciate it. I feel so bad."

"I'm sorry I came down so hard on you. The stuff you know about the criminal mind and murders makes me forget you're not a trained cop, just a damn good writer. We'll get you through this. Call us when you get home."

Chapter 3

The media frenzy over the next few days drove Maggi insane. She could not believe the headlines, "Mystery Writer Maggi Morgan Offers Mail-Order Murders!"

"Maggi, you have to leave to go to New York for your next show," pleaded Teddi.

"I can't. I don't want to. I don't want to make a fool of myself."

"It's a little late for that. You can't take back what you said. I think you should just hold your head high and agree with Warren and the publisher that it's the world's most clever marketing ploy. If you play it right, you could come across as brilliant. Not that you're not," Teddi added, just in case Maggi was in a sensitive mood.

Maggi sat on the floor brushing the dogs. She seemed to be ignoring everything Teddi was telling her. Touching her dogs' thick black coats caused stress to melt away. After a while she came back to the real world, having been lost in a more peaceful place in her mind with her dogs. Being a writer allows her to leave the world, as she knows it, to go off to secret places where no one can follow. Sometimes it is difficult to return.

Teddi packed Maggi's black leather luggage then placed it near the door. This time they would fly first class for added privacy. She called for a taxi to drive them to the airport so they could be dropped at the door without having to park and ride a shuttle. Teddi was doing everything in her power to protect Maggi from her fans until this crazy mess simmered down.

Maggi chose a black pantsuit with a black scarf to cover her hair and most of her face. She looked as if she were in mourning.

When Teddi saw her, she said, "Are you sure you should be dressed like that? You look like you're trying to be in disguise. Don't you think that outfit will draw more attention?"

Maggi stopped to view her slender mysterious image in the full-length mirror. The lady in black looking back at her brought laughter. "I look like a damn black widow!"

Teddi laughed with her. "Wait, wait you forgot these." She handed Maggi a pair of large black sunglasses.

Maggi put them on as she strutted in front of the mirror, viewing herself from every angle.

"You're right, Teddi. This completes the look."

Humor was what this situation needed. She went to the closet to find something more appropriate to travel in. She chose a winter-white suit with a pale pink blouse.

With her perfect figure, anything she chose to wear looked wonderful on her.

"What do you think, Teddi? Should I go for this publicity thing full force? Should I wear that black widow outfit on the show?"

"Oh, Maggi, I'm not too sure about that," warned Teddi.

"Where's your sense of adventure? I got myself into this; I might as well have some fun with it. Come on, what do you think? Let's pack it."

Teddi pulled out another small suitcase to pack the strange black outfit. Maybe it'll get lost at the airport, accidentally on purpose, she thought to herself.

The sound of the taxi's horn warned the girls that the time had come. Maggi ran next door with the dogs while Teddi and the driver loaded the luggage.

As Maggi and Teddi boarded the plane, they heard whispering. Many of the passengers recognized her. That probably would not have happened had she not recently been on Oprah. She followed Teddi's advice about holding her head high, pretending to enjoy the publicity she was getting. One thing about it, Warren told her that her book sales skyrocketed.

In the hotel lobby, while waiting to check in, a small group gathered around her for autographs. She wondered how they knew she would be there, until she looked up and saw the staff standing there with her books, waiting for their turn for an autograph. She assumed these were friends and family of the people who worked for the hotel.

Maggi was gracious as always, as she signed her name with her graceful, flowing signature. She had a way of making the name *Maggi Morgan* look whimsical on paper. She was proud of her signature that took weeks to master after her first book was published.

A young woman with dark circles under her eyes followed them to the elevator. "Bless you, Miss Morgan, and thank you. I will be forever grateful to you for your help." She slipped a wrinkled piece of paper into Maggi's pocket then left the elevator the first time the door opened.

It was obvious from her tattered appearance that she was not a customer at the hotel. The pain Maggi saw in her eyes sent a shudder through her body.

"What a sad little woman. I wonder what she meant by that?"

"She slipped a piece of paper into your pocket. Didn't you notice?" asked Teddi.

Maggi turned to look into her right jacket pocket when the elevator bell chimed. The door opened onto the floor where Maggi and Teddi were staying. They stepped off and headed towards their room, while the curious piece of paper remained in her pocket.

The bellhop followed them into their room. He set their luggage on the luggage rack then went to the windows and opened the drapes. He turned on the light in the bathroom.

"Can I do anything else for you, Miss Morgan?"

Maggi placed a twenty-dollar bill in his hand. "No, thank you. We'll be just fine."

When he left, Maggi plopped down on one of the beds while Teddi went to the window to see what kind of a view they had. A large bouquet of flowers caught Teddi's eye. She assumed they were for Maggi from the show she would be on later that night. To her surprise, the card read: *Roses are Red, Violets are Blue, With You in New York, I'll Have to be Too, Love Peter.*

Teddi read the card a second time, out loud, to Maggi.

"Oh brother, it's easy to see why he's not making it as a writer."

"Maggi, that's a nasty thing to say! I think he's sweet. Do you think he'll be here?"

"Oh probably. He seems to have a weird way of always showing up when we're on the road somewhere. I think he's stalking us," she teased.

Teddi did not think she was funny. The phone rang, Teddi answered. "Sure, she's right here. It's Warren."

"Yes, Warren?"

"Just wanted to wish you luck this evening and don't forget to play up this mail-order murder thing. If he doesn't bring it up, you have to. We're counting on you."

"I brought a black widow outfit to wear on the show. What do you think?" She shot a smile at Teddi.

"Perfect. Do it."

"Okay, bye."

"He thinks I should go with the look. Can you believe it? I think I will, just for the hell of it. After all, tomorrow's Halloween."

"Fine, do it. But I think it's a foolish idea." Teddi went into the bathroom to draw a bath.

Maggi changed into a pair of burgundy silk pajamas to relax in until the time approached when they needed to prepare for the show. As she gathered her suit from the bed to hang it in the closet, a corner from the piece of paper caught her eye. She dropped the clothes back onto the bed then sat down next to them on the tapestry bedspread that looked as if it had been chosen to match her sleepwear.

The paper was crumpled as if it had been retrieved from the trash then used to write the note. The handwriting was beautiful. Maggi wondered how such a tortured soul could produce such magnificent marks on paper. The note read:

Dear Miss Morgan,

I am living with a terrible man. Tony beats me almost every night when he comes home drunk. He's just started beating the kids too. I left a good family and a good life when I was just a teenager to follow this man. My parents told me if I didn't break it off with him not to bother to come home. I chose him. Miss Morgan, I'm afraid he is going to kill me. The beatings are getting worse. We live in number five in the third apartment building from the north, just off of Mason Street. I think if you just poison his beer or something similar, that might be the best way to do it. Thank you so much for helping.

I'd better not sign my name.

Maggi was stunned. It was as if the letter was glued to her hands. She could not put it down. She read it repeatedly. She always wrote about murders and evil people, but never truly knew a victim like this woman. It made her think about how she was making her living entertaining the masses with stories about crime and murder. Guilt crept up through the sadness. She stood, tossing the letter onto the bed as if it were about to bite her. She walked to the window in an attempt to get far away from it.

Reality hit. This poor woman was putting her faith in Maggi to remove her from the pain and suffering she knew as her daily life. She put her future in the hands of a mystery writer. How desperate this woman must be. There had to be some way to help, some way other than killing this man who abused her and her children.

Teddi stepped back into the room after her bath. She spotted Maggi at the window. She thought it unusual for Maggi to be enjoying the view. Maggi turned to her, but before she could say a word, Teddi read her face.

"Oh my God, what happened? Are the dogs okay?"

Teddi thought that would be the only news that would cause Maggi's face to look so pale and depressed.

"The dogs are fine. Read the note from the lady on the elevator," she said, as she pointed to the letter looking so small on the king-sized bed. That tiny bit of paper crushed the un-crushable, Maggi Morgan.

Teddi picked up the paper slowly, not quite sure she wanted to read whatever it was that hit Maggi so hard. Tears filled her eyes as she read the words so carefully scripted onto the paper.

"Oh Maggi, that's terrible, the poor woman. Why doesn't she just go to the police?"

"Teddi, the police are overworked in New York. This is just another of thousands of domestic abuse cases. Until someone ends up dead, there's not much that can be done. Even when the neighbors call the police in an attempt to help the victim, usually a woman, she is too frightened to press charges. If she does press charges, she knows she will be in for a bigger beating when he gets out. And he will get out, in just a couple of days."

"Can't she go to a shelter?"

"I'm sure she could, if they had room. From some of my research, it's only temporary, until you can make plans to move on. They are overcrowded the way it is."

"Maggi, there has to be something we can do. There has to be some way we can help."

"We can always kill her husband. Society sure wouldn't miss the creep."

"That's not even funny. I can't believe you said that!" Teddi looked around the room, as if somehow someone could hear Maggi making a death threat.

At that moment, there was a firm knock on the door. Teddi jumped, knowing if they were in a movie that would be the police at her door. She froze. The knock at the door repeated, only this time it grew louder.

"Open up, it's the police!"

Maggi and Teddi burst into laughter. Maggi ran to the door.

"Glen, you son of a bitch, you startled us! Hi, Debbie. What are you two doing here?"

"Debbie has family in New York that we've been meaning to visit for the last few years. We thought it would be fun to go to the show tonight and watch you stick your foot in your mouth again," he laughed.

"If you want the truth, Maggi, he also wants to be sure you're gonna be safe after the show," explained Debbie.

"Come on in. Make yourselves at home. We'll be leaving for the show in ..." she looked at her watch, "...about an hour. You might as well ride along with us."

Debbie looked at Teddi, then at Maggi. "What's up with you two?"

"Up? What do you mean?" asked Teddi.

Glen looked at Debbie then searched the faces of the girls. Being a seasoned detective, reading faces was second nature to him.

"Debbie's right. What has the two of you so shook up?"

Maggi did not want to tell Glen for fear she would hear an "I told you so". Teddi's eyes darted to the bed where the paper lay, hoping to figure out a way to get to it and hide it from Glen. He followed her eyes to the slip of paper, walked directly to it then began reading it out loud.

Debbie gasped, "Oh my, that poor woman."

Glen turned sharply, "Shit, Maggi, this is just the thing I told you would happen. How did you get this?"

Before Maggi could speak, Teddi confessed, "We were in the elevator with this woman and she slipped it into Maggi's pocket."

Debbie knew that look of concern on her husband's face. She was frightened for Maggi herself. She was very glad they were there so Glen could keep an eye on her. Maggi was one of her best friends; she was pleased that her husband was qualified to take care of her.

"Does this show you how vulnerable you are? That slip of paper could have just as easily been a knife. Are you not watching your back like I told you?"

"Glen, really now, calm down. Why would anyone want to harm me? They want *me* to kill the problem person in their life. I'm not making the connection."

"I think it's this rapist thing," said Debbie. "Glen, Maggi's right. The readers need her, no one really wants to harm her."

"They might if she doesn't follow through with their requests. Take this woman for example. What if her drunken husband comes home and kills one of the kids. She's going to blame you for not stopping him. She could go off the deep end and hunt you down."

Maggi sat on the bed. She was obviously disturbed. "I guess I never thought about it that way."

"Maggi, like I said before, you're one hell of a good writer, but you're just not seasoned enough to rationalize the dangers in the real world. The fiction you write is just that, fiction. You know it's not true; you can laugh and tease about it. If you were covering crime scenes and writing up those stories for real, your outlook on society and your safety would take on an entirely new attitude."

The phone rang, interrupting Glen's lecture.

"Maggi, the car's here to take you to the studio," said Teddi.

Maggi jumped up to get dressed. She looked at her black widow outfit that she had planned to wear. She quickly vetoed it, scooping up her clothes off of the bed. She looked at Glen.

"I guess this is my cue to leave. I'll meet you ladies in the lobby," he said.

Teddi and Maggi dressed quickly then shared the mirror to freshen their makeup. Maggi was not too concerned about hers since they would re-do it at the studio.

They rushed down to the lobby where Glen waited. Together they rode in the black limousine sent to the hotel by the show.

Teddi showed Glen and Debbie around backstage before she took them to the green room to wait. Debbie was bubbling with excitement, she had never been at any of Maggi's television interviews before.

Maggi returned to the green room all made up and ready to go. When the producer came to escort her to the stage, Maggi instructed her to be sure to seat her friends in the audience.

Maggi's portion of the show was short. The entire interview lasted less than ten minutes. It went exactly as she thought: questions about her books, her years of writing, what got her started, even her love life was not mentioned. Nearly the entire interview centered upon her mail-order murders. Now, two talk shows exposed her little mistake to the world. Unfortunately, anyone who missed the Oprah Show, but caught this show, would be able to send her emails.

Maggi was greeted backstage by Warren, and Brad from her publisher's PR department. They were thrilled with her interview.

"What are you guys doing here?" she asked.

"You're one hot commodity now. We need to spend more time following you around when you're in the public eye," beamed Warren.

"I'm trying to get you booked on more talk shows," Brad chimed in. "We've got to strike while the iron is hot."

"No, absolutely not. This has to stop. I owe you one more show, but that's it. I don't want to follow through on this anymore."

"I don't think you've got much choice," Brad told her.

"Please, speak to Detective Karst before you book me on any more shows. He has something important to say about the dangers of this stunt," she begged.

The three of them returned to the green room to wait until the show ended, before Debbie, Glen and Teddi would be able to join them. Since Maggi was in the second half of the show, their wait was short. She did not speak to either of the men while they waited.

Glen escorted Debbie and Teddi into the room.

"Thank God. Glen, tell these two that this has to stop. Tell them what kind of danger I could be putting myself in. Tell them to just go away!"

Debbie went to Maggi. She helped her gather her things. Glen took the men out into the hall to explain the situation from a law enforcement point of view. Maggi stormed past them on her way to the limousine. Teddi followed closely behind. Debbie slipped her arm into Glen's to encourage him to end his conversation, although that gesture was often futile if he was not ready.

Shortly after the four of them returned to the hotel room, Brad and Warren knocked at the door.

"Maggi, I'm sorry if you think we're putting you in any danger. That's not our intention," apologized Brad. "This is just one great story you've got going. Maybe we can work something out. I'll talk to the guys at the office about it."

"Can we take a peek at that letter you got from the elevator woman?" asked Warren.

Maggi looked surprised. "How in the hell did you find out about the letter?"

Warren looked towards Glen.

"Glen, how could you? I thought you were on my side."

"Maggi, I am on your side. I was trying to point out to these two that bad things were already happening."

She went to the bed, picked up the letter and tossed it to them. Brad held it while Warren read over his shoulder. Brad folded the letter, following the original creases, then slipped it into his pocket.

"I don't think so buddy," said Glen. "I believe that belongs to Maggi. I'm not gonna let you use it for more publicity." He held his hand out, waiting for Brad to return it.

"Come on Karst, give us break," said Brad. "It'll be much easier if we can show it to the big wigs at the publishing office to convince them to take your concerns seriously."

"Good try, but no." said Glen.

Teddi's cell phone rang. "Hi, Doll, I'm downstairs. Can you slip away for the rest of the evening?" asked Peter. "I'd like to show you New York City by night."

"Why don't you come up to the room? There's a few people here I'd like you to meet. Room 714. See ya in a minute."

Teddi was aglow.

"That must be Mr. Wonderful," teased Debbie.

"Oh hell, just what I need to complete this party. Peter!" complained Maggi.

"Why do you dislike him so?" asked Teddi.

"I'm sorry. I just don't like my past following me around."

"He's not following you around, he's following me. I'd appreciate it if you wouldn't run him off," Teddi snapped at Maggi.

Debbie smiled at Glen. They both thought Maggi walked on Teddi a little too much. They wished she would learn to stand up to Maggi. This was the first evidence of it happening.

Teddi was holding the door open, waiting, when Peter stepped off the elevator down the hall. When he met Teddi at the door, he kissed her sweetly, not minding his audience.

"Peter, I'd like you to meet Debbie Karst, and her husband Glen. Actually, if you've read Maggi's books, you'd know him as Detective Karst. This is Warren, Maggi's agent, and Brad from the publishing company."

Peter nodded to each of them as Teddi introduced them.

"Did I barge in on something?" asked Peter. He sensed the tension in the room.

Teddi quickly showed him the note before Glen or Maggi could stop her.

"Whoa! So, Mags, what are you gonna do about this? Are you gonna do the guy in?"

"First of all, don't call me Mags, you know I hate that. Secondly, I'm not going to do a damn thing about it. These three gentlemen are going to handle everything for me."

"Hey, Doll, let's go before she kills *me*," he laughed, as he guided Teddi out the door with his hand on the small of her back.

Maggi was steaming as he closed the door behind them.

"Back to this note, Glen. How can we reach a compromise here?" asked Brad.

"There is no compromise to be made and I'd better not find out you guys are using this with no regard to Maggi's safety."

Warren and Brad left the room feeling defeated.

"Glen, I have a big favor to ask of you," said Maggi.

"Uh oh, that could mean trouble," he teased.

"No, seriously. Can you call the police department here and check out the address that lady gave me?"

"Already did. The whole detective thing, remember?"

Glen called during the show and was waiting for a call listing from the records division. After his call came in, he joined the ladies.

"She's had a tough go of it all right. Her name is Linda Harmon; her husband is Tony. They have four little girls. Seems this jerk broke her jaw last year, a few months ago it was her ribs. He beats her on a regular basis. The neighbors called it in once but she refused to tell the truth to the investigating officers. She said she fell down the stairs. The neighbors filled in the story but without her cooperation it's all hearsay. She's right though; it's just a matter of time before he kills her."

Glen stopped talking to look at Maggi. She was off again in one of her worlds. Debbie looked first at Glen then followed his stare to Maggi.

When Maggi became aware of the silence, she said, "Thanks, Glen."

Debbie asked, "Maggi, what are you thinking?"

"What would happen if we took this woman and her kids and moved them away from him? We could set her up somewhere until she could get on her feet. We could help her find a job and start a new life far away."

"Oh, Maggi, it might be better if you don't get involved," warned Glen.

"Hell, I'm already involved. She came to me for help. You know I can't kill her husband, but damn it, I have enough money to help her start a new life. I do have the ability to make *that* happen for her."

"Okay, so what if you help this woman? Then what will you do for the next one, and the one after that, when more letters and emails come in? This case is one of millions of hard-luck abuse stories. Maggi, you can't help them all," he explained.

"I know I can't help them all, but the others won't be looking into my eyes pleadingly, thanking me for my help. The others will be faceless names and stories. Glen, if I don't do something to help this woman, her face will haunt my dreams. I have to do this. I need your help."

"Glen, do something. You can help her, can't you?" begged Debbie, as tears were filling her eyes.

"Oh shit, you women and your tears. Makes me wonder why a woman like this Linda person never learned the fine art of manipulating men."

"Her husband is no man, he's an animal. No woman would have a chance against someone like him. No, you know what? Animals are better than he is. I can't

61

come up with a good word to describe what he is," Maggi fumed.

Maggi jumped onto the bed, crossed her legs Indian style then looked up at Glen. "Okay, how do we start?"

"You're asking me? I thought you had a plan already in mind."

"I do. I just thought you might have a better one."

"Let's hear what you've got."

"First, I thought maybe I could ask Teddi to check with Peter about his small house in California. He says he's almost never there. He spends most of his time traveling in search of some elusive story. He's just lucky he was born to a wealthy family that can support his carefree lifestyle. Maybe we can talk him into letting this woman and her kids stay there for a few months, until she can get a job to support herself and the kids."

"Do you think he'd go for that?" asked Debbie.

"He'd look pretty cold and selfish in Teddi's eyes if he said no. Don't forget she was with me when this woman approached me. She saw the shape she was in emotionally."

Glen asked, "So, if Peter agrees and we have a house, then what?"

"That's where you come in. Can you go to where she lives, maybe ask the neighbors about her? Find out her schedule and when the loser is away from the apartment. Once you know when she and the four girls will be alone, I was hoping you'd flash your badge and ask them to leave with you."

"Maggi, this is out of my jurisdiction. I can't do that."

"Oh come on, Glen. As abused as she is, you know she'll not argue and go with you willingly. She won't even check your badge to see you're from Colorado. You really don't think she's going to turn you in for saving her life, do you?"

"No, Maggi. Ain't happening."

"Okay, if you won't, I will."

"Damn it, woman, you're going to get yourself killed."

"I thought you were here to make sure that doesn't happen."

Glen paced around the room, running his fingers through his sandy brown hair. He walked to the window, pressing his forehead against the cool glass. He strummed his fingers on the sill.

As softhearted as he was toward abused women, and as much as he cared for Maggi, he just couldn't bring himself to do something that would not be appropriate for his career as a detective.

"No Maggi, I'm sorry."

Maggi pouted.

Debbie felt sorry for Maggi. She also knew her next course of action would be to force Teddi to do it. Teddi was not very brave, nor capable of pulling this

63

situation off. Before Debbie had met Glen, she herself had been through the police academy. She felt she knew how to take care of herself.

"I'll do it," suggested Debbie.

"Hell no you won't," said Glen.

Debbie stood up to him.

"Glen, if it were me in this situation, wouldn't you want someone to go out on a limb to help me?"

He tapped his foot on the floor; he knew he was not going to talk Debbie out of this one.

"Okay, but you be careful and you check in every step of the way, do you understand?"

"Yes sir," Debbie saluted him. She smiled at Maggi.

Maggi ran across the room and threw her arms around Glen's neck.

"Thank you, thank you, thank you. I knew you wouldn't let me down."

Glen glanced at Debbie sitting on the bed with a huge smile on her face. He rolled his eyes while he peeled Maggi's arms from around his neck.

Maggi ran to the phone to call Teddi. She explained the plan, then waited while Teddi ran the idea past Peter.

"Maggi, he says he'll help. How soon are you going to do this?"

Maggi covered the phone, "How soon are we going to do this?" she asked Debbie.

"I can interview the neighbors in the morning, I guess."

Maggi put the receiver back to her ear. "Debbie's going to start the ball rolling in the morning. Is that okay with Peter?"

She waited again while Teddi spoke with Peter.

"He says when he brings me back tonight, he'll give you the address and his key. He says we'll stop somewhere tonight to get a second one made."

Now Maggi felt badly that she was so negative toward Peter. "Give that man a big hug and kiss from me."

"Okay, Peter will give us a key tonight. Debbie, if you can find out when you can grab that family, we might be able to have them on a flight to California tomorrow."

"Great. Now can we eat? I'm starved," said Glen.

Glen was not quite sure how he had let those girls talk him into this ridiculous scheme but he was glad he did. He was such a softy that he really wanted to help her any way he could. He was not going to reveal his true feelings to the girls. Little did he know they already had him pegged for the tenderhearted man he was and knew exactly how he was feeling.

Maggi offered to take them out to dinner at the restaurant of their choice. Glen wanted a huge steak. Since none of them were familiar with the streets of New York City, they asked at the front desk. Soon they were seated with the waiter taking their order. Maggi had experienced such an emotional day; she did not realize how hungry she was. She ordered the same large cut of steak as Glen.

Debbie kept her promise. She took a cab to the neighborhood where Linda lived. The neighbors were more than happy to tell all they knew about the woman-beating scum who lived in that apartment with her and the little girls. She learned that he leaves every day at one o'clock. He works until ten then hits the local bars until he closes them. That is when he returns home to assault Linda.

Debbie called Glen with her information. He relayed it to Maggi.

"Tell her, I'm going to call the airport and book a flight for them. I'd really appreciate it if she would accompany them to Peter's house."

Glen was about to repeat Maggi's comments when Debbie interrupted. "I heard her. Somehow I knew that was going to be her plan."

Maggi called the airport, the perfect flight left at four o'clock. That would give Debbie three hours to get them to the airport. The neighbors told her the kids would be out of school early today because it is Halloween. The city elementary schools only hold them until lunchtime then release them. Their school was just around the corner from where they lived.

Debbie returned with a cab shortly before one o'clock. She watched Tony leave the building. She felt the blood in her veins boil. She felt nothing but contempt for a man that would hit his wife and little girls. The urge to have someone show him how a beating feels was overwhelming. She tried to be more like Glen who took pride in the fact that, no matter what the circumstance, no matter how despicable the low-life, he could maintain his composure.

Shortly after Tony left, the four little girls appeared outdoors to play. She approached the building, looking in every direction to be sure Tony was not returning. She went to apartment five then knocked at the door. There was no answer. She knocked again. From where she was standing, she could see the girls gathered in a huddle near a dumpster, afraid to speak. The third time she knocked, she heard the chain rattle as the door opened a crack.

"Yes?"

"Ma'am, would you step out here please? I'd like to have a word with you." She glanced over both shoulders again to be aware of her surroundings.

Linda stepped out into the hall.

"Ma'am, are you Linda Harmon?"

"Yes."

"Ma'am, is it true that your husband has been abusing you and the girls?"

"No, I told that to the policeman that was here the other night."

"Linda, I'm not a police officer. I'm here to remove you and the girls from this property to safety. I can give

67

you a few minutes to pack up some things but we must get going quickly."

She backed into the apartment without saying a word and closed the door. Debbie stepped outside onto the steps. She leaned her back against the brick building making the area surrounding her totally visible. She was not sure if Linda was planning to go with her or not. She did not give Debbie any indication of her intentions.

Her fears were soon put to rest when the door opened. Linda stood in the doorway with one suitcase and two small trash bags. It broke Debbie's heart to think that she could fit all the prized possessions for herself and her girls into such small parcels.

She raised her hand in an attempt to help her down the stairs. Linda pulled back. A natural response from an abused woman, she thought. The girls watched silently from behind the dumpster.

"Girls, come here now," she directed.

Obediently, the girls arrived at her side in single file. They followed Debbie to the cab. She opened the back door. Linda and all four girls piled in. Debbie sat up front with the driver.

"Airport, please."

Once they were a few blocks from the apartment building, Debbie called Glen for the flight number.

Maggi had made all the arrangements. She lied to the ticket person about the situation. She explained there was a death in the family and that Linda and the girls

68

needed to fly to California immediately. She told him that they did not have time to get proper ID.

Debbie wondered how she was going to get past security. She should have known Maggi had a plan. Everything went smoothly. The girls took turns sitting by the windows. Debbie and Linda took the aisle seats.

Linda listened intently while Debbie told her the entire story from start to finish. She was grateful to Maggi Morgan. Linda sat back in her seat knowing she would never be abused again.

Debbie kept her promise to Maggi. She spent a couple of days with Linda and the girls. She took them shopping for clothes and groceries with the money Maggi wired to her. It was fun to help the girls with the shopping; they were so appreciative. She laughed when she thought how awkward that part would have been for Glen. Next Debbie, according to Maggi's instructions, purchased a small car. She did not want Linda and the girls to have to rely on buses to get around.

Finally, Debbie stopped by a church in Linda's new neighborhood; which, thanks to Peter, was a nice one. She asked for assistance in finding a person to look after the family. Once that task was finished she headed back to Denver, feeling proud.

Chapter 4

Word mysteriously leaked out about Maggi's generosity to the abused woman. She was rendered temporarily speechless when the host of the talk show from California began asking her questions about Linda. She explained the discretion needed for the situation and refused to offer any comments. Maggi pulled off the look of a confidently, cool attitude while inside she was fuming; wondering who could possibly have exposed her story.

The remainder of the show was a brief carbon copy of the previous one. The main interest of the host remained the mail-order murders. Final applause from the audience, coupled with dimming lights, marked the end of the show. Maggi ripped her microphone from her collar then reached under her blouse to remove the wires and box. Once free of the connection to the public, she stormed off of the stage where she bumped into Teddi, waiting near the exit door with all of her things. She knew Maggi well enough to know she was not going to want to stick around for chitchat.

Quietly and swiftly they made their way out of the back studio door where a car was waiting to return them to their hotel. The driver, a tall elderly well-groomed gentleman looked up in surprise when they approached the car. He assumed they would remain inside to visit after the show. He stood against the shining black limousine reading a newspaper. He tried to fold the paper before opening the door, but was forced to drop it in order to help the impatient duo into the car.

He returned to the spot where he had been standing to retrieve the paper. He slipped into the driver's seat.

"Would you like to return to your hotel now?" he asked, politely.

Maggi was still too angry to speak.

"Yes, please," responded Teddi.

"Maggi, how do you ...?" started Teddi.

Maggi raised her hand motioning to Teddi to drop it. She was not going to have a private conversation anywhere an extra set of ears could listen in.

Teddi barely had a chance to close the door to their hotel room when Maggi rushed to the phone.

"Hello."

"Glen, something terrible has happened," bawled Maggi.

"Maggi, are you and Teddi okay?"

"Yes, we're fine. Glen, someone leaked about Linda. I just went through an interrogation on national television."

71

"No shit? Maggi, I'm so sorry. I have no idea who would've leaked the story. Debbie did just like you asked. She told Linda not to speak to anyone about it. She didn't use your name on any of the paperwork."

"I'm not blaming her, Glen, but someone told the show before I arrived. When this thing airs, I'm dead. I'll never be able to get people to drop this thing."

"When are you coming home?"

"I plan to have Teddi change our itinerary to get us out of here on the first available flight. I don't care if I have to go by way of the moon!"

"You're not still planning to connect with Linda to see how she's doing, are you?"

"No. I'm so glad I didn't reach her to tell her I might visit. I'm finished with that chapter. I'm not going to call her and I hope she sticks to her promise never to contact me."

"She's so grateful. She'd never do anything you didn't want her to do."

"Thanks, Glen. I feel better. Tell Debbie hi from us and we'll see the two of you when we get back."

Teddi nearly had everything packed by the time Maggi hung up the phone. Maggi dug through the luggage looking for a pair of blue jeans and a sweater. She peeled off her stage clothes then slipped into the soft purple sweater and jeans. Teddi handed her a cup of tea then picked up the phone in an attempt to make travel changes. A flight leaving for Denver in three hours would take Maggi far away from her unpleasant situation in California.

"I hope Brad hasn't booked me on any more shows," complained Maggi, on their way to the airport. "No contract is going to force me to repeat today. I'll just do one of my disappearing acts and tell him I'm too busy writing."

"I've been meaning to ask you about that," said Teddi.

"About what?"

"You've been wanting to be alone a lot more lately. Are you okay?"

"Yeah, I'm fine. I just need a little more privacy these days. I think it's the pressure of all this new publicity."

"Alright if you say so. Not being able to reach you for days on end is something I'm not accustomed to. You've always made yourself available to me in the past."

"I trust you, Teddi. I know you can make decisions on my behalf without having to call me about every detail. The books are doing well; we have a good system. I think we can stand to be apart a little more. Besides, this will give you more free time to spend with Peter when he's in town. I'm really surprised he didn't show up today for the shoot."

"He said if his schedule allowed, he'd be here."

Maggi turned to study Teddi's face. Disappointment covered it like a veil.

73

"Teddi, you can stay if you'd like. I'm perfectly capable of flying home alone. If you and Peter have a few plans here, please follow through with them. Don't let me come between you."

The expression on Teddi's face lightened, "Do you mean it?"

"Sure. When you drop me off, just go back to the hotel. Hell, stay a week; charge it to me. I'm not going to be very sociable anyway. Enjoy yourself. Oh, do me a favor though."

"Sure, anything. Just name it."

"I didn't do any shopping for Debbie on this trip. Would you find something nice that represents California?"

"You bet. I'll find something nice."

Maggi reached into her handbag to retrieve her credit card for Teddi's mini vacation.

Teddi helped Maggi out of the hotel courtesy car with her luggage. Once she felt she could handle the rest on her own, Teddi climbed back into the car to return to the hotel.

The timing could not have been better. Peter was at the front desk speaking to the man behind the counter when Teddi walked up behind him, slipping her arms around his strong frame. He reached down to touch the hands around his waist. He recognized the ruby ring Teddi always wore. It was a gift from her grandmother.

74

While holding onto her hands, he spun in a slow circle to face her and then kissed her.

"I was under the impression you girls had just checked out."

"We did, but Maggi sent me back when she learned you might be here. She didn't want me to miss out on spending some time with you. She's not in the greatest mood; a little solitude will be good for her."

"Great. Do you still have your room here?"

"I will in a minute. Maggi said to charge it to her. Just give me a minute to register then our fun can begin."

"I'm so glad you've returned," said the desk clerk. "The young lady that checked you out neglected to give messages to Miss Morgan. Would you like to take them?"

"Yes, thank you."

He gathered the messages from the slot for their room. He sealed them in a large white envelope before handing them to Teddi.

Maggi asked the cab driver to set her luggage on the step while she ran next door to gather up her beloved dogs. As she entered the house she heard Brad's voice on the answering machine, telling her about new ideas he had for more shows. She pretended not to hear him.

She ran up the large winding staircase to her luxurious Victorian bedroom. She dumped the contents of the suitcase onto the bed, and picked through the items, tossing some of them back in. She went to her closet and gathered an armful of sweaters and jeans. Tossing those carelessly into her suitcase, she zipped it closed. It bumped hard against her leg as she lugged it down the stairs while trying to run.

She carried it into the garage then returned for her dogs' bag. She always kept extra water bowls and leashes, as well as a doggie medical kit packed for her kids. She opened the trunk and tossed it all in. Then she went to her pantry to find dog food and some treats. With her arms full of treats she could not manage the forty-pound bag of dog food. She made a quick return trip for that.

She walked back into the kitchen, breathless from dragging the dog food bag and heaving it up into the trunk of her white Lincoln Continental. The dogs' care came first. She took a moment to search the pantry for goodies for herself. She filled a box with cookies, chips and small cans of fruit. She added tea and juice boxes. She believed in a very healthy diet but considered junk food a reward for eating properly.

The dogs were running back and forth with her as if her high-speed packing was a game. A few times she nearly fell over the top of Bailey. He was not quite as quick to move out of her way as was Bridgette.

She checked her voice mail. She had twelve messages. She chose not to listen to any of them. She locked the front door, turned on the security system then left through the garage. The dogs happily jumped into the backseat. They loved to go with her when she went away to write.

As the sun began to set, Maggi thought she should find a place to stay for the night. She spotted a Quality Inn Suites sign up ahead. She pulled into the parking lot. Quickly, she filled out the paperwork and waited for the key. She drove around to the backside of the building where there was a field adjoining the parking lot. She slipped a leash onto the collar of each dog. They jumped out of the car, pulling her towards the field. After the dogs were finished with their business, she walked them to their ground level room. Once they were safely inside, Maggi brought in the luggage. She unpacked the dogs' food dishes then returned to the trunk to scoop food from the large bag. She had no intentions of dragging the bag in and out of the car.

The dogs gobbled down their food while Maggi called Glen and Debbie.

"Deb, it's Maggi. I just wanted to tell you and Glen that I'm fine but need to get away for a couple of days. I'm not sure where I'm going or what I'm doing. I just don't want anyone to be able to reach me. I gave Teddi the week off."

"Glen told me what happened. I don't blame you for wanting to get away."

"I'll check my voice mail on my personal cell phone. Only you two and Teddi have this number. I'm not going to check my messages at home and I didn't bring my other cell phone. I'll let you know when I'm finished hiding."

When Peter and Teddi returned to their room after dinner, Teddi picked up the white envelope containing Maggi's messages from the desk clerk. She opened it carefully and was about to pour the contents onto the bed when Peter stopped her.

"Hey, if Maggi says this is your vacation time, then damn it, don't do any work."

"This isn't work. I'm just curious about her messages. There could be something important in here."

Peter took the envelope from her. "It can wait. If you two would've gone home together it would've had to wait anyway. Go slip into something more comfortable and let's go for a moonlight stroll."

Obediently, Teddi went into the bedroom of their suite to change. When she returned, Peter was watching TV.

"Just what I thought. You were too good to be true. Now you're going to ask me if we can stay in. Right?" she teased.

Peter pressed the button on the remote, "Not on your life. Let's go."

Peter kept his promise about a romantic moonlit walk. When they returned to their room, the romance continued. They made love until the sun's glow could be seen out their east window.

He called for breakfast to be delivered to their room. He ordered orange juice, croissants, fruit and champagne. Teddi was not accustomed to all of the attention. Maggi was the one that got all the special treatment while Teddi watched on, choosing for herself the gifts and flowers that did not appeal to Maggi. This was so much better. She did not want this week to end.

It was during breakfast that Peter broke the news. He had no idea Maggi was going to give Teddi the week off. He made arrangements to stay for only one night. He had business to attend to later that day. His flight was scheduled to leave at noon.

Teddi was sad but did not try to make him feel guilty. His work schedule had been set before her vacation. She decided to stay on one more day to shop and see the sights.

They made the most of their last couple of hours before Peter left. She walked him to the lobby where they said their good-byes. Teddi yawned as she turned to walk away. Maybe going back to sleep was the best way to begin the rest of her day. She crawled back into bed for a nap.

It was three o'clock in the afternoon before she awoke. There was not much daylight left for sightseeing and shopping. Oh well, she thought, I guess I'll just have to stay an extra day. And she did.

Police cars lined the street as Glen crossed the yellow crime scene tape waving in the breeze. A uniformed officer stood guard at the taped line. Glen flashed his badge as he crossed. Neighbors stood in a group, trying to piece bits of the story together.

79

It was an older, quiet neighborhood that, until now, seemed oblivious to the crime happening in the rest of the city. A young woman in her twenties was found dead in the backyard of this house. The residents were away for the winter, in Arizona. One of the neighbors found her while walking his dog. The dog left their normal path to run into the backyard.

Glen took his time checking the body. He was extremely thorough. He believed in starting big and working his way into the crime scene, not missing the slightest detail. The other officers canvassed the area for any leads. Glen took notes on the position of the body while he analyzed the travel path possibly taken by the perp. At this point, there was no way of telling whether his rapist was to blame. Her nude body showed signs of a beating, the one piece of the puzzle that matched the others. He was anxious for the lab results. They desperately needed a clue.

Next, Glen went to the man and his dog seated in the back of one of the cruisers. He was quite shaken by the discovery he had made earlier that morning. The man repeated his story to Glen. There really was not much to it. The other neighbors confirmed that he did live in the neighborhood and walking his dog down this street was a daily occurrence. After taking down his statement and information on how to reach him, he was free to go.

Glen followed the ambulance carrying the body to the Medical Examiner. Other members of the crime scene crew remained behind searching for that elusive piece of evidence, the one lead they were hoping for.

Shortly after he arrived, a brother of the victim showed up to identify her body. Her name was Sharon Fulton. She was visiting from Oregon. When her brother awoke this morning, he discovered she was not there. She was staying in his guestroom on the ground level of his house. The screen had been cut, allowing the intruder to unlock the window and climb in.

As Glen listened to the story her brother told, it fit the M.O. of the previous rapes. The assailant would take women from their homes or vehicles. Since this girl had only been in Denver for two days, it meant that he did not spend much time searching for his victims. The attacks must be spur-of-the-moment, random choices.

From the time Sharon arrived, she was either with her brother or his wife. Last night she sat on their porch, alone, enjoying the crisp cold air after they had gone to bed. The assailant must have been driving around looking for a victim when he saw her. Chances are he parked his car and waited, watching the pattern in which the lights were turned on and off in the house, to learn in which room to find her.

He probably waited a fair amount of time until he was sure she was asleep before letting himself in. The one thing that puzzled Glen and the others was, the women never screamed. How was he able to gain entrance to their homes, overpower them then take them away

81

without screams? He had to be armed, forcing them into silence.

Glen was anxious to get back to his office. He wanted to look again at the map showing the hits by this guy. Up until now, locations looked rather scattered. Glen removed the red pins from the areas where the women had been abducted from their homes. There was no way to tell for sure about the ones taken from their cars. He replaced those pins with blue ones. He then removed the red pins from the abandoned cars, replacing those with yellow pins.

A pattern began to develop. His victims abducted from cars were chosen in Aurora. The victims he took from their homes were from Littleton. After his assault, the victims, dead or alive, were found in or around Lakewood. His car victims were taken by day, his house victims taken by night. It was not much, but it was a start.

"Hi Biscuit, any word from our missing Maggi?" asked Glen. He called Debbie over his lunch break. It would not be fair to call it a lunch hour. Not only did he frequently skip lunch, but also he rarely took the entire hour with so much work to do.

"No, I haven't heard from her. Is there a problem?"

"Our rapist hit again last night. I feel better when I know where you three are. Any word from Teddi?"

"No, I heard she's spending time with Peter in California, so I'm sure she's safe. Maggi promised to

82

check her voice mail at least once a day, if you want to leave a message for her."

"Why don't you call her and just ask her to check in. Better go, love ya." But before he could hang up, he added, "Hey, don't go anywhere without letting me know. Okay? At least until we catch this guy. And keep your car doors locked, and ..."

"Glen, chill. I'm okay. I won't do anything stupid. You don't have to remind me every day."

Teddi returned home to hundreds of emails for Maggi.

"Oh my God! I can't believe this." Letter after letter from people wanting Maggi to write their story into one of her books were bulging her email account. Hundreds of unhappy people, wishing someone would die.

Teddi started to read through them, but then she stopped, deciding it might be best to let Maggi do it. I wonder why Maggi hasn't called? That's not like her. She usually has an errand for me to run. No sooner had the thought popped into her mind than her phone rang. She checked her caller ID; it was from Maggi's personal cell phone.

"Hi, Maggi."

"Hi yourself. I hope I'm not interrupting you and Peter."

"No, I'm back home. Actually, I'm in your office going through emails. You should see ..."

83

"Why are you back home? Didn't Peter show up after all?"

"Oh, he showed up but he only made plans to stay the night. He didn't know I'd have extra time; he made prior commitments. So I stayed over a couple of extra days to relax and do some shopping. I just got back today. Where are you?"

"I'd rather not say. I'm hiding. It's kind of fun to be unreachable. If you need me for anything just leave voice mail. But spare me any work. Brad's trying to get me to do more shows, so I thought it best if you can honestly tell him you don't know where I am. If I don't answer my phone and he can't find me, he can't make me commit to something I don't want to do."

"Oh, Maggi, you're gonna make him really mad. I think you push him a little too far."

"Yeah, well, let Warren deal with him. That's what I pay an agent for. Speaking of Warren, he doesn't know where I'm at either. He probably thinks I'm with you. You'll probably be hearing from him, too."

"Gee thanks. I love listening to them when you piss them off."

Changing the subject, Maggi asked, "Is there any business that you think I should know about? I mean, something really important that can't wait."

"I thought you were hiding out to avoid all of this."

"I am, I am, but I'm still curious."

84

Teddi thought about telling her of the hundreds of emails she received then decided against it. Maybe she does need some time away from this mess for a while. It could wait until she returned.

"No, nothing special. Oh, when I went back to the hotel they had some messages for you that they forgot to give us when we left. I'm sure by now it's too late to answer any of them."

"You mean you haven't read them?"

"I started to after I tore the envelope open but Peter wouldn't let me. He said not on my vacation. I put them into my briefcase unread. Would you like me to get them?"

"Sure, why not?"

"Hang on a minute while I grab them." She set the phone down. She walked across the room to the chair where she had tossed her briefcase when she entered the room earlier. Maggi did not like to do any work out of her home if she could avoid it. She wanted to keep her personal life and her business life separate. That is why she always went away to write. She rented a nice office in Littleton not far from where Teddi lived. That is where they met to handle most of her work.

Teddi loved this little office. Since she would be the one spending most of her time there, Maggi allowed her to do the decorating and kindly paid for it. She chose to keep it quaint and feminine. Lots of lace and soft colors, not exactly Maggi's style, but it made Teddi happy.

85

"Okay, I've got it," said Teddi, as she emptied the contents onto Maggi's desk.

"Let's see. Here's a note from the studio thanking you for your appearance on the show. Here's a note from Glen and Debbie wishing you luck, another from Brad, same thing, one from Warren. There's one in a sealed envelope. It's not on the same message paper as the others from the hotel. Someone must have dropped this one off in person."

"Well, open it. Now you have my curiosity aroused. Do you recognize the handwriting?"

Teddi studied the handwriting then gasped.

Maggi heard the gasp, "What? Who's it from?"

"I'm not sure, Maggi, but it looks an awful lot like that Linda woman you helped. Remember how beautiful her handwriting was?"

"She probably just wanted to thank me for all I've done. She obviously keeps tabs on my personal appearances. Since these shows always broadcast which hotel they put their guests up in, it's not hard to find me."

Teddi opened the outer envelope. Maggi was right. It was a thank-you card.

"Would you like me to read it to you?"

"Sure."

Dear Miss Morgan,

How can I ever begin to thank you for all that you have done for my girls and me? The house you have chosen to put us in temporarily is beautiful. The girls love the yard to play in. Your friend is very generous for allowing us to stay here until we can get a place of our own. Your friend, Debbie, was very kind.

So let me thank you for the house, the car, the clothes and the new job that I will be starting next week. Debbie made arrangements for someone to help us out. The girls started school today. They love it. The new clothes they have to wear make them feel so special.

Just when I thought I had all anyone could possibly ask for, you fulfilled your promise to me by killing Tony. I'm not sure how you did it exactly but my friend *from back home. I'm sorry, I know I promised not to make contact with anyone, but I felt she needed to know since we were so close. Anyway, she called me with the news. I wanted to thank you in person but they told me you'd already left the hotel. Since I didn't have your address they said they would send my note with other messages they had for you. I stopped in their gift shop to find the perfect card to send you. I hope you like it.*

Thanks again for everything. May Tony rot in hell,

Linda

"What in the hell?" said Maggi.

"Maggi, what does she mean?"

"Sounds like someone did the jerk in and she's giving me credit for it."

"Doesn't that give you the creeps?"

"No, actually it makes me feel pretty good. Now I know he can't find her again. She's really safe to start a new life. Besides, I worried that if he found out what I'd done, he'd be looking for me."

"I guess you could look at it that way but it still gives me the creeps. Maybe you should tell Glen."

"Absolutely not! If he finds out I was that close to a real murder, he'd freak. The guy's dead, so let's just let it be."

"Okay, if you say so."

"Hey, I'm coming home. This was such good news I feel like I can face the world again. Do me another favor though. Do an Internet search and try to find out the details surrounding this guy's death. Could make for an interesting read. See ya tomorrow."

Teddi hung up the phone. She shuddered as she wrapped her arms around her body, rubbing her hands up and down her arms as if she were cold. She looked around the room nervously, as if she expected someone to reach out and grab her. She felt this way sometimes when she would read Maggi's unedited manuscripts. She learned to never read them at bedtime, unless she wanted to stay up all night.

Teddi followed Maggi's instructions and searched for the story of Tony's demise. The story she found was vague. It was in yesterday's paper.

Local Factory Worker Found Dead

Police were at the home of factory worker, Tony Harmon, who was found dead by co-worker, Lyle Brown, when he failed to show up

89

for work. According to Brown, Harmon had never
called in sick or missed a day in the eight
years they worked together. When officers
arrived on the scene they found the body of
Harmon in his bathtub. An electric hairdryer
was found in the water with him. Authorities on
the scene presumed Harmon died from
electrocuting himself attempting to dry his
hair while in the bathtub.

Chapter 5

Teddi paced around the office, surprised at how easily Maggi took the murder of Tony Harmon in stride. With Linda gone, who had the motive or the means to kill this guy? Murder in Maggi's books and real life murders are entirely different. Her adrenaline was rushing.

It was obvious to her that she was not going to get any work done today. She glanced at the computer email screen. The awareness that hundreds of people were plotting deaths, with their stories only a keystroke away, added to Teddi's agitated state. A chill ran down her spine, causing her to shudder. She left the office to drive home. She looked over her shoulder expecting to see a mysterious figure dressed in black following her, watching her every move.

Inside of her cozy home, Teddi locked all of the doors and windows. She closed the drapes, even though it was mid-afternoon. Now she wished she had dogs like Maggi, or better yet, she wished Peter were there to protect her. Living alone never bothered her until she took the position of Maggi Morgan's personal assistant. Murder has a way of unnerving a person.

She took a deep breath to gather her wits. She went into the kitchen to fix a nice hot cup of cocoa. Chocolate will help calm my nerves, she thought. She put a Brandenn Bremmer CD on the stereo. Soon the soothing sounds of Brandenn's piano filled the house. She lit a fire in the fireplace then curled up on the sofa sipping her chocolate, as a feeling of calm crept slowly throughout her body.

Her mood lightened. She looked around at the tightly closed drapes. She chuckled to herself. How silly she felt now. Why would she be in any danger? Tony, a real loser from New York, was killed in his home. How could that possibly affect her, tucked away in her home in Littleton?

The chocolate tasted good. She preferred making her own from cocoa rather than the pre-packaged type. Today she added a bit of hazelnut syrup to it, instead of vanilla. After taking one more sip she went to her bedroom to slip into her pajamas. As long as she was going to curl up in front of the fireplace to relax, comfort should be an issue.

Back in his office, Glen discussed his findings with the other detectives on the rapist case. The new clues showed he was a creature of habit. How did it begin? What would put him in Aurora by day and Littleton by night? If he were attacking the women by day in their homes, one would think he was a repairman or salesman of some type. Instead, all of his home attacks took place at night with forced entry, usually through a window. The victims did not know him. So what would cause them to allow him to approach their car and go with him?

Those were the questions being tossed around by Glen and Bill.

"Do you think he's a mechanic or something?" asked Bill.

"No, I feel that he's approaching them away from places where people would recognize him," answered Glen.

"You know, we're both pussyfooting around the possibility this guy is a cop gone bad. If he's using a badge or uniform, he can easily get these women to go with him."

Glen bit his lower lip. He was such an honest cop that the thought of one of his own doing something like this tied his stomach into knots.

"Maybe he's not a cop, but looks like a cop. Maybe he pulls the cars over or approaches a parked car when the woman is just returning to it. If she looked up and saw the uniform, she wouldn't be frightened or on guard, like she would if he looked like a stranger."

"We know the women, to the best of our knowledge, aren't connected. The families don't seem to know any of the other victims. All of the car women were alone. Most were out running errands. The same story with the house women, no connection," Bill pointed out.

"I guess we should go talk to these women ourselves. The police reports say that they don't want to talk about him. Seems the last thing they remember before passing out was he threatened to return if they worked with the police. Had these women not been tied and gagged, we probably would never have found out about the rapes at all."

Glen jotted down their addresses and phone numbers in the notebook that he always carried with him. The two men left to further their knowledge of the rapist.

One by one, Glen and Bill visited the women. The story was the same with each of them. They were all reluctant to discuss even the slightest detail with the detectives until they realized they were not the only victim. Glen convinced them there was no way this guy would find out they spoke to the police. He would not know which of his victims talked and there is no way he would take the chance of returning to all of them. The women and their families would be more on guard now, so he could not use the element of surprise a second time.

By the end of the day, they had interviewed seven women and the families of the three dead victims. His violence towards these women was escalating. With each rape, the beatings became more severe and with the last one, it appeared he murdered her more quickly. Maybe he decided a dead victim could cause him no harm.

The facts were falling into place.

Glen was correct with the home attacks being at night in Littleton. The day attacks were from cars in Aurora. Not one of the women could give a description of their attacker. They all agreed it was just one man. He was tall and strong. He used a type of chloroform to drug them. The women were putting packages into their cars when the man came up from behind, putting a cloth soaked with chloroform over their nose and mouth. In seconds they were unconscious. The next thing they remembered was waking up in a strange place. All of the women were discovered outdoors in an area that had bushes or trees for cover. He would beat them and rape them while they were unconscious then tie them up and leave.

The women who were abducted from their homes had the same story. They were asleep when attacked. When they revived, most of them managed to squirm and wriggle their way out of the vegetation to an area where they could be discovered.

"Damn, this guy has some real hatred toward women. He obviously enjoys the beatings as much as the rape itself. He's having some fun with us on this. He wants the women to be found rather quickly or else he'd take them off into a wooded area that is more secluded. There they could die more easily from exposure, as time would pass, without being found," Glen pointed out.

Armed with their new information, the two detectives returned to their office to attempt to piece together more of the puzzle.

Teddi was up bright and early the next morning. She listened for sounds most of the night while she tried to sleep. It reminded her of the nights she used to read Maggi's manuscripts in bed. Thinking about real life murders had the same effect on her sleep.

She was planning a big breakfast of eggs, waffles and juice. She dressed in her favorite sweatshirt with kittens on it and a pair of blue jeans that had been worn to the soft threadbare stage. She thought maybe after breakfast she would work in her yard.

Two bites into her breakfast the phone rang.

"Morning, Teddi, are you ready to go to work?"

"Morning, Maggi. I guess this means you and the dogs made it home safe and sound last night."

"Actually, we weren't that far away. We only made it to Fort Collins. Did you find anything more about that creep's death from the Internet?"

"Yeah, the story was there. Do you want me to read it to you now or can I finish my breakfast first?"

"Sorry. Go ahead and eat. I'll meet you at the office in an hour or so. See ya then."

Teddi always hated the way Maggi would end a conversation by just hanging up the phone without saying good-bye. Sometimes Teddi would be mid-sentence when she would hear the dial tone.

Teddi returned to her breakfast. The scrambled eggs were cold. She sampled the waffles and they were cold as well. She scraped her plate angrily into the garbage disposal. She gulped her juice while loading the dishwasher. She was reminded that her choice of clothes for the day would not meet with Maggi's approval as she wiped her hands on her jeans to dry them. She parted the yellow ruffled curtains over her kitchen window and sighed as she gazed out over her backyard. When would she learn not to make plans of her own unless Maggi was off writing? For someone as independent and strong as Maggi, she sure seemed to need Teddi for every little task.

Teddi arrived at the office one hour after their phone call. She started the coffee and opened the blinds. Two hours later, Maggi arrived.

"Show me what you found about Linda's husband," said Maggi, as she burst into the office without an apology for her tardiness.

Teddi looked up from her desk. The silence of the office was broken.

"It's on your desk. I printed it out."

"Thanks."

Maggi went into her office and closed the door. She picked up the printed article and read it.

"Yes! Rot in hell, Tony, this one's for Linda."

"What? Did you say something?" came the voice from the outer office.

"No. Sorry. I'm just talking to myself."

Maggi joined Teddi.

"Things appear pretty quiet here. Are you ready to help with some editing on the new book?"

"I'm ready when you are, but I think there's some business you should attend to before we get started."

"Sure. What?"

Teddi turned her computer screen toward Maggi. She opened the email screen. Now there were three hundred and twenty five emails from her fans.

"Fan mail, so? I thought you handled that for me. Is there something different about these?

"Read the first one."

Dear Ms. Morgan,

I'm the mother of two beautiful kids. My husband is a good provider financially but that's where it ends. He's a lousy husband and father. He spends all of his spare time at the golf course. He's a golf instructor, that's how I met him. I had an affair with him then left my first husband for him when I became pregnant with his child. He didn't want to marry me but I threatened to turn him in at the country club where he worked. I was foolish to think he would ever stop his womanizing ways.

He keeps a tight rein on the kids and me. To those on the outside he appears to be Mr. Perfect. I'm his slave. His meals must be on the table on time I must be dressed to the nines when he shows up. The kids must be fed and prepared for bed before he gets home. If his meals are not warm enough, or my hair does not meet his approval, he beats me.

I'm not allowed out of the house except to shop for groceries. He fears someone will see the bruises. Life has been this way for the past ten years. Now he brings his girlfriends home and I must stay in the guest room while he has sex with them in our room.

I know I should leave him, but I'm afraid to. I have nowhere to go. He made sure I have no friends and of course, I have no money. All of the accounts are in his name he gives me an allowance. The only document with my name on it is his life insurance policy.

So when you offered to kill the problem people in our lives, I thought if I was one of the first people to email, you might put me at the top of your list.

Please consider helping me.

It should be easy for you because I live in Denver. I remember reading somewhere that you have a home in Denver.

He comes home every morning about eleven to shower and have lunch before he returns to the club.

All of the neighbors work and we live on a cul-de-sac. A quick drive-by shooting and you could be gone before anyone notices a thing.

Sincerely,

Elizabeth Malone

99

"This is a joke. Right?" asked Maggi.

"I wish it were. There's more."

"What do you mean, there's more?"

"There are hundreds of emails for you and I'm guessing it's all more of the same."

"That's insane. How can so many people misunderstand my comments? There can't be that many stupid people in the world."

"Desperate people do stupid things."

"Oh come on. They really can't be serious. Are they just having some fun with me? How many of them have you read?"

"Just the first few. What are you going to do about it?"

"Nothing. I'm going to do nothing. I'm just going to ignore them."

"Okay, if that's what you want, but I don't think that's gonna stop them. Maybe we should call Glen."

"No! I mean, let's not bother Glen with this. In time I think it will just stop on its own."

"What do you want to do about Warren and Brad?"

"The same thing. Nothing. Wait, what do you mean?"

"Warren called yesterday to find out if we were getting any feedback on the mail-order murders."

"You didn't tell him anything, did you?"

"You never told me not to. I told him the emails were coming in by the hundreds. He wanted me to move them to a special folder then send them all to him and Brad as they arrived."

Maggi dropped into her chair and tossed her head back, looking up at the ceiling as if the answer to her problem would be written there.

"I'm sorry, Maggi, but we never discussed it. You never told me to keep this quiet. After all, everyone knew you'd get responses. Even Oprah told you to expect it."

"I know, I know. I'm not blaming you. I'm just trying to figure out how to make it all stop."

"As long as you're stressed out about this, let me add another layer. Warren and Brad are flying in this afternoon to visit with you about the publicity angles."

"When did all of this come about?"

"They called this morning while I was here waiting for you to arrive. I couldn't very well stop them. I can't tell those guys what to do."

Maggi stood up to pace.

"You don't think anything will go wrong, do you? You don't think I'm in any danger?"

"Remember what Glen said. He thinks these are desperate people that aren't reasoning straight, that could go nutso and come after you if you don't help them."

"That's what I mean. You don't think that could really happen, do you?"

"Maggi, I wish I could tell you that there's nothing to worry about, but Glen does know more about people like this than we do. I'd be worrying if I were you."

101

The phone ringing interrupted their conversation. Teddi answered the phone, while Maggi sat at the computer scrolling through the messages.

"Brad and Warren are on their way over. They just wanted to be sure you were here."

"Great, just who I wanted to see," said Maggi, sarcastically.

"Do you still want to work on some editing before they get here?"

"No, suddenly I'm not in the mood to work."

"Do you want to read through more of the messages?"

"No, I want to make them go away." Maggi highlighted them and hit delete before Teddi could stop her.

"Why did you do that? You know that's not gonna help. Besides, I have them saved in the Outbox to Brad and Warren. Please, don't make more work for me on this one. Don't delete any more of them. I'm having enough trouble sorting them from your normal emails and saving them, then sending them on. It a real pain."

"Sorry. I sure hope Warren or Brad can come up with a good solution."

"Why don't you stay here and wait for them and I'll run out for sandwiches. Knowing those guys, they'll be starved when they get here."

Teddi went to Schlotzski's Deli around the corner from the office. She knew the favorites of the guys. They were just getting out of their car when she returned to the office, "Go on in. Maggi's inside."

Brad held the door open for Teddi, while Warren helped lighten her load by taking one of the bags.

It was obvious Maggi was stressed. Domestically, she began preparing her desk for the lunch. She even refrained from tossing insults at the guys.

"If I didn't know better, I'd say maybe she's glad to see us, Brad. What do you think?"

"I know, Warren, I think she's damn glad to see us."

The teasing did not improve the mood Maggi was in. If anything, it only irritated her more.

Teddi passed out the sandwiches. Everyone knew it was best to let Maggi be until she was ready to speak. They ate in silence.

They were right; soon Maggi broke that silence.

"I'm assuming you guys have a plan of action that's been cleared by the big guys in New York?"

"Well, not exactly. They're pretty excited though, with the feedback you've been getting. They love the stories from the messed up people wanting you to off someone. They're quite entertaining. Did you read the one from ...?"

"I've only read the first one and I fail to see the humor in it. I think it's tragic. Now what are your plans to stop it before it goes any further?"

103

"Here's the word from the top. They want you to write a new book, or should I say, series of books. They want you to go with the media idea and call them the *Mail-Order Murders* series," said Brad.

"No way! You've got to be kidding!"

"Maggi, wait. Just hear him out," suggested Warren.

Maggi glared at him.

"Okay, I'm all ears," she responded, with disgust.

"They thought you could use some of the ideas from people that wrote to you, just like you suggested on Oprah's show. Remember, you started all of this. We could follow up with lots of ads and publicity about how you were inspired by your readers to create the series. Although you couldn't perform the murders in real life, you could on paper. We wouldn't give the last names or addresses of the characters, just their stories. We'd encourage the readers to buy all of the books to see if you used their story in one of your scenes."

"Do you promise to push the fact that it's all in fun and that there will be no real murders?"

"What? Why would you think there would be real murders? That's absurd. Of course this would be all in fun. You don't really think these people are serious, do you?"

"Yes, as a matter of fact, I do."

Warren said, "Maggi, Maggi, Maggi, get a grip. This is all in fun. No one is serious about this."

He put his arm around her shoulders, as if that would somehow comfort her.

Teddi looked up at Maggi from the chair where she was sitting. Maggi's eyes met Teddi's. They were both thinking of Linda Harmon and her dead husband, Tony. Someone already took this seriously. Even though the scumbag actually killed himself, Linda would never believe Maggi was not involved.

"Just exactly how many books are we talking about here?" asked Maggi.

"We figured we could ride this wave for four, maybe five books in a series, before it starts to fade. What do ya think?"

"Am I going to have to sign a contract for four or five books?"

"Yep," answered Warren. "Really Maggi, it's a good thing. Think how much easier they'll be to write with the plots already planned out for you by your fans. This will be a real kick in the pants for sales."

"I'm already getting hundreds of emails. Does this mean I have to read every damn one and pick out the ones I want to write about?"

"You've got Teddi here to help you," Brad pointed out.

"Teddi has enough work to do without taking on this project."

Teddi was relieved Maggi came to her defense. She kept eating while she watched the discussion. Her eyes followed the conversation back and forth as if she were watching a tennis match. She was hoping as long as she kept her mouth full of food, she would not have to participate.

"Tell you what," suggested Brad. "Why don't we stop the emails, say in about two weeks. We'll just change your email address or add an automated response to it saying that we are no longer taking requests. In the mean time, we'll put together that small staff we spoke about earlier to help sort. We could send out answers reminding people these are just for stories; no one will actually be harmed."

"Okay, two weeks. Then it has to stop."

Maggi glanced at Teddi. Teddi nodded in agreement.

"Where will this staff come from?" asked Teddi.

"We were hoping the two of you could put together a small staff here in your office. That way you can have your thumb on the entire operation. Also, we were hoping to keep this extremely confidential. We can't afford any leaks about which stories will make it into the books. We don't want any of the readers getting inside information, nor do we want someone from the inside contacting the people who wrote in to let them know their story is being used."

Maggi sat down at her desk. She leaned into her high-backed black leather chair. She was thinking.

"How many people do we need for this small staff? And who's going to pay for it?"

"We thought two or three people, besides you and Teddi. The publisher will pay their wages, handsomely I might add. They just need to be sure whoever you hire can be trusted to keep it confidential."

"Can the two weeks start from the day of my first email? Which was ..." Maggi turned to her computer to check the date "... three days ago."

Warren looked at Brad. Brad nodded.

"Sure, we can agree to that," said Warren.

"Okay, gentlemen. You have a deal. I have to work on emails that come in for eleven more days. You will take it easy on me with the tours and talk shows in exchange for me finding a suitable staff and producing four, not five, new books for the series."

Brad stood to shake hands with Maggi.

"Agreed."

"Now, get the hell out of my office. We have work to do."

Teddi escorted Brad and Warren to the door.

"Any idea who we should hire to work with us?" asked Maggi.

"I hope whoever it is, we can get along with them. This is not a large office."

"I wonder if Debbie would like to make some extra bucks for the Christmas holidays?"

"Hey, that's a great idea. Maybe I should ask Peter if he'd like to help out."

"No, I'd rather not have Peter in on all of this."

"Maggi, I thought after what he did to help you with Linda that you'd ease up on him."

"I have, Teddi, I have. But I would prefer to have an all girl staff here."

"Okay, let me make a few calls to some of my family and friends to see if anyone has any free time."

"Great, you do that. I'll call Debbie."

There was no answer on Debbie's home phone, so she tried her cell.

"Hello."

"Deb, it's Maggi. Where are you?"

"I'm grocery shopping. Why?"

"How close are you to my office?"

"Not far. Why?"

"Can you stop by here?"

"When?"

"As soon as possible."

"Is everything okay?"

"Oh yeah. We'll talk when you get here."

Teddi continued to make calls until Debbie arrived. No one wanted to take the position. They either had other commitments with their own jobs or just did not want to tie themselves down.

"Hi, Debbie, glad you agreed to this," said Teddi, as Debbie walked into the office.

"Agreed to what?"

Maggi stepped into the room. Teddi shot a glance at her.

"Agreed to what?" asked Debbie again.

"Teddi, get Debbie a cup of coffee."

"Debbie doesn't want coffee. Debbie wants to know what you two are planning that involves me."

"We need to pull together a small staff of people to answer emails and help with some publicity stuff for a couple of weeks. My publishers are going to foot the bill. Confidentiality is a big issue, so I thought of you because I knew we could trust you."

"You mean you want me to get up every morning and come in here to work with you two? Do you think I'm nuts?"

"Yes," answered both Maggi and Teddi, simultaneously.

Debbie had to laugh.

"You're right. Sounds like fun. Count me in. When do I start and what do I do?"

Maggi looked relieved, but not surprised.

"Before we can hire you, we need your promise of total secrecy, even from Glen."

"Why? Glen reads all of your books before they get published anyway. Or doesn't this have anything to do with your books?"

"Can't tell you until you promise," teased Maggi.

"Is he going to get angry at me when he finds out?"

109

"Maybe," said Maggi. "So you don't have to say yes if you're worried about causing problems with Glen."

"This is legal, isn't it?"

"Of course. Do you think my publishers would be paying for something illegal?"

"Okay, count me in. I'll deal with Glen later. Who else is on the staff?"

"We don't know yet," answered Teddi. "Do you know any retired or unemployed people we can count on?"

"Well ...," Debbie paused.

"Who? Do you have someone in mind?" asked Maggi.

"Well, how about Jean? She's retired. You obviously trust her or you wouldn't let her baby-sit your dogs. She lives right next door so she could ride into the office every day with you."

Teddi held her breath knowing that Maggi and Jean had a rather strange relationship.

Maggi looked back and forth from Teddi to Debbie. She bit her lower lip.

"I guess it's only for a couple of weeks or so. I think that might work. I'll talk to her tonight when I go home."

Maggi and Teddi spent the rest of the afternoon filling Debbie in on the details of the task ahead. Debbie was having second thoughts about getting involved because she knew how Glen felt about this publicity stunt. Maggi convinced her it would be a good idea to join them because if anything went wrong, she could break her confidence and bring Glen into the circle. So without dragging Glen into it from the start Maggi felt comfortable knowing he would be close by if and when they needed him.

That night Maggi spoke with Jean about the job. She quickly agreed to it. Maggi could not tell if she hastily agreed because she was lonely, needed the money more than Maggi knew, or if it just sounded like a fun thing to do.

The next morning the four ladies began the grueling task of reading, sorting and printing the heartbreaking emails.

Teddi sorted the new ones, organizing them by date. Debbie and Jean read through them, tossing out the really bizarre ones or redundant story lines. Then they would take their stacks into Maggi, who would read through them again, tossing out the ones she knew she had no desire to write about. This went on day by day for three and a half weeks. They sorted and read through over four thousand emails.

The final stack was narrowed down to one hundred and fifty. Brad kept his promise and stopped the flow of incoming emails. The girls then had to re-sort according to topic, such as cheating husband, abusive husband, tyrant bosses and so on. Maggi was so trusting of the girls that she allowed them to make copies of the final one hundred and fifty to take home in folders to work on, even though they seemed to have every story memorized. Debbie had to be extra careful not to let Glen find her folders.

Maggi went away to sort through, in her mind, how she wanted to write the series. Once again she told no one where she was going. She took her dogs and her personal cell phone.

Debbie heard Glen come in while she was working intently on the folders, trying to pick the most interesting and unique stories.

"Hi, Honey. I'm in here," she said, as she slipped the folders into her desk.

Glen joined her in the office.

"You're home early."

"Yeah, I needed a break."

Debbie slid into his arms for a hug and a kiss. He kissed her but his mind was not focused on her. She slipped out of his hold then went into the kitchen to fix him a drink. She could tell this was a bourbon time.

"So what happened?"

"Some poor guy got blown away today and so far, we've got nothing."

"Why? What makes this one so tough?"

"He's a nice guy, no enemies, great neighborhood, has a couple of kids and no witnesses."

"What happened?"

"He was a golf pro or instructor or something. He was walking up his driveway with his clubs on his back, heading into the house to have lunch with his wife. Someone blasted him."

"How can no one see or hear anything like that?"

"Turns out this happened in a new neighborhood on a cul-de-sac and all of the neighbors work. His wife was in the house fixing lunch and didn't hear or see a thing. We talked to everyone that knows him and they all had the same things to say about him. He was a great guy, great father and husband. They say his wife never complained about anything he did. She was really shaken up."

"Do you think this was a drive-by gang thing or something like that?" she asked, with a trembling voice.

"What's up with you?" asked Glen, picking up on the change in his wife.

"Nothing. It just reminds me how vulnerable you are out there."

Glen put his arms around her, pulling her close to him.

"Debbie, I told you I know how to take care of myself. Don't worry so much."

He held her while he continued to talk.

"This one was so strange."

"Strange how?"

Glen released his hold on Debbie. He walked to the kitchen counter to take a drink from his glass. He stared out across the room.

"Strange how?" she repeated.

Glen looked deeply into her eyes. He knew he could share his experience without fear of judgment.

"When I arrived at the scene, I glanced through the crowd at the spot on the driveway where the body lay. I saw an officer on his knee, studying the body and taking notes. Next to him stood a witness, I assumed, telling his story."

Glen paused to take another drink. He ran his fingers through his hair.

"I saw this man talking to the officer," he repeated. "He was bent slightly over, pointing to the body while he spoke. I was a little confused as to why the officer was not responding to him. At first, I thought he was taking his statement when I saw him writing. He never spoke back to the man, nor did he make eye contact with him. I thought if this guy has something important to say, I wanted to hear it. I kept my eye on the man to be sure he didn't leave before I got there. I cut through the crowd and slipped under the crime scene tape.

"Debbie, when I walked the last twenty feet to join the two of them, he was gone. I scanned the area to see where he went. I couldn't believe he slipped away without me seeing him. My eyes were glued to him, except for the moment when I bent down to slip under the tape.

"I was about to ask the officer where he went when I looked down at the body on the driveway." Glen stopped again to take another drink. This time he drained the glass.

"When I looked down at the body I realized the dead man was the same man that I watched standing next to the officer."

At first Debbie thought he might be teasing her. Then she could tell by the troubled look on his face that he was dead serious.

"What do you mean they were the same man?"

"Just what I said. The dead man and the man I saw visiting with the cop were the same man. There was no denying it. Debbie, I saw this dead man's ghost."

"Whoa, Glen. Are you sure?"

"Hell yes, I'm sure. I know what I saw."

"Did anyone else see him?"

"If they did, no one said anything."

"What do you suppose it means?"

"I'm not sure, but it freaked me out enough I took the rest of the afternoon off to sort through it. You know, since working with Jennifer Parker on that lost kid case, I have a greater respect for psychics and gut feelings. Something's up with this case."

"Maybe you should give Jennifer a call and discuss this with her."

"That's what I was planning to do."

He took his phone from his pocket and placed the call to Jennifer.

"Glen, good afternoon. It's nice to hear from you."

"Hello, Jennifer."

"What can I do for you, Glen?"

"I had a strange thing happen today and I just needed to talk to you about it."

There was a long pause on the other end of the phone.

"You had an experience today, didn't you?"

"Yes. I was at the scene of a shooting victim. I saw him standing over his own body."

"Glen, you are growing. The other side is opening up to you. Remember when you saw your friend Dave from the other side?"

"Yes."

"He was your friend; the connection was strong. Now that you've been able to see a total stranger shows your abilities are getting stronger. Congratulations, my friend."

"Why me? Why did this happen?"

"He had something to tell you, only you are not ready yet. You still need to be more open. What do you know about this case?"

"Not much yet."

"I can tell you that this case, this man's death, will touch you in a personal way. This is not just another homicide. You are to be drawn into this emotionally. Study this case well, for you will be more involved in this than most. If, by chance, you see him again, ask him if he has a message for you."

"What do you mean talk to him? What kind of message?"

"Glen, you will know what to do when the opportunity presents itself. Go with the instincts that you police officers possess. You will be just fine. I must go now, please feel free to call again if I can be of any assistance."

Glen hung up the phone, shaking his head.

"What'd she say?" asked Debbie.

"The next time I see this dead guy; I'm supposed to talk to him. Now I'm *really* confused."

Chapter 6

Early the next morning, Teddi was startled by a knock on the door. She fumbled with her robe on the way to answer it. She was unaccustomed to early morning visitors. Actually, she was unaccustomed to visitors at all. Working for Maggi consumed most of her life.

At the door she hesitated for a moment then pulled back the curtain on the side window that ran the length of the door. There was a man standing at her door; her heart raced. She thought of the rapist. He had his back to her; totally unaware she was studying him through the window. Suddenly, he pounded on the door with greater force, causing Teddi to jump back.

"Teddi, it's Peter. Are you up yet?"

Realizing she had not been breathing, she took a deep breath and quickly unlocked the door. When she opened it, she surprised Peter by leaping into his arms knocking him off balance. With his large frame, he returned to his center of balance before he and Teddi tumbled to the ground.

"Are you that excited to see me or are we playing football?"

Teddi blushed a bright red.

"Sorry. I was just relieved and excited to see it was you. Glen has all of us a little goosey with warnings about the rapist in the area."

"What rapist?"

"Come on in and I'll tell you about him over breakfast."

"Sounds good to me."

As Teddi led the way into the kitchen, she turned to Peter and asked, "What are you doing here? I didn't know you were coming to Denver."

"I thought I'd come help you finish those silly emails you've been reading to me so we can go out and have some fun. I've got a few free days, and you said Maggi was doing one of her disappearing acts again. I thought we could double-team them. She'll never have to know you took time off."

"Okay, but make sure she never finds out that you've been helping me. She'd kill me."

Peter crossed his heart and gave her the Boy Scout hand sign to confirm it.

At the Karst house, Debbie was trying to remain calm until Glen left for work. Sometimes she thought it difficult to be married to a detective. Surprises were hard to pull off; as were keeping secrets. After what seemed like an eternity, Glen put on his holster, slipped the chain with his badge over his head and was ready to leave. Debbie tried to coax him to stay a little longer. She knew he would not, but she thought it might help cover her uneasiness if she did not make it look as if she were anxious for him to leave.

She stepped out onto the sidewalk to wave good-bye. She reached down to pick dead leaves from her flowers along the house, once again trying to make it look as if she did not have a worry in the world. Glen blew her a kiss and waved good-bye. She watched his pickup until it was out of sight.

She rushed inside to call Maggi.

Damn, she thought. Maggi is not answering her phone. She left a message.

"Maggi, when you get this message, call me immediately. It's important."

Next, she tried Teddi. When Teddi's phone rang, Peter stopped her from answering.

"Sit down and enjoy your breakfast. I'm sure it can wait that long."

Debbie paced around the kitchen, wringing her hands. She leaned up against the counter. Her leg was violently shaking from frustration. Jean, I could call Jean, she thought. No, there's nothing she can do.

She ran into the office and pulled open the drawer where the folders were hidden. She started to put them on the top of the desk but she was too nervous; her hands were trembling. She dropped the folders onto the floor, spilling the contents of most of them. She dropped to her knees to begin straightening the papers as though they were a deck of cards.

Once the sheets were arranged in nice, neat piles, she sat on the floor to begin sorting through them. She recalled the story of the woman married to the golf instructor being the first one Maggi gave her to read. It was the first one they all discussed as a group. Although she knew most of the stories, that one was the most vivid in her mind.

"Where is it? Where is it?" she whispered.

She sorted the papers as quickly as her eyes could scan them.

"Here it is."

With her back leaning against the wall, she re-read the email request.

The facts were just as she remembered. Glancing across the room at the clock, she wondered what time the newspaper was delivered. Before today she never gave it any thought. Standing up, she dropped the email to the floor as she rushed to the front door in search of a paper. There was none. She glanced next door, no paper there either; it must be too early, she thought.

With her arms wrapped around her torso, trying to keep warm, she walked to the end of the sidewalk for a better view. There was no sign of the paper carrier approaching. She jogged back into the house to her room, where she changed into warmer clothes.

She tried calling Maggi again, but still no answer. She double-checked her messages to be sure she had not missed the call while she was outdoors.

Returning to her desk, she sat at the computer. She thought about playing solitaire to keep busy while she waited for either Maggi or Teddi to contact her. Her fingers drummed the keys lightly without adequate pressure to cause a key to function.

Her eyes drifted from the stack of papers to the monitor.

"Oh, come on Debbie," she mumbled. "Get a grip. Check the Denver Post online for the story."

Quickly her fingers typed the URL for the Denver Post. She scanned the news. There it was.

"**Denver Man Victim of Drive-By Shooting**"

Debbie's eyes searched the article. Finally, the name and address of the victim appeared. Slowly, she sat back in her chair. She could not believe what she had just read. It was he.

Too twitchy to sit still, she left her office to brush her hair and teeth. She managed to apply her makeup without being aware she was doing it. The phone finally rang. She dropped her lipstick into the sink as she ran for the phone.

"Hello."

"Good morning. As a valued Visa customer, we would like to take this opportunity to offer..."

"Not today," Debbie slammed the phone down. Generally she was a little more kind to the phone solicitors, knowing it was a tough job, but today she had no patience.

With phone in hand, she decided to call Glen to tell him what she knew. The promises she made to Maggi would have to be broken. This was serious stuff now. Her thoughts drifted to Maggi. She wondered how upset she was going to be.

Her question was about to be answered. Her phone rang before she had a chance to dial Glen.

"Debbie, what's the big emergency?"

"Maggi, where in the hell are you?"

"My little secret, remember?"

"Don't play games with me, Maggi. We've got a problem, or at least you have."

"Why? What problem?"

"Have you read this morning's paper?"

"No. Why? Am I in it? Did Brad do something stupid about this mail-order murder stuff again?"

"Maggi, listen to me. Remember the very first email you showed me about the abusive golfer? The one where the wife wanted him killed by a drive-by shooting?"

"Yeah. So? Is that one of the stories you'd like me to work with? Is that what was so important?"

"Maggi, shut up and listen."

Maggi could tell Debbie was really upset; losing her temper was so out of character.

When Debbie heard silence on the line, she began again.

"Yesterday when Glen came home, he was upset about a shooting case with no witnesses. As he told the story, I thought it reminded me of the first email we talked about. It made me really nervous hiding it from him. He picked up on my nerves, so I lied to him. I never lie to him. I hated doing it."

"Debbie, dear, I'm sure Glen has worked on dozens of shootings. What's got you so upset about this one?"

Debbie took the phone into her office. She picked up the email.

"Just listen to the email."

She read it to Maggi.

"Okay, now listen to the story from this morning's Denver Post."

"Oh shit. Not again."

Debbie, surprised, said, "What do you mean, not again?"

"Debbie, double-check that address and name, will ya?"

"Don't you think I've already done that? It's a match. Now back up and tell me what you meant by not again?"

"Remember the note I got from Linda asking me to kill her husband, Tony?"

"Yeah, but this one's different; someone actually died."

"That's what I'm trying to tell you. Her husband is dead."

"Dead? Do you know what happened?"

"Teddi found the story on the Internet, seems the jerk tried drying his hair in the bathtub and electrocuted himself."

"That's an entirely different story. That was an accident. This is a homicide. A homicide that we were, or *you* were, asked to commit."

"I feel like they are connected. The fact that I was asked to kill both of those men and now they're both dead makes me look guilty."

"I see what you mean. Maybe Glen will be able to make some sense out of this."

"Debbie, you promised to leave him out of this."

"I promised not to tell him so you wouldn't get into trouble with him because of all of the emails you're getting. I promised not to tell him you were actually going to use them for your books. This is different, Maggi. We know who killed this guy; we have to tell Glen."

"So tell me Debbie, who killed this guy?"

"I guess his wife did."

"Did Glen tell you that?"

"No."

"How about if you don't tell him this minute and give me a chance to drive over to the office and meet with you and Teddi?"

"Teddi's not at the office. I tried her there."

"She's probably still working at home. I'll meet you there in an hour."

125

"Maggi, where are you? I thought you were off at your lodge writing notes."

"No, I found a nice little hide-a-way that's closer, but I don't want to tell you or anyone else where it's at."

Debbie looked at her watch. "Okay, I'll meet you in one hour, but I'm still gonna tell Glen today."

Debbie busied herself tidying up her office. She set the stack of folders on top of her desk. No sense in hiding these any more, she thought. An overwhelming sense of relief flowed through her body, knowing she no longer had to hide them.

She knew it would only take her fifteen minutes to get to Teddi's house. She also knew that Maggi was always late. Hunger pangs reminded her that she had not eaten breakfast. She poured a bowl of cereal and a glass of juice. After her small breakfast was completed, it was time to meet Maggi.

It looked as though Teddi was having a party when Debbie arrived. Two cars were parked in the driveway. The first one was a rental car and the second car contained Maggi. She had just arrived. She saw Debbie drive up; she waited before going to the door.

"Looks like Teddi has a guest," said Maggi.

"Maybe this isn't a good time to discuss this problem. Should we just go to your office?" suggested Debbie.

"We'll let Teddi decide," Maggi insisted.

Debbie shrugged her shoulders then followed Maggi to the door.

Maggi rang the bell and the two of them waited for Teddi to answer.

"Maggi? Debbie? What're you guys doing here?"

Teddi looked nervous about their appearance at her door. Before she could invite them in, Maggi charged into the dining room, where she found Peter sorting through her confidential emails.

"Busted," laughed Peter.

Maggi and Teddi did not agree with his sense of humor. Debbie wanted to be anywhere but there at the moment.

Maggi turned on Teddi.

"Teddi, what's going on?"

"Peter stopped by to take me out, but I had all of this work to do. He offered to help and I really didn't see any harm since they were going to come out in the books and publicity eventually," explained Teddi, breathlessly.

Maggi turned to Peter, wondering what he was really up to.

"Find anything interesting?" she asked, sarcastically.

"I found out there are lots of pitiful people in this world, living pitiful lives, and I'm glad I'm not one of them."

"I'm sorry, Peter, but I need Teddi to work for a few hours."

"Maggi, can't we just work here?" begged Teddi.

She was afraid if Peter left, he would change his mind about going out later.

Maggi knew this meant a lot to Teddi. She looked at Peter.

"Tell ya what. Why don't you ladies work in here? I'll just go make myself comfortable in the living room and read the paper."

He stood to leave the room.

Maggi felt all eyes upon her. She did not want to appear the villain in Teddi's eyes. Then she saw the pleading eyes of Debbie, not wanting to discuss this in Peter's presence.

"Let's work in the kitchen. Then our voices won't disturb Peter while he's trying to read," she compromised.

Teddi and Debbie gathered the folders to move to the kitchen. Debbie knew they would not need them, but Teddi believed they were going to work on them.

"Say, where's Jean? Isn't she in on this?" asked Teddi.

"No, we won't be needing her today," explained Maggi.

Teddi dropped the folders onto the table then removed coffee mugs from the cabinet. As she poured the coffee, she noticed Debbie and Maggi making eye contact with each other.

"Is something wrong?"

Maggi went to the kitchen door to close it.

Debbie said, "Teddi, you'd better sit down. We have, I mean, Maggi's got a problem."

Teddi was about to make a joke out of that comment when she realized by the concerned looks on their faces this was not the time. She set a cup in front of each woman, then a napkin, a plate of cookies, and fresh fruit for Debbie since she does not like sweets. The whole time she kept trying to read their mood. She waited patiently for one of them to begin. She could feel the tension mounting inside, anticipating bad news.

Teddi took her place at the table and stared at Maggi to enforce her desire for answers.

"Debbie called me this morning. Seems there was a drive-by shooting yesterday. Glen told her all about it when he came home from work," started Maggi.

"Gee, is it someone we know?" asked Teddi, now even more concerned.

"In a roundabout way," said Maggi. "The man that was shot was married to a woman that sent us an email to kill him."

Teddi chuckled, "Man, you two almost had me believing that. Don't you have anything better to do than pull practical jokes on me? Wow, and I thought it was something serious." She took a sip of her coffee.

"Why am I the only one laughing here?" she asked.

"Maggi's serious, Teddi. The story was in this morning's paper. When Glen told me about it yesterday, it was hard not to tell him about the emails. I had a rough

129

night waiting for the paper to see, if by chance, it was the same guy."

"You're telling me it *was* the same guy?" asked Teddi.

"That's what we're trying to tell you," said Debbie. "Someone blew this guy away yesterday around eleven while he was walking up the driveway of his home for lunch. Just like the email request. The name and address matched."

"Oh man. What did Glen say when you told him?"

"I haven't exactly told him yet. Maggi wanted me to wait until we all talked about it. But I'm telling him tonight when he comes home, no matter what."

"I, for one, don't want to be there. When you tell him, he's gonna blow."

"Thanks for those words of encouragement," moaned Debbie.

"So who did him in? His wife?"

"That's my guess," agreed Debbie.

"I'm not too sure about that," said Maggi. "Why, after all of this time, would she finally decide to kill him? She lived with him and his abusive ways for ten years. The coincidence is too great. Plus, if the police learned about the email she sent me, she'd look guilty."

"Maybe it's a husband from another woman he's giving golf lessons to, with freebies on the side," suggested Teddi.

"That's probably it," agreed Debbie, hoping there was no connection.

"Maggi, did you tell Debbie about Tony?" asked Teddi.

"Yeah, I told her. She doesn't see the connection. She thinks his death has nothing to do with this one."

"Hey, ladies, check this out," said Peter, as he burst into the kitchen.

All eyes were upon him as he set the newspaper down on the table, exposing the same headline Debbie read online a few hours earlier.

"What is it?" asked Teddi, trying to appear surprised and curious.

"Doesn't this sound like one of the stories from your email murders?" he asked.

Maggi glanced at the story.

"Oh, I don't know, it's just a drive-by. Happens all the time. Now we really do need to get back to work," complained Maggi.

"No. Wait. I remember this one because the woman said she was from Denver." He grabbed the folders before Debbie could stop him. He looked through the ones marked "abusive husbands". The girls looked at each other nervously.

"Here it is. I knew I was right." He read through the email. "That poor dead son of a bitch is the same guy from the email. The same address, the same time of day.

131

Okay, which one of you ladies offed this guy?" he said, jokingly.

His remark brought no laughter.

He looked up from his seat at the table with the email in his hand. The smile on his face soon melted away when he saw the looks on the girls' faces.

"I was just kidding. It's one hell of a funny coincidence, wouldn't you say?"

Still no response.

"It is a coincidence, isn't it?"

Teddi walked over to Peter. She massaged his neck and said, "That's what we're hoping."

"What else could it be?"

He reached up and took Teddi's hands from his neck.

"Surely you're not telling me one of you girls is a murderer now, are you?"

Maggi was quickly becoming annoyed with his teasing sense of humor.

"Peter, we really need to discuss this, if you don't mind," she said, hoping he would leave.

"Maggi, since Peter knows this much, another head thinking this through can't hurt," said Teddi.

Debbie nodded her head in agreement.

"Fine. He can stay," huffed Maggi, not appreciating being out numbered.

Peter said, "Let's lay the facts on the table. Maggi gets an email asking her to stop by and shoot this guy on his way up to the house at eleven o'clock. She suggested a drive-by shooting. So then ..." he paused to look at the email again. "So then, about a month later, a drive-by shooting kills this guy. I'd say it's relatively safe to assume it's not any of you. So who did it, and why?"

"That's what we're trying to figure out," said Debbie.

Peter turned to her. "Does Glen have any suspects or clues or anything?"

"No," said Debbie, shaking her head.

"Does he suspect the wife?" he asked.

"He always suspects everyone involved. They just don't have much evidence yet. Besides, if she did it, they wouldn't have trouble proving it. She'd have gunpowder residue on her hands. Glen would have told me if they found any."

"Well, since Maggi didn't do it, do you think his wife hired it done?" he asked.

"Now that's a possibility. Maybe she waited a month and when Maggi didn't follow through, she decided to have someone else do it. Maybe Maggi wasn't the first or the last person she contacted," added Teddi.

"Maybe she has a boyfriend," said Maggi.

Debbie felt better talking this out. Actually, they all did.

Maggi had to admit, but only to herself, she was glad Peter was there with his cool head to add some rational thoughts.

"I agree with where this is going. She's probably been trying to kill her husband for some time and we just happened to know her plan. His death has nothing to do with us," sighed Maggi.

"What do you want me to do about Glen?" asked Debbie.

"Honey, go with your conscience. If you feel bad hiding this from him then feel free to go ahead and tell him. Like you said before, sooner or later he's gonna find out what I'm up to with my new contract. The sooner I face the music with him, the better. I'll let you be the judge," said Maggi.

The mood in the kitchen relaxed. The girls sipped their coffee while munching on Teddi's cookies.

Peter asked, "So you're really gonna do this mail-order murder thing? What a cool idea. Wish I'd thought of it."

"I'm not so sure it's a cool idea. I'm backed into a corner with it so I may as well make the best of it. My agent and publisher are having some fun with it. We all stand to make a little money, if I can pull it off. Teddi did tell you that you must be sworn to secrecy on this project, didn't she?"

"Yes, ma'am. But I'm not above a little hush money," he laughed.

"Sounds like extortion to me," said Maggi.

He walked behind Teddi and put his arms around her when she stood up to get more coffee.

"If my little Teddi says I have to keep this under cover, than I guess I'll keep it under cover. Speaking of under covers, you girls should know about your friend here."

Teddi threatened to pour hot coffee on him while the room burst into laughter. Teddi turned every shade of red.

"On that happy note, let's leave these two lovebirds alone," suggested Debbie, as she rose from the table.

Maggi was quick to follow her lead.

As they strolled down the driveway together, Debbie remarked, "Aren't they a cute couple? I'm so happy for her."

"Yeah, well, I wish I knew what he was up to. Teddi's not really his type."

"Oh, give it a break, Maggi. People change. Look at you. You're not the sweet innocent young thing that we met ten years ago. You've become a little on the crusty side," Debbie said teasingly.

Maggi smiled, "Maybe you're right."

Debbie stopped at the store on her way home. She decided if tonight was the night she was going to confess to Glen, she wanted to prepare all of his favorites to soften the blow.

When he arrived home for supper, he was feeling badly because he was an hour late. Debbie had the grill fired up and the aroma of a freshly baked cheesecake filled the kitchen. There was bread baking in the oven, along with potatoes.

"Sorry I'm late. Do I have time for a quick shower before supper?"

Debbie was glad he was late; it gave her an edge.

"Sure, if you hurry. I'll season the steaks while you shower then you can grill them when you get out."

The table was set. The dogs were out in the yard playing while she guarded the steaks from them. Her little dachshund, Madison, was fine but Glen's shepherds, Cheyenne and Shawnee, might decide the steaks would be better off in *their* stomachs.

Glen showered quickly then joined Debbie and the dogs in the backyard. The evening was too cold for Debbie to stay out much longer. Glen took over the steaks while she tended to the remainder of the meal in the kitchen.

After dinner they curled up on their sofa with a nice fire. Debbie had a glass of wine; Glen had his favorite Buffalo Trace bourbon.

"Anything new on the drive-by case?" she asked.

"Spent the day doing interviews with everyone that knows him and learning all I can about his life. No banner discoveries. It's frustrating as hell."

"Believe it or not, I might have a lead for you."

"You? How could you possibly have a lead for me on this case?"

It was the moment of truth. Debbie took a deep breath.

"You know I've been working for Maggi for the last month or so."

"Don't tell me she's playing real life detective for me," laughed Glen, as he sipped his bourbon.

"Not exactly. Remember how you were mad at her for getting involved with Linda and her sad story?"

"Oh yeah, I remember. I came down pretty hard on her. But when she helped her out I felt pretty good about it. Oh hell, what's she up to now and what's it got to do with my case?"

"Her publishers sort of put her on the spot. They liked the publicity she was getting about the mail-order murders. So they asked her to sign a contract for four books in the series and call them the *Mail-Order Murders*."

"Don't tell me she agreed?"

"Glen, she really doesn't have much say. Signing with a publisher is like selling your soul."

"Deb, I'm confused here. What's this got to do with my case?"

"I'm getting to that. Emails started coming in shortly after she went public on Oprah. Her publishers want her to take the best stories and use them in her books for the series."

"What kind of stories are we talking about?"

"You know, like the Linda story. People are writing to her with names and stories about people they want to see dead."

"Are they just wanting to see these people dead or are they actually asking Maggi to kill them?"

Glen sat up, lifting Debbie from her position with her head on his chest. He turned to face her eye to eye.

"Debra Lynne, tell me. What's she gotten herself into?"

"Her publishers wanted her to hire a confidential staff to read through the emails and help her choose the best ones to use in the books."

"Debbie, you're avoiding my question. Do these people believe Maggi will kill for them?"

"I'm not sure if they believe she will, but they're asking her to."

Glen set his drink on the table near the sofa as he stood up to pace angrily around the room. He punched the soft bottom side of his fist on the mantle of their fireplace.

"Damn her. Is this why you've been helping her out? Are you part of her confidential staff?"

Debbie went to Glen to calm him.

"Yes, sweetheart, but I knew it was only a matter of time before she told you, because you'll still have to edit her books."

"Why in the hell didn't you tell me?"

"Glen, don't swear at me."

"I'm sorry." He pulled Debbie's head back into his chest and stroked her hair. "I'm so sorry, baby. Tell me the rest. I'll control myself. I promise."

"Anyway, the publishers wanted her to hire a staff, so it's me, Teddi, Maggi and her neighbor, Jean, who takes care of the dogs. We narrowed it down from a few thousand to one hundred and fifty. The publishers stopped any new emails and want to play up the publicity as soon as she has the first book ready to go."

"Okay, but my case?"

"The first email she got was from this woman in Denver. She was married to a golf instructor. Turns out this guy was a real loser and she asked Maggi to kill him. She suggested she do it with a drive-by shooting. When you came home and told me about your case I thought it was quite a coincidence. I wanted to tell you then, but I had this confidentiality thing about the job. You should be able to understand that with your work."

"Deb, lots of drive-by shootings happen. They just do. What makes you think this is connected?"

"It's from the same address the woman gave Maggi in her email."

"No shit! Where's the damn email now?"

Glen was no longer Glen Karst, Debbie's husband, but Detective Karst on duty. His entire demeanor changed.

"I have a copy in my office."

He followed her. She handed it to him.

"I've got to take this in. We need to go with this lead. I'm so glad you were honest with me. Sorry I lost my temper."

139

He kissed her and held her close again.

"That is the end of the story, isn't it? There are no more dead bodies for me to worry about, are there?"

"Just one, but I don't think it's connected."

Glen felt the anger rising under his skin. He was angry with Maggi for putting his wife in such danger. He wanted to keep his promise to Debbie and control his temper. One thing Glen had was the ability to stay cool at work. This conversation was more on the job, than in his living room, he convinced himself.

As calmly as possible, he asked Debbie for more details.

She told him about Linda's husband, Tony. Much to Debbie's surprise, he did manage to keep his cool.

"I'm going into the office for an hour or so. I need to turn in this information. Thanks for telling me."

Glen climbed into his pickup. He drove down the street with his music booming inside. Around the corner, once he was out of sight of his house, he stopped then climbed out in the dark and stomped around, kicking his tires. He was livid.

At the station he turned what he had over to a couple of the other detectives that were on the case with him. They planned to work through it in the morning.

Before leaving, Glen went to his computer to look up Harmon's death. He called the precinct handling the case and spoke with the detective in charge.

"This is Detective Karst from Denver PD. I'm interested in what you might have on the death of a Tony Harmon. What I have here shows it listed as *cause of death under investigation*. Why would an accidental bathtub death be under investigation?"

Detective Morrison, on the other end of the phone, asked, "How are you connected to this case?"

"My wife knows his ex."

"I'll just fax over what I have, if that's okay with you. We're kinda busy here tonight. If you want to call back to discuss this, I'd be happy to at another time."

"Sure, not a problem. Thanks."

Glen waited for the fax.

He read the details:

> **White male, Tony Harmon dead in tub with hair dryer.**
> **Cause of death electrocution.**
> **Pronounced dead at scene.**
> **Possible homicide.**

"What the hell?" said Glen.

He went to check the fax machine for a second sheet.

> **Officers on scene found body in tub. During routine search of the apartment, officers found a book, *Intrusive Deaths* by Maggi Morgan, on his table in the kitchen opened to chapter twelve, page 235. Morgan describes in great detail**

the death of the victim when an intruder enters the bathroom, tossing a hair dryer plugged into a wall outlet into the tub with vic.

Glen slid down into his chair, running his fingers through his hair.

"Holy shit! Maggi, what have you gotten yourself into?"

Chapter 7

While Glen was at his office, Debbie called Maggi.

"Hello, Maggi. Just thought I'd let you know I told Glen and he's actually taking it pretty well. He was a little upset at first but he calmed down surprisingly fast."

"Glad he's taking it so well. Now maybe he won't let me have it the next time I see him."

"I think you're pretty lucky. I really thought he'd be more angry."

"Hang on a minute, someone's trying to beep in," said Maggi.

"Hello."

Glen's voice answered on the other end.

"Maggi, I'm at the office now. I'm heading home. I suggest you get your ass over there right away. I mean it Maggi; don't screw around with me. I'm pissed."

"Okay."

Maggi heard the click of the phone as Glen hung up on her. She clicked back to Debbie waiting on the line.

"I thought you said he was okay with this?"

Debbie answered surprised, "He is. Why?"

"That was him on the phone telling me to get my ass over to your house right away. He's on his way home."

"Uh oh, something's happened. He must've found out something when he went into the office. Guess I'll be seeing you soon. It's already late, why don't you plan to stay the night."

"No way am I planning to spend the night at your house as mad as Glen is. I'll leave the dogs here so I have an excuse to go home. See ya."

Debbie was watching television when she heard Glen pull up. She stayed seated, not wanting to admit she knew he was mad at Maggi. She thought it best if he did not think they were talking and doing things behind his back.

He headed straight to the kitchen and poured himself a drink.

Debbie called out, "Hi honey. There's a good movie on. Do ya wanna watch it with me?"

Glen walked to Debbie, reached down and gave her a kiss.

"I'm not in the mood; Maggi's coming over to talk."

"Did something happen at the office?"

"I don't want to talk about it 'til she gets here."

Glen looked at his watch.

Debbie pretended to be interested in the movie to give Glen a chance to gather his wits and calm down.

Finally, Maggi rang their bell.

Debbie leaped up ahead of Glen to let her in.

144

Maggi searched her face for a clue.

Debbie bit her lip and shrugged her shoulders in an attempt to warn Maggi he was still mad but she did not know why.

Maggi hung up her coat then walked to the kitchen in the same manner Glen had done when he arrived home. She opened the refrigerator and removed a bottle of white wine.

Debbie handed her two glasses.

Maggi filled both glasses. Keeping one for herself, she handed the other to Debbie.

Maggi looked across the room at Glen sitting in front of their fireplace, staring into the flames. He did not acknowledge she had entered the house. It was so unlike him. Glen is always a cordial host. She knew whatever she did to make him mad was probably the worst thing she had done since she met him ten years ago.

She took a big gulp of the wine then refilled her glass.

"Glen," Debbie said, "Maggi's here."

She led the way into the living room, with Maggi at her heels.

Glen stood, took another sip of his drink then walked to the fireplace. He placed his glass on the mantle. Slowly he opened the screen on the fireplace and began poking the logs, causing sparks to rise.

Maggi curled up on the sofa. She grabbed a pillow, squeezing it tightly to her chest. She took a deep breath.

"Okay Glen, I can't stand it. What did I do wrong?"

"Maggi, I don't know where to begin. I just can't believe one person can continue to get herself into so much trouble. This time you've involved my wife. I have to tell you that really pissed me off. Thank God Debbie and I have such a good marriage. She came to me with the whole story. Well, at least she thought it was the whole story."

Now Debbie was interested.

"Did you find out more?" she asked.

Glen looked at his wife sitting in the chair nearest to Maggi, as if she were poised to protect her friend.

"Let me begin with the drive-by. It wasn't exactly a drive-by shooting. The shell casings were too close to the body. Someone had to be waiting for this guy, probably hiding behind a parked car. Since everyone works, the only parked car would be the one belonging to the shooter. Anyway, someone had to walk up behind this guy to blast him then go back to the car and drive away. Pretty damn gutsy, if you ask me. This person had to know there was not a soul around who could see it happen."

"Do you think his wife is connected?" asked Maggi.

"Hell yes! But then, so are you!" snapped Glen.

He paced back and forth in front of the fireplace while he talked, occasionally stopping at his drink to take a sip.

"Let's put that story aside. Why in the hell didn't you tell me Linda's husband was dead?"

"Glen, as upset as you were about Linda in the first place, I was afraid to. There was nothing you could do about it. The guy was dead; I didn't want to face another soapbox lecture from you."

"Hell Maggi, don't you know I worry about you. For God's sake, you write murder mysteries. You're putting yourself out there for the weirdoes the way it is then when you pull this asinine publicity stunt; you're making yourself a sitting target. On top of that, you drag Debbie into this behind my back."

Glen stopped to regain his composure.

"Okay, I'm not going there right now," he paused. "I called the precinct about the investigation into Harmon's death. I was fortunate enough to speak to the detective in charge. He was working late tonight. He was swamped so he faxed me the file. We never had a chance to discuss it."

He took another drink. Maggi's eyes were glued to him, as were Debbie's.

Glen tried now to ease his voice. He needed to find a way to tell Maggi without terrifying her. He was angry, but still very much concerned about her well-being.

He went to the two girls, who sat leaning forward, listening to his every word. He squatted down in front of them. He looked into Maggi's eyes.

"Maggi, at the scene of Harmon's murder ..."

Maggi cut him off. "Murder? Who said he was murdered?"

147

Debbie reached her hand out to touch Maggi's arm.

Glen started again, "At the scene of the murder, your book, *Intrusive Deaths*, was on his kitchen table. The book was opened to the page where you write in detail about an intruder killing some guy in the tub by tossing in a hair dryer. Maggi, it was highlighted. Someone intentionally left it there for the police to find. I'm surprised they haven't contacted you or your agent by now."

Maggi stared at Glen speechlessly. She leaned back into the soft sofa. She clung more tightly to the pillow she had pressed to her chest.

Glen noticed her grip on her glass of wine loosening. He took the glass from her hand, placing it on the table next to the sofa. Debbie was motionless. The news shocked both women into a state of total numbness.

He joined Debbie on her chair, balancing himself on the armrest. He rubbed her shoulders gently as the words he spoke slowly sank in. Debbie reached up to touch his hand.

Glen Karst, the husband, was back now that Detective Karst said his piece.

"Maggi, are you okay? I'm sorry, but I had to tell you," he said in a soft caring voice.

Maggi did not answer.

Debbie moved to the sofa to comfort Maggi.

Maggi spoke, "Glen, are you sure? Are you absolutely sure he was murdered?"

148

"No Maggi, it's under investigation. The connection to you and Linda and Harmon is so ironic. How can it be anything else?"

"Who do you think killed him?"

"That's just it. I don't know. With Linda in California, I'm not sure who else would have the motive. From what little I read on the report, the guy obviously gets along with everyone at work. I don't think he was much of a troublemaker, just a wife beater when he was drunk. Which seemed to be every night. Hell, he was loaded when he was in the tub. I suppose he could've been passed out when someone tossed in the hair dryer."

It was Maggi's turn to get up and pace.

"Okay, no one knows about the connection with Tony and no one knows about the connection with this Patrick guy, the golfer. I should be okay. No one has to know. We'll just all keep quiet until it blows over," she said.

"Maggi, it's not that easy. I have to let them know in New York about Linda and her letter to you. Shit, I even have to let them know Debbie's the one that moved her to California."

"No Glen, please don't," begged Maggi.

"Are you sure you have to give them the information?" asked Debbie.

"Look you two, I let you manipulate me about moving Linda. That made me involved. There's no way you two are gonna whine and get your way now. How bad

149

would it look if the investigation went further and the fact that my wife moved her came out? Or, heaven forbid, the police in New York consider Maggi a suspect. I'm not going to withhold evidence. No way, end of discussion."

Glen went back to the fireplace for his glass. He tipped it, emptying the contents, before returning to the kitchen for a refill.

Maggi looked pleadingly at Debbie.

"It's no use, Maggi. When it comes to doing his job, he's not gonna give in."

"You've got that right," he said, joining them.

"Glen, I'm scared."

"You should be scared. You should've been scared a month ago when I told you to watch your back. Look, I'll call the guys in New York. I'll ask them what they know. I'll tell them I know the writer personally and will handle her from here. Let's hope since Harmon was such a loser that they'll be more than happy to let me work it from here for a while. They've got a hell of a lot more cases to work than we do. I'd be surprised if they don't take me up on my offer."

"Thanks Glen. I know you have to do what's right. I'm sorry I didn't listen to you about this whole mess before it got out of hand," said Maggi.

"It's late. Why don't you stay over? I've got to get some sleep. Tomorrow will be a big day between the New York death, the shooter from yesterday and the rapist; my plate is full."

150

"Thanks, but I've got to take care of the dogs."

Glen kissed Debbie on the top of the head.

"Guess you won't be seeing much of me for a while."

He went off to bed.

"Are you going to be okay?" Debbie asked.

"Yeah, I still can't believe any of this is happening. How could one stupid television interview turn into my biggest nightmare?"

Maggi went to the closet near the door to retrieve her coat. Debbie walked with her.

"Why don't you call me when you get home?" she asked.

"No, I'll be fine. I don't want the phone to wake Glen. I'm gonna need him rested and clear headed to get me out of this."

Maggi kept her window open on the drive home. The cold night air helped her to think. Everything will be fine, she convinced herself. There is no way I can be convicted of anything. Getting my name dragged through this can only help with book sales. I don't have anything to worry about.

By the time she arrived home she was feeling much better. She noticed that Jean's light was still on when she pulled into her yard.

No sooner had Maggi gone inside than her phone was ringing. It was Jean.

"Maggi, I thought you'd gone away to write. Then I heard the dogs barking when I took my trash out. I let myself in to check on you when you didn't answer your phone. While I was there I let the dogs out. Good thing too, they really had to go. I wish you'd let me know when you're leaving them alone like that. I worry about them."

"Sorry Jean. I was at Debbie's house. I hadn't planned on being gone very long."

"I thought you always take them along to play with Glen's dogs."

"Normally, I do, but tonight I just didn't feel like hauling them with."

Jean knew this did not sound like Maggi. She never left the dogs if there was a possibility they could be with her.

"Was everything okay?"

"Sure. Why?"

"I don't know. You left the dogs, you're getting home late and you sound funny."

"What do you mean I sound funny?"

"I don't know, you sound like you had some bad news or something. If you need to get away or want some quiet time, the dogs can come over here."

"No, that's fine. Thanks for letting them out but they'll be fine with me."

"Okay, if you say so. Do you want me to take my own car tomorrow or should I ride with you to the office?"

Maggi had totally forgotten about her commitment to the book project. Maybe work as usual would be the best thing for her.

"No, I'll drive. I'll be at your door at eight."

"Goodnight."

Maggi hung up the phone. She wished she had never allowed Jean to find the dogs for her. She loved her dogs dearly but having Jean right next door watching her every move, making her feel inferior as an owner, grated on her.

They were Maggi's dogs, not Jean's. When will she understand that? She has dogs of her own. Why the fascination with Bailey and Bridgette? Maggi was surprised she had not turned her into the Humane Society to get a few complaints on file. The dogs could be removed from her care and Jean could adopt them.

Maggi called the two dogs to join her on her bed. She slept soundly, considering the rough day she had.

When Maggi pulled up in front of Jean's house the next morning, Jean was waiting, her arms loaded with the folders needed for her day at work. She likes this more than I would ever have imagined, thought Maggi. I wonder what the fascination is for her?

Jean climbed into Maggi's car.

"I didn't notice you walking the dogs this morning. What time did you go out?"

Maggi had not walked the dogs. She let them out into her fenced backyard. She felt obligated to lie to Jean.

153

"Oh early, I didn't really look at the clock."

Debbie and Teddi were waiting at the office when Maggi and Jean arrived.

"Debbie told me about your meeting last night with Glen. That's unbelievable."

Jean dropped her folders onto the desk in the front office.

"Why? What happened?"

Teddi said, "Do you remember the first email we discussed here from the woman who had the golfer for a husband and wanted someone to shoot him? Someone did and Glen's on the case. Debbie had to tell him about the email and he was pissed at both Maggi and Debbie for hiding it from him."

"What happened?" asked Jean.

"It played out just like the email. Someone shot him as he walked to the door, carrying his clubs. Turns out the name and address matched the email."

"You mean it really happened just like she wanted?" pressed Jean.

"Yes, just like the email," added Maggi, wishing the subject would change.

Teddi picked up on the tone of Maggi's voice.

"Your two favorite guys are in town," announced Teddi.

"Oh great, Warren and Brad? What do they want?"

"Seems someone called the publisher about one of your books. They didn't want to give me any details over the phone. They're on their way over."

"That doesn't make any sense; people call about my books all the time. Why does this time warrant a visit?" complained Maggi.

"You can ask them yourself; here they come," said Jean.

Brad and Warren entered the office that seemed smaller than usual with all the women present.

"Morning, ladies," said Warren. "Maggi, we need to talk in private."

"Right this way, gentlemen," she said, as she escorted them into her office.

Brad closed the door behind him.

Maggi sat in her chair behind the desk. Warren pulled a chair from across the room closer to Maggi's. Brad did the same.

"Maggi, we were here visiting with another writer when Brad got this call about one of your books."

"Go on," said Maggi, impatiently.

Brad continued the conversation, "The home office got a call from the New York Police Department. You're gonna love this. Seems that guy that beat his wife and kids, you know, the loser from New York. Oh hell, what was her name? You know, the woman that handed you that note on the elevator. Anyway, her old man is dead. She's nowhere to be found. My guess is they think she

155

did him in. But the clincher is, *Intrusive Deaths*, was found in his apartment with..."

"I know, Glen already told me. So why is it that you're here?"

"Publicity, Maggi, publicity," said Brad.

"Warren, tell me he's not serious. I don't want my books connected to such an unfortunate death," she complained.

"Maggi, honey..."

"Don't Maggi honey me. I don't want to get involved."

"Too late," said Brad. "The big guys want you to fly to New York to visit with the police. They want a camera crew there and reporters from the New York Times. Maggi, you're gonna be the biggest thing to hit the literary world since Harry Potter."

"No! Read my lips. N-O. I won't do it. I know from my research that killers use stories from mystery books all the time to commit crimes. What makes mine so different? I'm not gonna do it."

Warren said, "I'll give it to you straight, Maggi. The office told them about your letter from his wife. They think the connection is too coincidental. They want to talk to you about it. We're trying to get them to allow a camera crew and reporters in on it and offering them the last say on what gets out to the public."

At Glen's office, he found out the news about the same time Maggi did. He called the detective he visited with the night before to tell him about his and Maggi's connection to the case. The detective already knew about the letter. Maggi's publisher told them. They did not know about Debbie moving the wife to California. That secret had been kept from Warren and Brad, so the publisher was unaware.

Glen learned from his New York counterpart, Morrison, that Maggi was going to be brought in for questioning. He suggested Glen accompany her to discuss the case with him.

Bill was sitting in Glen's office while he made the call.

"Is that beautiful babe we had lunch with in trouble? Or are you just slipping away to New York with her for a fun weekend?"

Glen took his marriage just as seriously as he took his work, so he took offense at Bill's remark.

"Grow up asswipe, this is about work."

"Whoa, what has you so worked up? Is something seriously wrong?"

"Seems someone used Maggi's book as inspiration to kill some jerk in New York. She needs to go there so they can talk to her about it. The bad thing is she knew the vic's wife."

"So the wife probably had a copy of Maggi's book. Is she a suspect?"

Glen leaned back into his chair. He strummed his fingers on his desk while he looked at Bill. There were

157

things Glen did not like about Bill, such as his lack of respect for women and the institution of marriage, but he was a damn good detective. He knew eventually he would have to tell Bill the whole story, as they would be working the golfer case together.

"Grab a cup of coffee and a chair. It's story time," said Glen.

Obediently, and with much curiosity, Bill followed orders.

Glen told him the whole story about Maggi's screwup on the Oprah Show. He told him about the elevator lady and how Debbie helped Maggi move her to California. Then he explained the death of her husband and why the wife would not be a suspect because she was not present when it happened. She was with Debbie. He told him how the police found the book and the passage that was highlighted. Then he told him about Maggi's publisher sending her to New York to be interviewed about the death, all the while wanting to use it for publicity.

"That explains why you need to go with her to New York. You know, if you have trouble getting away I would be more than happy to be her bodyguard any time you need one."

"Oh yeah, and who should I hire to protect her body from you?"

"From what I saw of her at the restaurant, I think she can take pretty good care of herself. So when are you leaving?"

"I don't know. I have to call Maggi and find out what the schedule is."

"How do you think we should proceed with this dead golfer?"

"Well, we do know that somehow the wife is involved. We know she wasn't the shooter, but that doesn't mean she didn't hire someone to do it," said Glen. "We've got her under surveillance while we wait for more info on the computer analysis."

"Why don't you hand me the email you brought in last night from his wife to Maggi."

Bill read it while Glen poured himself another cup of coffee. He checked the clock on the wall. He should give Maggi a call to find out when they need to leave.

"Says here the woman hasn't had access to a dime of his money. How was she going to pay a hitman?" asked Bill.

"My guess is from the insurance policy. She doesn't say how much it was for, but it was probably enough for some low-life to buy drugs with."

"I think I'll go pay her a visit today. Wanna come along?"

"Let me make a couple of phone calls first, then I'll let you know."

Maggi asked Warren, "How soon do I have to leave for this trip?"

"Tomorrow. You have to be in New York City, ready for your interview at four p.m."

Brad stepped out to use the bathroom.

"Maggi, I have to warn you. They want to play this up big. If they can pull it off, your name and your books will be plastered over every news channel and newspaper they can get it into. Watch your step and choose your words carefully. I really tried to stop them, but money talks."

"Thanks Warren. Somehow I didn't think you were in total agreement with Brad."

"Maggi, they may own you, but I know you can fire my butt at any moment. I'd never do anything that would jeopardize my job with you as your agent. We've been through too much together. There've been a lot of good times, but now I think we're in for some rocky times."

Brad popped his head back into the room.

"Are you ready to go? We've got a flight to catch," reminded Brad.

"I guess we'll see you in New York tomorrow. Don't be late. Oh, I almost forgot. This letter came for you. It was in a larger envelope addressed to me. The sender said your email wasn't working and wondered if I would forward this on to you. I didn't open the inner envelope. Maybe it's some fan. You could use the cheering up."

Warren handed her the envelope then left with Brad.

160

Maggi tossed it onto her desk. She went into the outer office where her staff was gathered going through the remaining emails, narrowing them down even further.

Teddi asked, "Maggi, is there any special way you want us to eliminate emails? Would you like an even number of men and women killed? Do you want to do a series of husbands or keep them in the same vicinity?"

"I'm not sure. I guess I've not given it much thought," she replied.

Jean said, "Might I make a suggestion?"

Maggi seemed surprised. "Sure."

"Since most of your murders have always taken place in Colorado, it might be nice to keep that theme in your series. It would make it easier for your sleuth to handle the cases if they're all in his backyard."

"That is a good idea," agreed Teddi.

Maggi tried to draw herself back into the work at hand. "You know, that would make my writing easier if I didn't have to have my killer or killers gallivanting all across the U.S. Are enough suitable stories happening in Colorado to make it work?"

"That depends," said Debbie. "How many murders do you want to happen in each book?"

"Oh, I don't know; five or six should be enough."

"We'll keep the titles for each stack and remove everyone that's not from Colorado. If we come up short, we might dig back through some of the others that were close to being chosen. I think we can do this. Besides, we could just pretend they all take place in Colorado. They don't really have to be. Remember, this is fiction."

"Yeah, fiction. I have to keep reminding myself of that," said Maggi.

Maggi's phone started to ring. Teddi jumped up to answer it.

"No, that's okay, Teddi. I'll grab it in my office."

She was not in the mood to work and did not want to put a damper on the ambition of the others. They were all feeling comfortable that the connection was just a strange coincidence. Reading and helping Maggi with her books made these stories, although they were really happening, seem like made-up stories for the books. Surprisingly enough, even Debbie was at ease. Probably because she knew Glen was on the case.

"Hello," said Maggi, as she picked up her phone.

"Maggi, Glen."

"Hi Glen. Do you want to talk to Debbie?"

"Oh, that's right. She's at your office. Not right now. I need to talk to you first."

"What's up? Did you find out anything new?"

"I found out what your publisher did to you. I plan to go with you to New York for that interview. Do you know when you have to be there?"

Maggi, with relief in her voice, said, "I'm so glad you're going along. They need me there by four p.m. tomorrow. Will that work for you?"

"I'll make it work. They want to talk to me too since Debbie was involved with moving the wife and I know you and the story about the emails."

"Is Debbie going with us?" asked Maggi.

"Hey Maggi, hold on. I've got another call."

Maggi played with the pen on her desk while she waited for Glen to come back on the phone. She ran the pen over the letters spelling out her name on the envelope Warren had given her. She picked it up to look at it. Glen was still not back on the line, so she decided to open it and read some happy fan mail.

Dear Ms. Morgan,

I tried to send you an email but it got kicked back, so I am sending this letter to your agent. I hope it gets to you.

I am so indebted to you for helping me out. After some time went by, I wasn't sure you were going to shoot Patrick. Thank you so much. My life will be so much better without him in it. I had nowhere else to turn. I promise to never tell a soul that you were involved. The police have been asking questions, but I'm sticking to my story that I have no idea who could've killed him.

Thanks again,

Elizabeth Malone

"Hey Maggi, are you still there? Sorry about that. I had to take that call. Now where were we?"

"Glen, I just got a thank-you note from Elizabeth Malone. She thinks I shot her husband. What do I do? I thought she hired someone else."

"Tell Debbie to stay there with you. I'm on my way over."

Chapter 8

Debbie was sitting in Maggi's office with her when Glen arrived. Jean and Teddi were out to lunch. Maggi handed the letter to him before anyone had the opportunity to speak. Glen's eyes caught Debbie's. His look reassured Debbie, who felt immediate calm knowing he was there. It is one thing to have a kind husband or a handsome husband. Glen, along with those attributes, was a fearless husband that could protect her. Not a day passed that she did not remind herself how lucky she was that they met.

Glen picked up the envelope. He turned it over.

"Where did this come from? It obviously wasn't mailed like this."

"Warren gave it to me. He said she sent it to him when we stopped emails to my current email account. He was here earlier today."

He carefully folded it, placing it back inside the envelope from which it came.

Maggi watched the careful manner with which he handled it. Evidence, she thought. She opened the lower drawer to her desk and removed a large envelope.

"I don't have any plastic bags but this should work until you can get it to your office," she said, handing it to him.

"Thanks." She never ceased to amaze him. Even during her time of stress, she still thinks like a cop. Her research into the workings of the police department has become ingrained into her subconscious mind, just as if she had been through the academy.

"Maggi tells me you are going with her to New York. Can I come along?" asked Debbie.

"There's really no need, hon. We're just gonna fly there, talk to the guys on the case, then fly back. They won't even let you in during the interview."

"I guess you're right. I'll stay here and take care of the dogs. Does that mean you guys are leaving in the morning and will be back tomorrow night?"

"That's my plan. What about yours, Maggi?"

"Sure, whatever you think, Glen."

Maggi looked at her watch.

"Teddi should be back from lunch any minute. I'll have her make the flight arrangements."

"Why don't you let me take you ladies out to lunch? By the time we return, Teddi will have made the arrangements; then we'll know our schedule."

Maggi did not have much of an appetite but went along anyway. She did not want either of them to know she was nervous about being on the other side of an interview.

166

Debbie was thrilled to have lunch with Glen. With his busy life it does not happen very often.

When they returned to the office, Teddi handed them their flight schedules.

"Great," said Glen. "I'm gonna drop this letter off with Bill to run it for prints to be sure it's from Mrs. Malone. We'll probably spend a few hours working before I head home. I'll swing by and pick you up in the morning around nine."

Maggi wished she had not driven Jean to work. She desperately wanted to leave the office to return home and stay there. Then she remembered her dogs, she'd use them for the excuse.

Glen and Debbie were walking out to his pickup when Maggi jumped up to run after them.

"Glen, can I catch a ride home with you? I'll leave my car here for Jean."

"No problem. Are you ready?"

"Just give me five minutes."

She ran back inside, gathered her handbag and a notebook from her desk.

"Jean, would you mind driving my car home when you're finished today? I'm going to ride home with Glen. I want to take the dogs for a walk. You guys should be able to get along fine without me."

She turned to Teddi.

"I'll see you in two days. Keep up the good work. Maybe you'll be finished by the time I return."

Debbie waved good-bye to Glen and Maggi as they drove away.

When Debbie went back inside to work, she saw Jean watching from the window.

"I can't believe you trust her with your husband," she said.

Debbie looked shocked. She trusted both of them; there was no reason not to.

Teddi said, "Jean! I can't believe you said that."

"Well, they're only human you know. Maggi is good looking, and so is Glen for that matter. I'm just saying if he were mine, I wouldn't be trusting him alone with Maggi, especially going away together to New York."

Debbie replied, "It's a good thing for them that I'm not you then, isn't it."

She knew Maggi and Glen so well. The thought never crossed her mind that anything would ever happen. They were both too loyal to her. She did not want to give any more thought Jean's nasty comment.

They made great progress on their project; they worked a few more hours than planned. It was obvious that soon they would have the list compiled for Maggi to begin her series. She could definitely start writing the first one at any time.

When Debbie arrived home she found Glen packing his overnight bag.

"I thought you were coming home tomorrow night?" she asked.

"So did I, but when I called the detective in charge, he asked if I could stay over to offer some assistance on the case. The hours tomorrow will be filled with the interview."

"What about Maggi? Is she staying over with you?"

"I don't know her plans. I haven't told her mine yet. I need to call her right away to tell Teddi to change my tickets."

Debbie undressed to slip into sweats for the night. Glen watched her while he dialed the phone to call Maggi. Debbie changed her mind, slipping into a slinky nightgown instead. She enjoyed watching Glen watching her. He blew her a kiss while the phone was ringing.

Maggi answered.

"Maggi, Glen. I'm gonna stay over an extra day to help out on the case in New York. Can you have Teddi change my tickets and book a room for me?"

"Sure, I'll call her right away. See ya in the morning."

Glen hung up the phone; his eyes searched the room for Debbie. She had left their bedroom to shower. He watched her through the shower doors for a moment then stripped off his clothes to join her. He made love to her in the hot steaming shower. When they stepped out into the cooler air of the bathroom, he wrapped an oversized towel around her then carried her off to bed. He tucked her, in telling her to stay put. He clicked the television on. He returned shortly with sandwiches and drinks. He crawled into bed next to her where they talked, ate and watched television until they could barely keep their eyes open. He fell asleep first. Debbie shut the television off then curled up into his arms and slept until the alarm woke them in the morning.

Glen reached over to turn off the alarm. Debbie was waking slowly. He did not have to pick up Maggi until nine and it was only seven. He made love to Debbie one last time before getting up to prepare for his trip.

Debbie remained in bed while she watched him dress. She was feeling badly for letting Jean's comment cause her concern about Glen telling her he was staying over. He loved her, it was obvious. Maggi would never do anything to jeopardize their friendship. Jean must just be an unhappy busybody, thought Debbie.

When the plane landed in New York, Maggi's uneasiness became apparent to Glen.

"Maggi, don't worry. You haven't done anything to be concerned about. This is just routine questioning. I'll be with you the entire time. Try to relax. You don't want to look guilty," he teased, trying to make her calm down.

"Tell me Glen, what's routine about being questioned regarding a murder case with cameras in your face?"

"I keep telling you, they're not gonna allow that."

She turned to watch out the window. They waited in their seats for most of the passengers who were in a bigger hurry to depart.

170

Suddenly, she felt something cold on her wrist and heard a click; she turned to see what it was. She looked down at her wrist to see she was handcuffed to Glen.

She looked at him as he burst into laughter.

She raised her arm with his hand dangling from hers.

"What in the hell is this for?" she asked.

"Since you're a suspect in a murder case, I thought you might like to get a little more into the mood. Might even help you with your writing."

"Ha, ha, ha, very funny. Unlock these damn things before I lose control completely and embarrass both of us," she threatened.

"Hey, won't bother me. I'll just flash my badge around and everyone will think you're nuts or something."

Glen let her sit there and stew for a while longer, watching the looks they were getting from the passengers moving down the line. He hung his badge around his neck before he put the cuffs on her. He opened his jacket to expose the badge, confirming to the other passengers that Maggi was his prisoner.

Maggi was no longer nervous. Now she was getting upset with Glen. She laid her jacket over their arms to hide the cuffs.

She whispered, "Glen, you son of a bitch, get these off of me. Now!"

As he reached into his pocket to take out his keys, one of the passengers bumped his arm sending the keys out into the aisle amongst the feet of the passengers. When he leaned down to pick them up, he nearly pulled Maggi from her seat. He missed the keys.

This time she held her arm over so he could lean further into the aisle. A passenger, anxious to get off, accidentally kicked them further down the walkway. Glen sat back in the seat and burst into his hearty laugh. Normally, Maggi enjoyed his laughter, but this time she was too steamed to appreciate it.

They had to wait until there were no longer passengers behind them before they could work together to stand up then walk sideways to the aisle. There she had to continue walk sideways behind Glen while he looked for the keys. They were two seats down and had been knocked into a row. Maggi's wrist hurt from being dragged around by Glen as he finally managed to retrieve his keys. Maggi was not sure which made her angrier, the pain from the cuffs or the fact that he could not stop laughing. Either way, she was not nervous about her interview any longer.

Glen grabbed his carry-on bag from the overhead compartment then stepped back so Maggi could exit the plane ahead of him. The stewardesses had seen the two of them cuffed together, looking for the keys. They watched every move Maggi made as she left. Glen chuckled again as they walked up the ramp to the waiting area for their gate.

"Did you see the looks I got back there?" she asked.

She finally saw the humor in it. She punched Glen in the arm. He put his arm around her and walked her the rest of the way, still laughing as he thought about the entire cuff episode.

Once outside he flagged a cab for them, giving the driver directions to the precinct station. Maggi had visited many police stations, including FBI offices, for research for her book. Instead of being nervous when they got out of the cab, she felt calm. She was surprised and pleased with the change in her mood.

She allowed Glen to take charge. Inside the building, Maggi prepared herself for the media.

"Glen, there's no camera crew or news reporters here."

"I told you they wouldn't allow it. Your publishers were just hoping to get their way. It's imperative to the case that they don't allow the media to have the information. They don't give a damn about lining the publishers pockets at the expense of a case."

Without the media in her face, Maggi was now looking forward to the interview, hoping to memorize questions and facial expressions to use in one of her books.

Maggi was disappointed with the questioning. Glen was right; it was very routine in nature, boring actually. They really did not consider Maggi a suspect at that point. They were concerned about who might be setting her up. They agreed that if Maggi were involved in any capacity, she would not leave such a blatant clue behind. Someone was playing with the police on this one. They ran prints on the book, but that was worthless. The book came from the library, checked out by Linda, so there were literally dozens of partials on it. They even found Tony's prints on the cover. Maybe it was not a homicide after all. He could have committed suicide. His wife and kids did leave him. Maybe in his drunken state he did himself in, taking the idea from Maggi's book.

"What can you tell us about this letter from his wife?" asked Detective Morrison.

"She put it in my pocket on the elevator. I felt sorry for her and decided to move her away from him. She seemed so desperate ... so helpless."

"Desperate enough to kill him?"

"I suppose so."

Glen butted in, "She was in California with my wife, getting settled in, on the night of his death. There's no way she could've done it herself."

Morrison added, "We know his neighbors didn't like him but we're reasonably sure none of them would want to risk their own necks by killing him. He wasn't worth going to jail over."

"What'd the crime scene crew come up with?" asked Glen.

"Nothing we could use. Until you told us about his wife moving, we thought she would be our number one suspect. Most of her things were still in the apartment."

"Any signs of forced entry?" asked Glen.

"Nope, no sign of it. We figured he was too drunk to remember to lock the door or he answered it and let whoever inside."

"I don't suppose there was any way to tell if he put himself in the tub or if he passed out and was placed into it, setting him up for the hair dryer?" asked Glen.

"No."

"What about his buddy that found him? Did he say the door was locked when he went there?"

"He said it was unlocked, so he let himself in."

"From what I understand, other than beating his wife, no one had a motive to kill him, right?"

"That's right."

"Hey guys, remember me?" teased Maggi, feeling left out of the conversation.

"What about my book?"

"What about it?" asked Detective Morrison.

"Why would my book be there? Do you really think he was reading it and the idea came to him? Or do you think the killer had time to sit with him and read it to come up with the idea? I'm still having trouble making the connection."

Morrison asked, "Do you think there's any way he knew you were responsible for taking his wife and kids away?"

"I don't think so."

"Then I don't think the vic was trying to set you up. Now, if this wasn't a suicide, why would the killer be trying to set you up? Do you have any enemies that would want to frame you?"

"I suppose there could be someone that doesn't like me. That happens when you are in the public eye. I get prank emails once in a while from people who don't like what I write, but whoever did this had to know I wouldn't get blamed for it."

"Where were you that night?"

Maggi squirmed just slightly. "I ... I was here in the city that night."

Morrison sat up. "So you did have access to the victim?"

"Well, I guess so. But that doesn't mean I killed him."

"You were upset enough with him that you moved his wife and kids away earlier that day. Correct?"

"Yes, but I'm not involved with his death."

"Was anyone with you that evening?"

"Yes, Glen."

Detective Karst, were you with her all evening in the same room?"

Glen knew where this was going but had to answer truthfully.

"No, not all night. I stayed with my wife's family overnight."

"Miss Morgan, can anyone vouch for your whereabouts that night?"

Glen asked, "What about Teddi?"

"No, she went out with Peter that night. She stayed in his room with him."

"Look, Detective Morrison. I can vouch for Maggi; she'd never do anything like commit murder. She might write about them but she'd never actually do it. Besides, you already said, if she was going to do something like that, why would she set herself up by leaving her book as a clue?"

"You are one clever lady," said Morrison. "With a mind like yours you might use the fact that we would consider it stupid to leave a clue like the book so you would feel safe doing just that."

"That's bullshit," said Glen. "Maggi didn't do it."

Maggi felt ill. Could this detective really think she was involved beyond moving Linda to California?

"I'm not saying Ms. Morgan did it, but we have to consider her a suspect for the time being. She had motive, she had access, she had the vic's address and knew his habit of coming home drunk."

177

Glen knew that Morrison was just doing his job but was upset, just the same, that he was putting Maggi through this.

"Are we about finished here?" asked Glen.

"Sure, sure. Ms. Morgan, you're free to leave. Just keep in close contact with Detective Karst, in case we need to talk to you again."

Maggi stood to leave. She was surprised how her heart raced. Fear enveloped her but at the same time she wanted to remember the feeling to be able to write how a suspect might feel during an interrogation. Not having the press present brought relief.

Glen shook hands with Detective Morrison and said, "I'll stop by in the morning; we can discuss this a little further. I have a late afternoon flight back to Denver."

"Great, looking forward to it."

Glen placed his hand on the small of Maggi's back to guide her to the door. In the hall she pulled away from him and leaned against the wall; her legs too weak to take another step forward.

"Are you okay?" asked Glen, as he positioned himself in front of her, ready to catch her if her balance became unstable.

"Yeah. What just happened in there?"

"We'll talk later. Do you need to sit down?"

"No, but I could use a drink of water."

Glen's eyes scanned the hall. At the very end hung a restroom sign. He knew there would be a water fountain there.

"This way" he said, as he took Maggi's arm, holding on tightly to her forearm and elbow for support.

Maggi took a long sip of water then checked the time.

"Hey, I've got a plane to catch."

Glen realized they spent more time visiting with Detective Morrison than he thought.

He escorted Maggi outside into the fresh air; that is, if air in New York City can be considered fresh.

"Let me see your ticket. What time are you scheduled to leave?"

She reached into her handbag searching for the paper envelope containing her ticket. Glen took it from her then opened it to read the designated time.

"Maggi, you're not scheduled to leave until tomorrow afternoon; the same flight I'm on."

"What?" she said, taking the ticket back.

"Teddi must've misunderstood and changed the flight for both of us."

"Maybe that's not such a bad idea. You could use a good meal and some sleep before heading home tomorrow. I'd feel better not sending you on your way alone tonight anyway. I think today was a little more than you expected."

179

"You've sure got that right. Can we go to our rooms now?"

Glen hailed a cab.

At the front desk, he told the clerk they had reservations for two rooms. The clerk checked the records.

"I'm sorry, Mr. Karst, but we only have reservations for your room. There's nothing in your companion's name."

"Could you check again?" Glen asked.

The clerk obeyed scanning his records again on the computer.

The outcome was the same.

"That's okay, Glen," said Maggi.

She placed her credit card on the counter. "I'd like a single, non-smoking for the night, please."

"I'm sorry, ma'am, but we're booked solid. There's a Republican convention in town tonight. I'm afraid, without reservations, you're going to get the same story in most of the hotels near here."

"Come on Maggi, you can share my room."

"Why Detective Karst, I'm not that kind of girl," she teased.

Glen swatted her behind, saying, "Behave yourself, you know what I mean."

They took the elevator to the third floor. Glen walked ahead of Maggi, looking for room 326. He used the key card to open the door then stepped aside to let her in first. The whole time he kept his fingers crossed hoping for two beds. Sleeping on the sofa or the floor worried him. He was too much of a gentleman to take the only bed.

Maggi plopped on the bed nearest the door while Glen tossed his bag on the bed near the window. Maggi looked at his bag.

"Damn it, Glen. I don't even have a toothbrush with me."

"I might share my room with you but I'll be damned if I'm gonna share my toothbrush."

"What do you want to do about supper?" she asked.

"I don't care. Do you want to eat in or eat out?"

"To tell you the truth, I'd rather stay in, if that's okay with you?"

"Sure, I don't mind. There should be a menu around here somewhere for room service."

Maggi went in to use the bathroom. When she came out, Glen was reading the menu. He made his decision then tossed it to Maggi. She lay on the bed reading the choices.

"I'll have the chicken Caesar salad."

Glen picked up the phone, ordering a salad for Maggi and a large cheeseburger and fries for himself. He also ordered a bottle of wine. He needed to unwind and felt Maggi needed to as well.

Glen turned on the television to watch the news while they waited for their supper.

"How long will it take? I'd like to have a bath."

"They said about twenty minutes."

"I'll wait, I want a long bath."

Maggi placed her head on the pillow and dozed off to be awakened by the knock on the door when their food arrived.

She sat up rubbing her eyes while Glen signed for the meal.

He brought the tray to her then sat to eat while he continued watching television.

"Did you know you snore?" he teased.

"I do not!" she said. "Do I?"

Glen just laughed.

After they finished eating, Maggi filled the tub.

"Damn it," she said.

"What?"

"I don't have anything to sleep in."

"I sleep naked, why can't you?"

She threw a towel at him.

"I brought a fresh shirt for tomorrow; I suppose you can borrow that," he offered.

"I can't do that. I know how you are about your appearance. You'd have a fit if you had to work tomorrow in a wrinkled shirt."

"Really, Maggi. I don't mind under the circumstances."

"Liar. Just give me the one you're wearing."

Glen smelled the armpits of the shirt, "I don't think you'd want this one; I've been wearing it all day."

"It's either that or you can go shopping for a pair of pajamas and a toothbrush for me, because I'm not going back out tonight."

"Okay if you don't mind, I don't mind. Tell ya what, I'll go down to the gift shop to buy you a toothbrush and see if they have anything you can sleep in."

"Really, Glen, your shirt's fine. But I could use that toothbrush," she said, as she stepped into the bathroom, closing the door.

She slipped into the tub and heard the door close, knowing he'd left the room. No sooner had he left than the phone rang.

"Damn."

Maggi wrapped the towel around her and ran to the phone in case it was important.

"Hello."

"Maggi, is that you?"

"Debbie, hi. You just missed Glen. He ran downstairs to buy a toothbrush for me."

"I thought you were coming home tonight."

"I was, but Teddi messed up the tickets and scheduled my return flight for tomorrow with Glen. We only found out a couple of hours ago, when Glen was about to take me to the airport."

"Can I have his room number then?" she asked.

183

"Can you believe it? There's a convention in town and all the rooms were booked. Teddi changed my flight but didn't book a room for me, so I'm bunking with your hubby tonight."

"Where did you say he was?"

"Oops. Wait a minute; I think he's back. I'm sitting on his bed in a towel dripping wet, hang on."

Maggi dropped the phone then ran to the bathroom. Glen stepped inside, bumping into her before she made it to the bathroom.

As she stood there, dripping, she said, "Debbie's on the phone."

Glen handed Maggi her toothbrush then went to the phone.

When he picked up the phone, he heard the dial tone.

He assumed they were disconnected. He dialed back but there was no answer.

Debbie sat on the bed in their room, listening to the phone ring. Her heart raced as her body temperature rose. She felt sick to her stomach. "Damn Jean, damn her.

Chapter 9

Maggi stayed in the room when Glen returned to talk with Detective Morrison. His conscience forced him to tell him about the email and the second death in Denver. He wanted to think they were not connected but his gut told him otherwise.

"Karst, come on in," said Garrison, when he heard Glen's knock.

"Morning," said Glen.

"Sit down, sit down. How about a cup of coffee and a donut?"

Glen filled a cup then pulled up a chair. He studied the donuts, looking for his favorite jelly-filled with white frosting. He leaned back into the chair.

"I've been giving some thought about Ms. Morgan. Do you really think she's not capable of murder under the circumstances?"

"What circumstances?"

"You know the wife thing. Moving her all the way to California is a big step. Are you sure they weren't connected before that letter?"

"I'm sure."

"I just find it pretty hard to believe that this woman would run up to a perfect stranger on an elevator and ask her to kill her husband. The longer I thought about it, the less likely it seemed to me. I think maybe they've known each other for awhile and made up this story."

"I'm telling you, you're wrong. Don't waste too much time pursuing Maggi when you should be looking for the real killer or else call it a suicide."

"Well, can you explain how this story works for you, because it sure as hell is not working for me?"

"Let me back up and fill you in," Karst replied. "You are aware that Maggi is a mystery writer?"

Morrison nodded his head.

"For about ten years I've been helping her with her storylines where the police scenes are concerned. Hell, she even made me the sleuth in most of her books. She's my wife's best friend."

"Go on."

"A little over a month ago she went on the Oprah Show while on a publicity tour for her latest book. The two women were kidding around and Maggi was teasing the audience. She told them to write to her with the name and story about someone they'd like to see eliminated and, if Maggi liked the story, she'd write it into one of her books and kill the person with words."

"Sounds like she was asking for references for her victims."

"Sort of. Anyway, this Linda Harmon woman watched the show. She followed Maggi onto the elevator and slipped the note into her pocket. Maggi's assistant, Teddi, was with her. I already visited with her about it."

"How did she know where and when to find Ms. Morgan?"

"Maggi says at the end of these shows they advertise where the guests will be staying. On Maggi's website she lists her upcoming events, including booksignings and tours. Her show schedule is on there. It wouldn't be hard to figure out when she'll be in a city. My wife said Linda spent most of the day in the lobby waiting for Maggi. She recognized her from the show, plus there was a crowd around her getting autographs."

"I suppose all of that's possible but it's still pretty hard to swallow."

"I'm telling you, Morrison. Maggi didn't do it."

"Glen, I know you're friends with her but don't let that affect the way you approach this. Do you honestly believe someone would watch a television show then write in to ask Ms. Morgan to commit murder?"

Glen chuckled. "You're not gonna believe this but she received thousands of emails from people asking just that."

"No shit?"

"No shit. That's part of what I need to discuss with you today. We had a shooting in Denver a few days ago. I'm working the case. Seems his wife wanted him dead. She sent an email to Maggi giving her details on how to pull it off. I'll be damned if someone didn't blast this guy when he was in his own driveway."

"The wife's your main suspect, right?"

"Yeah, but we can't pin anything on her yet. She wasn't the shooter and we can't prove she hired someone. We're gonna keep close tabs on her, but other than that email, we don't have anything to go on."

"Nothing at all?"

"Maggi did get another note from her, thanking her for killing her husband."

"Can you get a match on the woman's handwriting?"

"No, it was typed on a computer. We already checked the printer in her house but couldn't say that it was printed there."

"What about prints?"

"Nothing there either, except Maggi's and her agent's."

"Why would her agent's prints be on there? Is he connected?"

"He gave the letter to Maggi. They stopped her incoming emails when she got so many requests. Elizabeth Malone, the vic's wife, sent a note to Maggi's agent because the emails weren't going through. She asked him to forward it to Maggi. He was in Denver a couple of days ago; so he gave it to her personally."

"Are you telling me her agent is aware of what's been going on?"

"He knew about Linda's husband being killed, he knew about Linda giving Maggi that note on the elevator but he doesn't know that Maggi moved her to California and he's unaware of this dead golfer, Patrick Malone, in Denver."

"Does he know about all the emails wanting people bumped off?"

"Oh yeah, he and the publisher are pushing this for a publicity stunt. They're sort of forcing Maggi into it. She has a contract with them to write four books using these emails to form her story lines around her victims."

"Nice guys to work for."

"She's pissed about it but her hands are tied."

"I can see why you believe she's innocent but hell, this ties her to two deaths now. I'm gonna have to keep her on my list of suspects."

"I understand; you have to do what you have to do. I'll do all I can to keep you informed as the case unfolds."

"Thanks, Glen, I really appreciate it. I hope we can come up with something to clear your friend before this gets more involved."

Glen shook hands with Garrison then headed back to the hotel where Maggi was waiting.

189

In the cab, on the way to the room, Glen tried Debbie again; still no answer. He was starting to worry. He wondered if she was okay or if she just forgot her phone again. He hoped Maggi talked to her this morning.

Glen knocked at the door of room 326. Although he had his keycard, he did not feel comfortable barging in on Maggi.

"Who is it?"

"It's Glen."

Maggi unlocked the door.

"Why did you knock, you have a key?"

"It's called manners, Maggi."

"Thanks," she said, feeling foolish.

"Did you talk to Debbie this morning?"

"No, but I talked to Teddi. Jean's been putting crap into Debbie's head about me being alone with you."

"Oh hell. You've got to be kidding."

"Nope, Teddi said it started the day before we came, when you gave me a ride home. Jean told Debbie in front of Teddi that there's no way she'd trust me with her husband, especially when he's good looking like you."

"She's right about the good looking part but she's way off base with the rest of it. How'd Debbie take it?"

"Teddi said she got testy with Jean and blew off the comment, but now I wonder if that's why you couldn't reach her last night. Hell, Glen, I told her I was sitting on your bed in a damn towel."

Glen sat on the bed, rubbing his hand on his chin. "I feel guilty and I have no reason to. I know Debbie is pretty sensitive about other women but I didn't think she'd worry about you. She knows most of the time I'm upset with you about something or other. You are, after all, her best friend."

"Glen, *all* women are sensitive when it comes to their husband and other women. That's the first commandment of womanhood."

"I'll see how she is when we get home later today."

"I'm pretty sure Teddi will be able to calm her down. She's going to explain her blunder about the tickets. And actually, that's not her blunder. She was with Jean when I called her and had Peter on hold. Jean offered to handle the tickets for Teddi so she could talk with Peter."

"Do you think that dame set us up?"

"I don't think so. My guess is she's just not as reliable with it as Teddi and just screwed up accidentally. I mean, really, what would she have to gain? She had no way of knowing I couldn't get another room. I don't think she did it on purpose. I really don't."

"If you say so. Let's check out and get some lunch then go to the airport. I'm anxious to get home to Debbie."

Teddi, Debbie and Jean were just about finished with all of the files by lunch.

"I guess that's it," said Teddi. "Jean, you might as well go home and take care of Maggi's dogs now. There's

191

no need to come back. You've been a great help. I'm sure you'll be getting a check from the publisher in the mail soon. It's been really nice working with you."

"I can come back if you need me, after I turn the dogs out. I really don't mind. It's been good to have some purpose in my life again. Retirement doesn't agree with me."

"Thanks for the offer but we really are finished here. Maggi will be back in a few hours. I think I'm gonna head home and treat myself to the rest of the day off. When Maggi gets back from a trip she's either wanting to take time off or work like crazy for a couple of days. I'm hoping she's going to opt for a few days off."

"Is Peter coming for another visit?" asked Jean.

"Yep, we've got dinner plans for tonight."

Debbie and Teddi watched out the window as Jean left.

"Do you really think she was just trying to start some trouble about Glen and Maggi?" asked Debbie.

"Debbie, come on. Glen and Maggi. You've got to be kidding. Maggi spends most of her time avoiding Glen because he's always on her case about something. He's not her type. Right now, no man is her type. She's still pretty bitter about Daniel, you know."

"I know, but now I feel bad that I've been avoiding Glen. I even hung up on him last night."

"Hey, that's a natural reaction. I'd feel the same way if it were Peter."

192

"So if Peter and Maggi got stuck sharing a room; you'd be upset too?"

"Of course, at first, until I realized how foolish that would be. Can you actually picture Maggi and Peter together?"

"There must've been something that attracted them to each other, for a little while at least, when they were together."

"What do you mean, when they were together?"

"Maggi and Peter used to see each other after her divorce from Daniel. I thought you knew all about that?"

"No, how did you find out?"

"Oh, I don't know. Maggi and I were talking about you and Peter when she told me. But that was a long time ago. Glen and I knew at the time she was seeing someone but we never met him and then it was over. She never talked about him and we didn't ask."

Teddi was feeling uneasy about the information, her face showed it.

"I'm sorry, Teddi, I really am. Maybe I shouldn't have said anything. Maggi probably didn't want to tell you because she didn't want to cause any problems between you and Peter."

"I can understand that. What bothers me is why didn't Peter tell me?"

Debbie did not have an answer for that.

That evening Glen went home to Debbie. Peter met Teddi at her house and Maggi went home to her dogs.

193

Maggi was not up to talking to Jean so she chose not to answer her phone. She turned on every light in her house so that Jean could not miss the fact that she was home and the dogs no longer needed Jean's care.

During dinner with Peter, Teddi was not quite herself.

"What's wrong?" asked Peter.

"Nothing."

"Oh, come on. Something's wrong."

"I said nothing's wrong. Maybe I'm just a little tired or maybe I'm coming down with something."

Peter studied Teddi's face. He knew something happened that upset her but he did not know what. Before tonight, every time they were together she was glowing and bursting with happiness. Tonight she seemed saddened by something.

"Did something happen at work today? Did Maggi give you a bad time?"

"No, I haven't seen Maggi since she returned. You think she's pretty hard to work with, don't you?"

"Sometimes she can be impossible, yes."

"Does Maggi having any redeeming qualities in your eyes?"

"Does it bother you that I complain about her all the time?"

"You didn't answer my question."

"Redeeming qualities of Maggi Morgan. Well...she's hard working, determined, and a hell of a good writer. Why? Where's all of this leading?"

"How about on a more personal level? Do you like her personality? Is she fun to be with when you're not working? Do you find her attractive?"

Peter was squirming in his chair. He did not want to give the wrong answer.

"I suppose away from work she can be fun and yes, she's attractive. So?"

"Peter, why didn't you tell me that you and Maggi had an affair?"

With his mouth hanging open, he studied Teddi's face. She looked away so her eyes would not meet his.

"Teddi, that was a long time ago. I didn't bring it up because I wasn't sure if you'd go out with me if you knew I'd dated Maggi for awhile."

He came up with just the right words. Teddi felt much better.

"Peter, next time you are trying to protect me from something that could be hurtful, don't. I feel like you were trying to hide this from me."

"Teddi, I'm sorry."

The waiter brought him their ticket. He paid then drove Teddi home.

"Can I come in?" he asked.

"Not tonight. I've got lots to think about."

Peter kissed her goodnight, then left.

Teddi was sad to see him go but wanted to make a point. She did not want him to think he could hide things from her and, no matter what, she would accept him. She sighed hoping she had not driven him away.

At the Karst house, things were a bit tense when Glen arrived home. Debbie was afraid he would be mad at her for hanging up on him and not answering the phone. She let Jean's comments get to her, even though she knew better.

Glen was afraid Debbie would be mad at him for sharing his room with Maggi, though it was not planned and nothing happened. Much to his surprise, when he walked into the house Debbie greeted him at the door. She smiled and he knew things were not as bad as he imagined. He smiled back; she breathed a sigh of relief knowing he was not angry with her.

"Glen, I'm so sorry I doubted you."

"Debbie, I really had no choice. I didn't plan to hurt you."

"I know. Teddi explained it all to me. I still can't believe I listened to Jean."

"Yeah, what's with her? She needs a life."

"How's Maggi?"

"A little hurt that you didn't trust her, but more shaken up about her visit to the police station. They're actually considering her a suspect at this point."

"No way."

"I don't know how to help her out of this one. I'm going to try to stay on the case from here, but hell, I'm not sure I can find out anything."

"Why are they not accepting this as a suicide or an accident?"

"I'm hoping they will eventually, but that damn book of Maggi's is slowing down the investigation."

"They don't really think she had anything to do with it because someone highlighted that page, do they?"

"They didn't, until they found out she paid to have you move Linda, and the fact that she was in the area on the night he was killed."

"I picked up a pizza. I'm keeping it warm. Want some?"

Glen kissed Debbie. "Thanks, Biscuit. I could use a bite to eat."

Debbie got the pizza while Glen grabbed a couple of beers.

He looked at his watch. After he and Maggi got back to Denver, he went to his office to check for messages and have Bill bring him up to speed on his cases. Bill was not there so Glen thumbed through the papers on his desk. Things looked calm. There was an interview from Elizabeth Malone, nothing on Tony's death and the rapist had been quiet.

He felt badly that Debbie had been holding the pizza so long, waiting for him to get home. He was tired and ready for bed as soon as they finished eating. He

197

made the rounds of the house, locking all the doors and checking with the dogs.

The phone rang at five-thirty. Glen jumped up to answer it, hoping it would not wake Debbie.

"Glen, Bill. We've got another body."

"The rapist?"

"Yep."

"Give me the address, I'll meet ya there."

It was a cold, windy morning in Lakewood. An early morning rain washed away much of the evidence, especially any footprints. Not that they had any from the previous cases; but they could hope.

When Glen arrived on the scene, Bill was already there with the crime scene investigators.

"What do ya have?"

"A white female, approximately thirty years old, beaten and probably raped."

Glen looked at the body lying on the wet ground behind a tool-shed in the backyard of a Lakewood residence.

"Who found her?"

"The man that lives here. He was taking out his trash when he saw her."

"Kinda early to take out his trash, wasn't it?"

"He normally leaves for work at six so his early morning trash is a standard routine."

"Any clue who she is?"

"Not yet. I'm waiting for someone to call in a missing person. If this is the rapist he nabbed her from a house in Littleton. Someone's gonna wake up this morning and find his wife or girlfriend missing."

"Unless she lives alone."

"If she lives alone, why would he bother to haul her away? Why not just do her there, where he doesn't have to deal with this shitty weather?"

"Any idea how long she's been dead?"

"Not yet. Sometime during the early hours is the best guess, before any work can be done on the body."

Glen and Bill returned to the office to get a grip on this case. Maggi's problem was going to have to remain Maggi's problem for the time being. Glen needed to put all of his focus into stopping this creep.

Teddi had an early morning knock at her door. It was Peter, soaking wet. Teddi quickly opened the door to let him in.

"Peter, what in the world. Why are you all wet?"

"Teddi, I feel really bad about last night. I've been out walking all morning. Please, tell me you forgive me."

"Peter, there's really nothing to forgive. Just don't ever hide anything from me again. Now go take a hot shower while I throw your clothes into the dryer."

Teddi returned to the bathroom while Peter showered. She noticed a scratch on his face when he stepped out.

"What happened to your face?"

199

"What? Where?" He looked into the mirror. "Oh that. It was pretty windy this morning when I was out walking. There was a low branch hanging over a sidewalk that blew down and scraped across my face. I'm lucky I didn't get hit in the eye."

"Where's your car? Why were you walking?"

"I came by here early this morning. It was too early to wake you so I got out and walked until I thought you might be up. When I came around the corner I saw your lights were on, so I knocked."

"Weren't you freezing in the wind and rain?"

"No, I didn't notice. I was too busy thinking of you."

Bill came to Glen's desk with a name, "Sheryl Hansen. This girl was missing from her room in a house in Littleton. Her roommate went in to find out why she wasn't getting up for work. We've got a car headed over that way to pick her up to I.D. the body."

"Do we think it's the same guy?"

"She said the screen to her first floor window was cut."

The phone rang in Glen's office. They finally had their first lead. Someone may have seen the suspect. He grabbed his coat and motioned for Bill to come along. Bill was talking to another officer at his desk. He jumped up to follow Glen.

They drove back to the scene, where one of the neighbors waited to talk to them.

200

"Tell me again what you told me on the phone," said Glen.

"I'm not sure it's important but I did see a man walking down the sidewalk in the pouring rain early this morning. I got up to use the bathroom then looked out to check on the storm. I thought he was nuts, out walking around in the freezing rain and wind. When I saw the police cars down the block, I called one of the guys I know that lives there. He told me about the missing woman. He thought I should give you a call. But like I said, it's probably nothing."

"Can you give us a description?"

"Tall, white and wearing a dark green jacket. Kinda like an army jacket or something. Maybe it wasn't green; maybe it was black. It was hard to tell. When he walked under the street light, I could tell he was white but the jacket was pretty wet so maybe it wasn't green."

"Can you tell us any more about him?"

"No, that's it."

"Was he alone?"

"Yes."

"Was he in a hurry or just casually walking around."

"He seemed a little bit of both. If I was out in that weather, I'd be walking a little fast, too."

"Did he have dark hair?"

"I don't know; it was wet."

"Did he have facial hair?"

"No."

"Was his hair long?"

"No, he looked like he might be clean cut if he were dry."

"Have you ever seen this guy before?"

"No."

"So you don't think he was one of your neighbors out for a walk or heading to work?"

"No, most of the folks on this block are retired."

"Exactly what time did you see him?"

"Around three or four. I didn't look at the clock. I just went back to bed."

"Okay, thanks," said Glen.

"What do ya think?" asked Bill.

"Could be him. But if it is, he's getting more careless. This time he let someone see him."

Maggi called Teddi later in the morning, "How far did you three get on those folders?"

"They're finished. You can start writing any time you'd like."

"Great. Are they at the office?"

"Yeah, they're on your desk."

"I'm gonna swing by and grab them. I'm leaving for a while. I need to get away. I'm not sure how much writing I'll get done but I'm gonna try. The sooner I get through with these books, the happier I'll be."

"Where are you going?"

"I'd rather not say."

"Okay, I know the drill. I'll keep things going at this end while you hide out. Just be sure to call or email like before."

"Oh, before I forget. Call Glen or Debbie later to tell them I've vanished again."

"Sure thing."

"Don't tell me Maggi's planning on putting you to work today," said Peter.

"No, she called to say she's going away. So my dear, I have the day off. Actually, I probably have as many days off as I'd like, as long as I keep up on the mail and phone calls."

"Damn, why is it every time Maggi gives you time off, all I have is a day. Then when I'm free, she works you like a slave. I've got to go out of town for a while. I'll try to cut my appointments short so I can get back to you sooner."

"Let's make the most of today."

Once there was a break in the rat race at the station, Glen gave Debbie a call.

"Hi honey, he hit again last night. I'll probably be working late today. I'll check in with you later. This time someone saw the son of a bitch."

"I sure hope you guys catch him. How bad was the woman beaten?"

"To death."

Debbie felt the hair on the back of her neck stand on end as she hung up the phone. She double-checked

203

the locks on the doors to be sure Glen locked them before he left that morning.

Maggi was pulling out of her driveway when Jean flagged her down.

"I see you have the dogs with you. Are you going away?"

"Yes, we'll be gone for awhile. I need to write."

"Are you going to start the first *Mail-Order Murder* book?"

"That's the plan," said Maggi, not wanting to speak with Jean. She was still angry about the grief Jean caused with Glen and Debbie.

Glen and Bill worked the case day and night. Three more detectives joined them when they could spare the time. Their leads went nowhere. They studied the evidence repeatedly. There just did not seem to be a pattern; except the one Glen found earlier, car abductions in Aurora by day, house abductions in Littleton by night. All the vics were found either dead or alive in Lakewood.

No DNA evidence appeared on the bodies . They knew his luck could not hold out much longer. If he was careless enough to be spotted he will be careless enough to leave behind DNA sooner or later.

Three days went by before Maggi reported in to Teddi.

"Anything going on that I should know about?"

"Not really. Warren's been in town for a while. He's been working with that new writer. He called but didn't stop by. Glen called to check on you. The rapist hit again. Maggi, it was right down the street from me."

"You're kidding."

"Not exactly down the street but only a few blocks away."

"Are you keeping yourself locked in?"

"Yes. Peter was here for a couple of days but he had to leave. I'd feel better if he were back."

"I'd feel better if he was there to look after you. You be careful."

Six weeks later, Glen and Bill were no closer to solving the case. The good news was he had not struck again. Maggi was still away writing. Detective Morrison was upset when he found out she could not be reached. Glen told him this was standard procedure for her with her writing and there was nothing to be concerned about. He guaranteed she would return.

During those six weeks of writing Maggi, checked in with Teddi every three days as planned. She faxed finished chapters to her to forward on to Warren for his approval. He and Brad did not want to wait for edited copy on these books. They wanted to see how well she was pulling off the whole concept knowing, she did not have her heart in it.

Maggi discovered not having to name her characters or make up the stories made her writing easier. The reporter part of her turned the crime stories into novel material. She treated the stories as if she had to write them up for the paper then expanded upon them. If only all her books could be so easy.

"Hi Teddi, when do you expect the slave driver home?" asked Peter.

"Any day now. She finished the first book in the series."

"Wow, already?"

"She was on a roll. Are you in town?"

"No, but I will be soon. I'm at the airport waiting to catch a flight to Denver. See ya when I get there. Better go."

"I'm back," Maggi told Teddi.

"When did you get in?"

"About an hour ago. I'm gonna take a long, hot bath. I've ordered Chinese to be delivered. The dogs and I are going to bed early tonight. I'll see you in the office in the morning. Good night."

"Just like Peter said," mumbled Teddi. "Maggi always needs me to work when he's here."

Maggi turned the dogs out in the back. She started the tub; the doorbell chimed. She paid for her food and popped it into a warm oven while she soaked in the tub. After her bath, she let the dogs in then took her containers of food to her bedroom with that day's paper.

She insisted the dogs stay on the floor while she ate. After savoring the first few bites of her chicken and Chinese vegetables in white sauce she opened the paper.

Denver Man Found Dead in Home

Maggi always read stories about deaths in an attempt to find new methods to use on her victims in her books. She knew the old saying, *truth was stranger than fiction,* fit when it came to accidental deaths.

Jack Anderson age 45, was found dead in his home by his housekeeper late yesterday morning. When Maria Sanchez arrived at the home to begin her duties as housekeeper she found Anderson dead in his home office. Cause of death is under investigation.

Maggi set the paper aside and dialed Glen and Debbie while she stuffed her mouth with her food.

"Hello," said Debbie.

There was silence on the other end while Maggi chewed quickly and swallowed.

"Sorry, I'm eating and didn't think you'd pick up so soon. I'm back. I was wondering if Detective Karst is around?"

Maggi always referred to him as Detective Karst when she was working on her books or needed to ask him about a case he was working on. The rest of the time he was Glen.

"Detective Karst is working late. Why don't you call him there."

Maggi dialed his cell phone. When he picked up the phone, she said, "Detective Karst, this is Maggi

Morgan. I'd like to speak to you about a case from the newspaper."

"Hi Maggi, when did you get home?"

"Tonight."

"What do you want?"

"I was reading about this guy"...she grabbed the paper. "Jack Anderson, can you tell me more than the paper?"

"I can, but I won't. We are still investigating."

"Please," she whined.

"No, Maggi, you'll just have to wait like the rest of Denver."

"Okay, be that way. Maybe I'll make you wait to read my latest book, too," she teased.

"Got another one done, huh?"

"Yep," she said, trying to talk and eat at the same time. "I killed my first guy with poison in his wine. He was a divorce attorney that was pretty ruthless. He made many a husband pay through the nose while he had affairs with the wives he represented. Somebody sent in an email wanting me to knock him off. Seems he thought he was some wine connoisseur so he wanted me to tamper with his collection, add a little poison, then all the ex-husbands of the world could rest easier."

Glen said nothing on the other end.

"Hello, Glen, are you too busy to talk with me? I can let you go if you're swamped."

"Maggi, are you bullshitting me about your first story?"

"No Glen. Why, don't you like it?"

Glen looked around the room to be sure no one could hear him.

"Son of a bitch, Maggi. You just described my vic's life and death."

Chapter 10

Jean watched from her window as Glen pulled into Maggi's driveway. Shortly after Maggi let Glen inside, Jean called.

Maggi checked her caller ID. "It's Jean. I'm not going to answer. I don't care if I ever talk to her again. I'm still mad about the crap she fed Debbie about us."

Glen poured a glass of bourbon for himself.

"I think I'll join you," said Maggi.

He poured a second glass.

The dogs were jumping all over Glen; wanting him to play. They knew he was a dog person and always enjoyed a good wrestle with him. Tonight was not such a night.

"If you start a fire, I'll put the dogs away so we can talk."

The phone rang again. It was Jean; just as before, Maggi ignored it.

"Where's your new manuscript? I want you to show me the part about this attorney and how you tampered with his wine."

Maggi opened her briefcase to remove the manuscript. She thumbed through the pages until she found the section then handed it to Glen.

He set his drink down, sitting on the floor in front of the fire. He leaned his back against the sofa.

Maggi watched him read as she paced. She never watched him read her material. She always sent it to him then he returned it with his corrections marked in red ink. She realized she had emptied her glass. As she was filling another she could not take her eyes off of Glen. It was painful to actually watch her work being read.

"Shit Maggi, this is exactly what happened. I mean, you can tell you embellished it a bit, but in a nutshell the attorney was found dead with traces of poison and wine in his stomach contents. During the investigation, we found the bottle that had been tampered with, but there were no prints other than his. Just like what you wrote in the story."

Maggi was frightened. "Glen, what's going on? Why are these people from my emails dying and who's responsible?"

"Hell Maggi, I wish I knew. I can tell you one thing though; we're going to get to the bottom of this. Someone is trying to set you up."

"It sure appears that way. But who?"

211

Debbie was asleep when the phone rang. She took it to bed with her so she would not miss Glen's call if he wanted to talk to her. He explained to her that he would be working late. He likes to check in when he leaves her alone at night.

Sleepily, she answered, "Hello."

"Hi Debbie, I hope I didn't wake you. I just wanted to check to make sure Maggi's alright," said Jean.

"Maggi? I guess so. Why wouldn't she be?"

"I've tried calling her a couple of times but she's not answering. When I saw Glen show up so late at night; I became concerned and called a couple of more times. He didn't answer either. I thought you might be able to shed some light on the subject for me."

Debbie was wide-awake now.

"I'm sorry, Jean, I don't have an answer for you. I'm sure if Glen is with her, all is fine. He would've called me if anything was wrong."

"Okay, if you say so. I guess I'll just go to bed. Everything must be fine."

Debbie tried to think of her earlier conversation with Glen. He told her he was working late but there was no mention of Maggi. She dialed Maggi's number. There was no answer. She felt that sick feeling in the pit of her stomach.

"Damn that Jean. Damn her. I'm sure there's nothing to worry about. Maybe Glen's not even there. Maybe she's just trying to start trouble," she whispered.

With a determination to prove Jean a troublemaker, she quickly dialed Glen's cell phone. He picked it up on the second ring.

"Hi Biscuit, what's up? Why are you awake so late? Is everything okay?"

"Glen, where are you? Are you working?"

"Yeah, I'm working on that attorney's death. Remember, I told you I'd be home late."

"Have you heard from Maggi? She called here earlier looking for you."

"I'm at her house right now. Do you want to talk to her?"

"I thought you were working?"

"I am. Maggi's new book has her first victim murdered with the same story as this case we're working on. I think, or at least we think, this is another email murder. Do you remember reading that one?"

"Vaguely, I'm not sure if I remember the email or the story you told me. The email might be one that Teddi or Jean worked on. Do you really think it's connected to the other two?"

"Deb, I wish I could say no, but I'm afraid so." He stepped out of the room. "I also think Maggi's in deep shit. I'm gonna hang around here for a while longer to talk this out with her then I'm going back to the station. This might be an all nighter."

"I guess I'll see you when you get in."

"Love ya. Good night."

213

Debbie knew it would be a sleepless night for her as well.

"Okay Maggi, let's get to work. Hand me that email."

Glen read the email. It was signed from "the good old boys club". The email was sent from a library computer. The email could not be traced beyond that. The previous two letters could be traced back to the two women whose husbands had been killed.

Maggi pointed out to Glen that Mrs. Malone, the wife of the golfer, denied writing the email and they could not trace it to her home. They were working on assumption there.

Glen took out his notebook.

"Maggi, give me the names of everyone who had access to those emails."

"Besides myself, there was Debbie, Teddi and Jean. Then there were the email folders sent to Warren and Brad."

"Is that it? Can you think of anyone else?"

"No, the emails would come to my computer. Teddi would send them to Warren and Brad. We printed, sorted and picked the top one-hundred and fifty."

"Could you have left them sitting out when you had maid service wherever you were staying?"

"No, I'm very careful about that."

"I know Debbie brought them home and I had access but I didn't read any."

"Did Jean take hers home as well?"

"Yeah, but she never has any visitors."

"Never?"

"Almost never. In all of the years I've lived here, she's only had a few. The last couple months there's been a car there occasionally. When I asked her about it she said it was some guy that wants to be a judge at dog shows. She's been giving him pointers."

"Do you know if he ever visited while she was working on the emails?"

"I don't know. I suppose he could have. To tell you the truth, I don't generally pay any attention to her house unless my dogs are there. Don't forget, I've been gone throughout most of this project."

"What about Teddi?"

"What about her?"

"Does she have company often?"

"Only Peter. Peter! He knows about the emails. I found him working on them with Teddi, even though she knew she wasn't supposed to."

"Do you think Peter could be involved somehow?"

"Peter? He's just a spineless, rich kid that never really grew up. I wouldn't think he'd be involved."

"We'll come back to him. What about Brad and Warren?"

"I guess they included others from the publishing company. Remember they wanted to use them for

215

publicity. That's why I'm stuck in this contract for four books."

"I suppose those emails could have been in dozens of hands at the publishing company's office building."

"I suppose, but it's unlikely. They wanted complete confidentiality on this. They were adamant about not wanting any leaks. I'd be surprised if they were careless."

"That leaves our list of suspects being you and me, Debbie, Teddi, Jean, Peter, Brad, Warren, and whoever else they shared them with in New York. Are we leaving anyone out?"

"That should be everybody. I guess the next step is to look for a motive, right?"

"The three main motives are money, love or jealousy. That leaves me out. I'm not mixed up in a love triangle with you, I'm not jealous of you and there's no money in it for me."

"Gee, Glen and I thought you cared," teased Maggi, trying to hide her fear.

"Next there's you. You don't know the men so there would be no love or jealousy there. You do stand to make a lot of money on these books if the publicity pays off."

"I'm comfortable with what I've got. I don't need money bad enough to kill for it."

"Debbie then. She wouldn't gain any money. She doesn't know the men and I doubt if she's jealous of you or is mixed up in some love affair."

"How about Jean? She hates me sometimes; she could use the money, she's retired. I'm not sure about a love affair with anyone other than her dogs."

"Teddi?"

"Oh come on Glen. This is ridiculous. Teddi could not possibly be involved."

"That leaves Peter, Warren and Brad and the New York gang. Money would be the only motive except for Peter. What exactly is your relationship with Peter?"

"We worked together and had a brief affair while I was divorcing Daniel, that I broke off. Now he's involved with Teddi. We might not be the best of friends but I can't see him having the balls to kill anyone."

"Maggi, you could be the number one suspect in this. You are aware of that, aren't you?"

"How could I forget? This is insane. I feel like I'm trapped inside of one of my books and can't get out."

"Maggi, bear with me. I need a few answers from you. I need to know where you were when the golfer was hit."

"Away writing."

"I know, but how far away were you?"

"Glen, you know how I feel about my privacy."

"Screw your privacy Maggi, you could be a suspect in multiple homicides."

"Okay, okay. I was in Fort Collins at the Quality Inn Suites."

"Is that where you were when the attorney was killed?"

"Yes."

"Shit, Maggi. I thought you drove for hours to go into the mountains to some lodge to write."

"I always have, but one night the dogs and I took off to get away from pressure. We stopped there for the night. I liked how quiet it was; besides they allowed my dogs. It was so handy with a field next door for the dogs to play in and the Olive Garden right down the street. No one knew why I was there or who I was. It was perfect and much closer, with the added advantage of not having to worry about snowy or icy roads during the winter months."

"Hell, that puts you in New York for Harmon's murder and close enough to drive over for the murders of Malone and Anderson. This doesn't look good. Do you have any witnesses or alibis?"

"What do you mean?"

"Just that. Can someone place you in Fort Collins during the time these two were murdered?"

Maggi buried her face in her hands. She started to cry. Glen had never seen Maggi lose control before.

"No Glen. No one saw me. I always used the back entrance. I tried on purpose to be invisible. I made a game out of it. It's part of the fun and mood I put myself in while I'm writing. I'm screwed, aren't I?"

"Not necessarily. Remember, you were not the only one that knew about the murders before they happened. Up to this point, we've not collected any evidence other than your book at the scenes. There is nothing to make you any more guilty than the others on this list," he said, shaking his notebook.

"Do you really believe that, Glen?"

"Look Maggi, I know you didn't do it. I'm gonna do everything in my power to prove you innocent. I'm gonna find out who's responsible and make sure he pays. You do trust me, don't you?"

She looked up with tears streaming down her face.

"Oh shit, Maggi. Come on, pull yourself together."

Glen sat next to her on the sofa, wiping her tears away with his handkerchief. It did not help. She put her head on his shoulder and sobbed. Glen stayed with her until she cried it all out. He knew the stress she was under.

Maggi raised up, feeling rather foolish. "I'm so sorry Glen. I'm usually in more control. I don't know what got into me."

"You've really gotta trust me on this one, Maggi. I'm not gonna let you take the blame."

Maggi left the room to throw cold water on her face. When she returned, Glen was going through his notes.

"Sure is a good feeling having Detective Karst on the case. You always save the day in my books. I mean, look at you studying your notes already."

"Actually, Maggi, these notes are on the rapist. He hit again early this morning. My time on your case has to be split with the time I need to put in on catching this son of a bitch. I hope I'm the one that gets to bring him in."

"What's happening on that case?"

"Not a whole hell of a lot. This slimy creep is pretty damn slippery. We have no DNA. The women are either too scared to talk to us or just plain can't remember anything. We're sure it's the same guy on all of the cases. He's getting more violent; he leaves no live victims now. With each new case, he has to know sooner or later he'll screw up. When he does, we'll nail him."

"Teddi told me this last woman came from her neighborhood. That's a little too close to home, Glen. I hope you catch him soon."

"We may have our first break on the case. A neighbor saw a man walking in the rain shortly after the woman was attacked. That could be our man. The problem is we got a partial description, nothing we can go on. It would've been better if he watched him get into a car so we'd have something to look for."

"It's late, Glen. Maybe you should go home to be with Debbie."

Glen looked at his watch. "Maybe you're right. I'm sure Bill's left to go home for the night. Give me a call if you remember anything that I can use to prove your innocence. I hate to say this, but I suggest you call your attorney in the morning. See if he can recommend a criminal attorney."

"I know a couple that I've interviewed for book research. I might give one of them a call."

Maggi walked Glen to the door. "Good night," she said, as she gave him a hug.

The next morning, Maggi made plans to meet Teddi in the office to work. She wanted to get her mind off of her potential problem.

Teddi brought a cup of coffee into Maggi's office.

"You look terrible. What happened to you?"

"I was up all night. I really don't want to talk about it right now. Are you up to some editing on this new book?"

"I guess. Where do you want to start?"

"I thought instead of you pre-reading, it we would just go over every page together. Is that okay with you?"

"How far did you want to go today?"

"Is Peter here?" asked Maggi.

"Yes. We had somewhat of a falling out a couple of days ago. We made up yesterday morning and I'd like to spend some time with him."

"I hope it wasn't anything serious."

"Now that you mention it, the problem was you."

"Me?"

"Why didn't you tell me that you and Peter were an item?" asked Teddi, angrily.

Maggi thought that on top of everything else going on in her life, she did not need to deal with this schoolgirl attitude about something that was ancient history.

"Teddi, that was ages ago and you seemed so happy with him. I chose not to hurt you. Did Peter tell you?"

"No, that's why we had a fight. He didn't tell me either. I felt like the two of you were hiding this from me. Debbie let it slip. I confronted Peter with it. He told me the same thing you did. It happened a long time ago and he didn't want to hurt me either. He thought I might not want to date him knowing he was one of your leftovers."

"He's not my leftover, Teddi. We barely had a relationship. Daniel made our lives so miserable, I chose not to continue. I wasn't ready for a relationship anyway. I'm still not ready. I hope you don't let that come between you."

"No, I've forgiven him. He was so sweet. Do you know he walked around my neighborhood all morning in the pouring rain? He just walked and thought about the two of us, hoping I would forgive him. By the time he saw my lights on, he was soaked clear through his clothes."

"What did you say?"

"I said he was soaked clear through his clothes."

"No, the part about being out walking in the rain."

"Yeah, he was walking in the rain thinking, until he showed up at my door."

"Did he mention seeing anyone else that morning?"

"No. Why?"

"With the rape in your neighborhood yesterday, I thought maybe if he saw someone or something strange, he could help Glen with his case."

"I suppose I can ask him, but he didn't tell me anything."

"You know what Teddi, I just remembered an appointment I made. Can you stay here and read this new manuscript until I can get back to work on it with you?"

"Can I just take it home with me?"

"No, I shouldn't be that long. Just wait here for me."

Maggi grabbed her handbag and rushed out to her car. She drove around the block then parked. She fumbled through her handbag looking for her cell phone. She was frantic that she had forgotten it. She finally found it. She turned it on to call Glen but it was not charged. She had left her car charger in her other car.

"Damn," she said, as she beat her fists against the dashboard. She looked at her watch. She did not know if she should drive to Debbie and Glen's house or head directly to the station to see if Glen was there. She was so accustomed to using cell phones, it never occurred to her to use a public phone. She opted to drive to the station.

223

Once inside, she told the officer behind the desk that she was there to see Detective Karst.

"He's not in yet but he should be any minute. Would you like to wait?"

"Sure."

Just then Bill walked in. He noticed a woman sitting on a bench along the wall. He could not miss an opportunity to flirt a little. As he approached the dark-haired figure, he realized it was Maggi.

"Well, if it isn't the beautiful and talented Maggi Morgan."

Maggi looked up and smiled, while thinking, oh great.

She rose to greet him. "Bill, isn't it?"

"I see I made quite an impression on you. You've remembered my name. Are you here to see me or Glen?"

"I was hoping to speak with Glen."

"Come on with me, you can wait in his office instead of out here."

Gladly, Maggi followed him through the door and down the hall.

Bill opened the door then stepped back to allow her to enter first. The room was overly warm from the radiator. Glen's desk was neat and tidy. Bill's desk looked as though it had been ransacked during a drug bust.

Bill poured two cups of coffee. He was handing Maggi a cup when Glen walked in.

"Maggi, what are you doing here? Did you remember something important?"

"No, but can I speak with you in private?"

"Is this about your case? If it is, we should let Bill stay. He's going to be working on it with me."

"No, this is about your rapist."

"Well, in that case, I'm definitely not leaving." Bill plopped down hard on his chair. Being overweight made the chair groan as he dropped into it.

Glen poured himself a cup of coffee.

"What do you have for me?"

Maggi was terribly uncomfortable speaking to Glen in front of Bill. She was not sure how much trouble she would get Glen into revealing that they have been discussing the case. She squirmed in her seat as she looked at Bill.

"Well?" asked Glen.

"I just thought you would like to know that Teddi said Peter was out walking in the rain in her neighborhood early yesterday morning. It's possible that he might have seen something. Maybe you should go talk to him."

Glen set his cup down as he stared intently at Maggi. Now he, too, wished he could speak privately with her.

"Peter was walking in the rain. Why?"

"He and Teddi had an argument the night before. He was killing time, waiting for her lights to go on so he could talk to her."

Bill's interest was peaked.

"I wonder what else he was killing that morning? Can you give me a description of this Peter?"

Now it was obvious that the three of them were sharing the same thoughts.

Maggi was searching Glen's face for clearance to talk openly about the case in front of Bill.

"Maggi, we have a witness that saw someone walking in the rain. We thought maybe it was our perp. Now you have me thinking it was just Peter."

"Maybe Peter and the perp are one in the same," said Bill.

"Where's Peter now?" asked Glen.

"I think he's at Teddi's," answered Maggi.

Glen looked concerned.

"Teddi's working at my office. Peter is waiting for her to get off work."

Glen scratched the whisker stubble on his face. He wanted to talk to Teddi. He wanted to question Peter. He wanted to include Bill. He also wanted to handle this with great tact, because he was dealing with a friend. Glen knew Bill could be cold and blunt.

"I think we should pay Peter a visit this morning. What do ya say, Glen?" suggested Bill.

"Maggi, why don't you go back to work? Bill and I will stop by and visit with Peter."

Glen felt comfortable knowing that Maggi would be with Teddi, so she would not be present during the questioning. He also wanted her with Teddi in case the worst could be true; that Peter could be their rapist.

The three of them left the office together. In the parking lot, they parted ways.

Glen drove while Bill began to ask questions about Peter.

"Peter is the man Teddi is seeing. Teddi is Maggi's personal assistant. Maggi and Peter go way back. She used to work for him years ago and they had a brief relationship."

"So is Maggi just bringing this to our attention because she holds a grudge?"

"No. Maggi wouldn't do that."

"Have you met him?"

"Yeah, he seems like a nice guy. I have to let you know up front, he doesn't live here. He has a home in California but he's rarely there. He travels a lot. He's a freelance writer. He goes off on a story and is gone for days at a time. Teddi usually doesn't know his schedule. He likes to pop in and surprise her whenever he can."

"Did she meet him through Maggi then?"

"Sort of. Maggi was in Germany on a booksigning tour. He was there on some assignment and stopped by to say hello. That's when he met Teddi."

"How much time has he been spending in the Denver area?"

"To tell you the truth Bill, I'm not sure. I met him for the first time in New York when he surprised Teddi there. He just comes and goes."

"So does he happen to come and go on the same dates as our rapist?"

Glen was wondering the same thing.

"I'm just not sure. I guess we'll have to find out, won't we?"

Glen pulled into the driveway of Teddi's house. He and Bill walked to the door. Glen knocked. There was no answer. He knocked again; still no answer.

"Peter. Are you in there? It's Glen."

The sound of the chain rattling on the door let the two detectives know that the door was about to be opened.

"Glen, Teddi's not here. She's working today."

"I know. We'd like to speak to you, if you have a few minutes.

Glen's eyes scanned the room out of habit. On the back of a chair hung a green jacket, army fashion.

"What can I do for you two?"

"Excuse me. Peter, this is Bill. Bill, Peter. We heard you took a stroll in the rain yesterday morning."

"Yeah, how did you know?"

"Maggi was visiting with us this morning about a case when she mentioned you were walking in the morning rain. You are probably aware that there was a rape and homicide that morning in the same

228

neighborhood and we were hoping maybe you saw something that could help us out."

"Like what?"

"Like someone else out walking or driving quickly or driving slowly. Anything at all that seemed odd to you at the time."

"No, I was pretty upset about an argument Teddi and I had. I really can't say I was focused on anything other than that."

"That's a nasty scratch on your face," said Bill. "Just how bad was the fight between you and Teddi? Did she let you have it?"

Peter raised his hand to his face to feel the scratch. He finished the movement by running his fingers through his silver gray hair.

"It was windy. I wasn't watching where I was going and a branch blew in front of my face, scratching me. I told Teddi I was lucky it wasn't my eye."

"What time were you out walking?" asked Karst.

"I'm not sure. I never drove home after I dropped Teddi off. I drove around and around her neighborhood. A couple of times I stopped and just sat in the car. I debated about going back to her house to clear up the misunderstanding. Finally, I drove to her house. When I got out to walk to the door I changed my mind about waking her then started walking. I really couldn't tell you the time or how long I was walking. It started to rain, but

I was so far from her house I had no choice but to walk back, getting soaked to the skin."

"Did you see anyone else?" asked Bill.

"No."

"Did you see anyone drive away from any homes during your late night walk?"

"I told you, if someone else was out, I didn't notice."

"Do you remember the route you took or the names of the streets you were on?" asked Glen.

"No. I'm not familiar with this neighborhood. I don't know the names of any of the streets."

"You had to remember something in order to find your way back."

"I guess I just followed my instincts and ended up back here."

"Good, then let's use those instincts and go for a walk together and you can show us the path you took," suggested Glen.

While on their walk Bill said, "Glen tells me you're from California. Bet this cold Colorado weather is pretty nasty compared to what you're used to."

"I travel a lot; I see all kinds of weather."

"Now that you're seeing ..." Bill paused to look in his notebook, "...Teddi. Do you plan to stick around Colorado?"

"I'm not sure. I guess I haven't given it much thought."

"How often do you get to stop by for a visit?"

"Not as often as I'd like to," he answered.

"When are you planning to leave again?" asked Glen.

"I'm not sure. I haven't made any real plans yet. Why?"

"I'd like to be able to talk to you again if we get any leads, to see if you remember anything that can help," explained Glen.

"Sure I understand. Teddi will be able to reach me if you need me."

"That's great, but we'd really like to find you ourselves without having to inconvenience Teddi. Could you please give us your cell phone number and your itinerary for the next few weeks? It would be a big help," urged Glen.

Reluctantly, Peter complied with their requests.

"Thanks for your time," said Bill handing him a card. "Just give us a call if you remember anything else."

Out in the car, Bill said, "Pretty damn cool. I sure as hell couldn't read him. What about you?"

"I'm not sure either. That scratch has me concerned. Let's swing by my house and talk to Debbie. Maybe she can give us a date or two when he was in town and see if we have any matches."

"Sounds good to me. Will she fix us lunch?"

"Probably, but I'm not going to ask her to. If you're hungry, we can raid my refrigerator."

231

Debbie was surprised to hear Glen come in so early in the day.

"Hi honey, what are you doing home? Oh, Bill, hi."

"We're gonna raid the refrigerator and talk to you," said Glen, as he kissed her.

"What do you want to talk to me about?"

"You're good with names and dates. Do you think it would be possible to think back over the last few months to how often Teddi's friend Peter was in town?"

"Oh Glen, I'm not sure."

"Just try, Deb. Was he around while you were working for Maggi? Do you remember Maggi going off to write and Peter spending time with Teddi?"

"I remember the day we went to Teddi's and Peter was there. When Maggi learned about the golfer's homicide. Oh, and then there was the time..."

Glen winked at Bill.

"Why don't we leave you alone to think about it and check your calendar while we make a sandwich," said Glen, as he escorted her to the office to jot dates down. Once he closed the door he grabbed her and kissed her a long passionate kiss. He ran his hands up and down her body. She playfully slapped him.

"Stop it, Glen. Bill's in the other room."

"I know," he teased.

She shoved him out of the door.

When Glen returned to the kitchen, Bill had emptied the entire sandwich-making contents from their refrigerator onto their counter.

"Do you have those dates in your notebook?" asked Bill.

"Yep," answered Glen.

They were sitting at the counter in the kitchen when Debbie returned. She had done a thorough job. She handed a slip of paper to Glen then went to make a sandwich.

"You two didn't tell me why you need this. Does it have anything to do with Maggi's case?"

"Not exactly. I'll explain tonight when I get home."

Bill looked over Glen's shoulder as he opened his notebook to compare dates.

"Debbie, how sure are you about these dates?"

"Pretty sure, why?"

Bill's cell phone rang, interrupting the conversation.

"Great. Thanks."

"What?" asked Glen, seeing the excitement on Bill's face.

"Seems we have a lead. The last vic that he killed had a good amount of skin cells and blood under one of her fingernails. She may have scratched the guy."

"Let's go," said Glen.

Debbie stood watching the two of them run out of the door. She was totally confused.

"Tree branch, my ass. Walking in the rain, pining over some argument. Can you believe how close those dates were? Most of them were right on," said Bill.

"Even those that were a day or so off could still mean he was in the area but hadn't connected with Teddi yet."

They sped back to Teddi's house. When they arrived, Peter's rental car was gone.

Chapter 11

The lab finished the work on the blood and skin cells from under the woman's fingernail. Glen and Bill waited outside the door for the results. The short time they were in Teddi's house, Glen managed to lift a hair off the shoulder of the army jacket draped over the chair. He dropped it off at the lab to be analyzed. It was not much, but it was all they had for the moment.

"Do you think we'll have a match? asked Bill.

"I don't know. My guess is we'll have to go back to Teddi's to find more traces of DNA. Maybe he shaved while he was there and used Teddi's razor, or maybe we can find his prints on a glass, or..."

Glen stopped wishing out loud when the door opened and the results were handed to him. Bill studied his face, waiting for his expression to reveal whether the news was good or bad.

His expression told Bill it was bad. Glen handed the report to him.

"Damn, I can't believe it, can you?" said Bill.

"I sure never thought we'd see these results. Looks like we're back to square one. That hair sample didn't do us a hell of a lot of good."

"I hear ya. Who would've thought the blood and skin cells would have been from the victim? She scratched herself. The report said she scraped a blemish, probably a scab or a pimple. I was hoping she had a piece of Peter's face under her nail," whined Bill.

"Let's get over to the office and run a background check on our friend Peter," suggested Glen.

Glen sat at his computer and began the search for Peter Eugene Hughes. It turned out he was a Junior. Maggi was right; his dad has lots of money. Glen waited, as the screen slowly, line by line, put up his record in chronological order, from the oldest to the most recent.

"Anything?" asked Bill.

"Some speeding tickets, parking tickets. Here's one for drug possession, marijuana."

Glen watched as the words appeared on his screen. He jumped forward in his chair to get a closer look. Bill rushed to read over his shoulder.

"Bingo! Seems little Peter was involved in a rape case years back," Bill said, with a bloodthirsty sound to his voice.

Glen jotted down the information then did a search to bring up the case.

"Hell, it happened right here in Denver. Let's pull the file," suggested Glen.

236

Reading through the file, they learned Peter was in his early twenties and the girl was fourteen. He was accused but once it made it to trial, not convicted. The charge was statutory rape. His high-paid attorney got him off. He convinced the jury his client had no idea the girl was fourteen and it was consensual.

"Hell, that's one of those he said, she said cases," complained Glen.

"Yeah, there's no telling if he really raped her or not. His record is clean after that. No other girls came forward at that time to help convict him. Do you think we can use it to pick him up for questioning?"

"I don't know, Bill, we really don't have anything. The guy was out walking; that's not a crime. He did have a reason to be in the neighborhood since he's dating Teddi. We don't know if he was around Denver every time our rapist hit and I doubt if even Teddi can confirm all of those dates for us. The eyewitness didn't tell us anything that could connect him to the victim, just that he was seen walking in the neighborhood. Even if he's our guy, without any evidence at the scenes or..."

Bill looked up at Glen, who was pacing around the room.

"What?"

"Let's get a photo of him to the women to see if we can get a positive ID. They said they couldn't give us a description but maybe, just maybe, they remember more than they think they do."

Glen sat back at the computer to find a drivers license photo of Peter. They gathered a few more pictures from their library to do a photo lineup to show the women. If one or more of them identify him then maybe the D.A. will allow them to issue an arrest warrant for him. They agreed it was worth a try.

One by one they visited the victim's homes. Not one of them could pick Peter out of a photo line-up. One thought there was a chance it could be him but then changed her mind because she was not really sure.

Glen called Maggi to find out if Peter was still in the area.

She informed him that when Teddi went home, later that day, he was gone and she had not heard from him since. She told Glen she would call Teddi to see if there was any news from Peter.

"Hello," said Teddi, when Maggi called.

"Hi Teddi. Any word from Peter?"

"I'm not sure I'd tell you if I did hear from him after you turned him in to the police as the rapist."

"Teddi, I just told Glen he should ask him if he saw anything that night while he was out walking."

"You think he's guilty and so does Glen!"

"You have to admit it does seem a little strange that he just disappeared after they spoke with him."

"I think he was just scared."

"Of what, unless he had something to hide."

"Look Maggi, I don't think I want to talk to you right now. As a matter of fact consider this our last conversation. I don't think I can work for you any longer, under the circumstances."

"Teddi, you can't be serious," Maggi pleaded.

"I couldn't be more serious."

Teddi hung up the phone.

Maggi was stunned. She phoned Glen.

"Did you find out anything?" he asked.

"Nope. She said even if she did hear from him, she wasn't going to tell me after I accused him of being the rapist and turned him into the police."

"She sounds pretty mad. I'm sure she'll calm down soon."

"I'm not so sure. She just quit her job."

"No shit?"

"Glen, what have I done? Do you think I was too hasty telling you about Peter?"

"No Maggi, you did the right thing. If he's totally innocent, he wouldn't have disappeared like he did."

"I hope you're right."

"Say, when am I supposed to read through your manuscript?"

"Oh, there's been a change of plans. The publisher took it and they are going to push through the editing for a speedy release. They hope to have it on the market within the month. They are already pressuring me to begin the second in the series."

"You know, I really don't mind helping you but I feel I can serve you best at this time by working on your case instead of your book."

The publishing company kept their word and her book was released in just six short weeks. Book tours and talk shows were already scheduled. Maggi's nightmare continued when one of the staff members from a talk show did a thorough job of her homework. She found the connection between the dead attorney and her first victim in her book.

The discussion soon turned to the coincidence between the two.

"Tell me Maggi, you live in the Denver area. What did you think when you learned that someone, an attorney no doubt, died from poisoned wine just like your victim? Did you take your story from the newspaper or was this one of your email murders?"

"I'm afraid he died while I was away writing. It was just a major coincidence."

"My researchers tell me that you received thousands of emails from readers asking you to kill someone for them after you made the offer on Oprah."

"I guess we received a few."

"Your publisher tells us that you're writing a series of books based on your requests from those emails. Is that correct?"

Maggi squirmed under the warm lights. She wanted to be anywhere but where she was at the moment.

"Yes, that's true. They thought it would be fun and entertaining for my readers to possibly see their story in one of my books."

"We also learned that you were in New York when a man was found dead in his apartment. It appears he died according to a scene in one of your books and that scene was highlighted and left open for the police to find. How do you explain that?"

"I can't."

The host shuffled through his cards on his desk.

"And there was the golf pro, also in Denver, that was shot in his driveway. Didn't you write that into one of your stories as well?"

"No, I didn't use that one."

"Oh, that's right. That was one of the emails you received. That makes three dead men that you are connected to. Tell us how that happened."

"I suppose you could pick up any one of my books or those of other mystery writers and discover a death somewhere that fits the same profile and storyline that was written. There are only so many ways to write murders in books. They're repeated over and over."

During the commercial break, Maggi removed her microphone and left the stage. She so wished Teddi would have been there to help her through this. She would have known the interview was going badly and would be prepared with Maggi's bags at the door to leave.

Maggi ran out the backstage door to hail a cab. She left her things behind. She went back to her hotel and sent a driver to retrieve her belongings. She was furious. Her publishers must have betrayed her for the almighty dollar.

She called Warren.

"What in the hell's going on?" she asked.

"Honestly, Maggi. I have no idea who leaked. I just talked to Brad and he said the same thing."

Maggi's phone was beeping, so she said good-bye to Warren to accept Glen's call.

"Maggi, how did the show go?"

"Glen, the word is out that I'm connected to all of the deaths."

"That's impossible. We haven't even, I mean the D.A. hasn't even built a case against you yet."

"Someone told the story to someone, because it's out."

"Who do you think it was?"

"Warren swears Brad and the publishing company had nothing to do with it."

"That leaves, Debbie, Jean, Teddi, and Peter."

"We know Debbie wouldn't say anything. Teddi is mad at me but I still think it would be highly unlikely that she would do something so hurtful. Peter, now that's a different story. Who knows, after his disappearing act, what he's capable of?"

"When are you coming home?"

"I'm flying back in the morning. I'm going to force the cancellation of the rest of my shows and my tour. I can't keep this up."

Most of the next day Maggi was on the phone with Warren and Brad, trying to get out of her commitments. She agreed only to take the talk shows that would promise to avoid the subject of the real murders that paralleled her stories in the book. That was not an easy task but by the end of the day they had reached a compromise.

Bill and Glen went to Teddi's house to question her about Peter's whereabouts.

"Any word from Peter?" asked Glen.

"No. Not a word, thanks to you and Maggi."

"Come on, Teddi. He needs to contact us so we can clear him."

"All he did was go for a walk in the rain and you want to connect him to a series of rapes and murders. Your imagination is just as wild as Maggi's. Maybe you should start writing fiction. The two of you have always made such a good team. Maybe you can outdo her."

"Teddi, your boyfriend was in the area when that last woman was raped and killed. According to our information, he was in Denver for most of the cases. Then there is the little detail of him being accused of rape in an earlier case. He was tried but not convicted," said Bill, in an attempt to shock her and read her face.

It worked. She nearly fell over.

"I don't believe you. Peter is not capable of such a thing. Why would someone like Peter want to rape anyone? We had a good relationship. Just look at him," she pointed to a picture of Peter on her fireplace mantle. "He's surely not had any problem over the years finding women who want to be with him."

"Rape isn't about sex, Teddi. Many men live relatively normal lives until this side of them surfaces. They can go years before anyone suspects them. All we want to do is clear Peter. If you hear from him, tell him to contact us. In the meantime, be careful, just in case."

Teddi looked up at Bill. She had tears in her eyes. She was hurt and angry.

"Please leave," she instructed, as she walked to the door to open it.

Glen put his hand on her shoulder.

"I'm sorry, Teddi. We just have a job to do. We really hope you're right and Peter has nothing to do with this."

Teddi closed the door behind them. She believed Glen. She knew he really wanted what was best for her. She started to rethink her decision to quit her job with Maggi. She thought maybe she was being too hasty. She convinced herself that for the time being she would take a few months off. If she felt she could forgive Maggi for breaking up her relationship with Peter then she might consider returning to work.

Her thoughts turned from Maggi to Jean. She had real regrets about talking to Jean about Maggi and the police. She seemed to call Teddi whenever she could not reach Maggi. At times, Teddi felt as if she was just pumping her for information. The day she quit her job with Maggi, Jean called. She caught her in a vulnerable mood and she told her things about the rapist, Peter, Maggi and Glen.

Oh man, she thought. I can't believe I shared that information with her.

Since that time, she always checks her caller ID and does not pick up when it is Jean. She tried to brush off that sick feeling about Jean by thinking warm thoughts about Peter. She really missed him. She was extremely hurt that he thought so little of her he could just walk away without a word. That was weeks ago. Deep down inside, she knew no matter how much she chose to blame Maggi that something else caused Peter to disappear. Was Bill right? Was he really accused of rape before? Could he be the rapist?

She hurried to her room to open her diary. She wrote down all the days she knew Peter was with her. She was not quite sure what she planned to do with it. She did not want to show it to Glen and Bill. She did not want to give them any more leads to help convict Peter. Thoughts continued to race through her mind. Perhaps, if they had these dates showing Peter was with her in New

York or California when the rapes occurred, that would clear him.

She closed her diary and carefully placed it in her drawer. She carried the piece of paper with the dates from room to room. She would glance at the telephone then decide against it. Normally, she would discuss this with Maggi. She felt she could not talk to anyone who could help her feel better.

She did not have Internet access on her home computer. She spent so much time at the office that she did not want emails or work coming to her at home as well. She wanted to do a search for the stories about the serial rapist in Denver over the last year. She thought about going to a library. She assured herself Maggi would not be working at the office without her. Maggi never went there to work alone. Teddi read in the paper that her book was released so there was no reason for her to be there.

She took her list then drove over to the office. It was late afternoon. The weather was cold and gray. The streets were slushy and the snow was black from exhaust. She hated this part of winter, when everything looked dreary and depressing. She drove around the block first to be sure there were no lights on and no sign of Maggi's car.

She stayed until early evening searching and reading the stories. She was matching more dates than she wanted to. When she was finished she decided to take them back to her house to spend more time working out every detail without having to look over her shoulder every few minutes, fearing Maggi might walk in.

She was feeling pangs of hunger as she was locking the office. She decided to pick up Chinese food so she would not have to cook. She had a little difficulty walking on the icy parking lot to return to her car. It was dark so she moved as quickly as she could while trying to remain upright.

When she arrived the lot was filled to capacity but now there was hers and just one other. She pulled out onto the street then stopped at the light at the corner. She glanced into her rearview mirror to see the small pickup pulling out of the lot she had just left.

As she drove along the streets to her favorite Hunan restaurant, she noticed the pickup was behind her. She was feeling uneasy, having read so many rape stories earlier. She shrugged the chill from her shoulders then pulled into the parking lot to pick up her food. She felt very foolish as she walked quickly to the front door and noticed the same pickup turning the corner, leaving the area.

She was relieved. For a tiny moment, she hoped it was Peter looking for her. Soon she was pulling out of the parking lot with the smell of hot and sour soup and almond chicken filling the car, making her hunger grow more intense.

She was nearly home when she happened to see that same pickup behind her. At least she thought it was the same. It was hard to tell in the dark and it was at least four car-lengths behind her. She tried to slow down to get a license number but he stayed the same distance behind her, adjusting his speed to hers.

She pulled over to let him pass, hoping to get the license number then but his plate was too snow-caked to allow her to read it. She jotted down on paper that it was a burgundy, Toyota pickup. She could not tell the year; she was not very good at that.

She pulled back into the street and headed home. The vehicle never returned to her line of vision. She carried her food to the kitchen then returned to her car for her paperwork. When she was walking back to the house; she turned to look at the street as the burgundy, Toyota pickup drove by. She ran the rest of the way. Once inside, she locked and bolted the doors and windows. She closed the drapes and turned on all of the lights.

She went to the front window to look out. The street looked quiet. Occasionally, one of her neighbors drove by. She tried to put it out of her mind. She started a fire then returned to the kitchen to find her hot supper had grown cold during the time she took to safeguard herself and watch out the window. She warmed it then went to the living room to eat in front of the fire.

Just before she finished, she spread out the information she had printed at Maggi's office about the rapes and began comparing dates. Uneasiness crept over her as she realized she could never give Peter an alibi. Not one rape happened while he was out of the state with her. That did not mean he committed them; it just meant she could not prove him innocent.

She stared into the flames, trying to decide what to do. Should she call Glen and tell him what she learned? She thought back to the Toyota that followed her tonight. Maybe she should call him about that. He was always complaining not enough people notify them of suspicious happenings. Then, after a crime is committed, they wished they had.

She looked at her watch. It was late. She decided to call him at his office in the morning.

It was a long night for Teddi. She tried to sleep but sleep never came. Her mind raced with thoughts of Peter and the Toyota. Every time she closed her eyes, she woke to every creak in the house. It did not help that the wind picked up, blowing frozen branches against the window in her room. She remembered how the rapist always entered through a lower level window by cutting the screen then lifting the window. She climbed out of bed repeatedly to be sure the window was locked and to reassure herself the sounds were truly tree branches.

Maggi was having breakfast in the kitchen with her dogs when her doorbell rang. She looked out to see a young man standing there with a large envelope. She opened the door as wide as the chain would allow.

"Are you Miss Morgan?"

"Yes."

"I have a delivery for you."

He handed the envelope and a clipboard through the small opening. Maggi signed for the envelope then handed the clipboard back to him.

"Thank you," he said. He turned to walk away.

Maggi returned to the kitchen, turning the envelope over to see if she could tell who sent it. There were no markings on it. She thought back to the mysterious letters she received before, connecting her to the deaths. She chose not to open it. She decided to give it to Glen and Bill instead.

She finished her breakfast then took the dogs out for a walk. The mysterious envelope remained unopened on her kitchen counter. When she returned, she planned her day.

First, she thought she would do her grocery shopping. She was making plans to disappear for the second book in the series. The first one, having only been out for a few weeks, was selling off of the shelves. The publishers could not be happier.

Next, she would stop by her office to check for messages and emails, since Teddi was not around to do it. She knew she should begin interviewing someone for office work but hoped Teddi would return before more time elapsed.

The weather was cold; Maggi decided to let the dogs go along. She knew they would not overheat in her

SUV. Errands went smoothly. Maggi and the dogs found themselves back home by mid-afternoon.

While she was putting away her groceries, the envelope caught her eye. She picked it up, feeling the contents inside. She considered opening it then decided to stick with her instincts to call Glen about it.

When she connected with his office he was out on a call but Bill was there. He managed to include himself in all of the conversations and investigative work that Maggi and Glen were working on. He liked to consider them a three-some. Actually, Maggi was growing accustomed to his interference and had no trouble sharing information with him. When she told him about the envelope, he offered to pick it up himself. She agreed.

Bill made it to Maggi's door in record time. She wanted to tease him about speeding but did not want to give someone with his personality any reason to think she was flirting with him or, worse yet, attracted to him. She kept their relationship as stiff as possible.

The two dogs came bounding into the room to see who was at the door. Bill stepped back against the wall, not sure how friendly the two huge dogs were. Bailey let out a bark so deep; it caused Bill to gasp.

Once Maggi assured him the dogs were fine, he followed her to the kitchen.

"Can I offer you a cup of coffee?"

"That would be great."

Maggi poured two cups of coffee while she watched Bill examine the envelope.

"How did you say you got this?"

"A messenger brought it."

"Do you know what company he was with?"

"No, I didn't notice."

"Can you remember anything about the advertising on his vehicle?"

Maggi thought for a moment.

"You know, I think he used his own car. It was an older small car. I sure couldn't tell you what make it was. It was dark and dirty."

Bill opened the end of the envelope with his pocketknife. He shook a letter out onto the counter.

Maggi did not want to read it at first.

Bill let out a whistle.

"Seems you have an admirer."

"Oh great!" said Maggi.

"It also appears you broke a date."

"Why? What do you mean?"

She walked over to the counter to read the letter.

Dear Ms. Morgan,

My compliments to you and your books. You are one very clever writer. We have much in common. I feel as though I am very clever with my work as well. I would like very much to meet with you in person. Let's meet today for lunch at "The Egg and I" nearest you. I'll meet you there at one o'clock. I do hope you come. You see, if you don't, you won't want to know the outcome. My rules are that you come alone and if you call or go to the police with this, trust me, I'll know.

Your brother in crime.

"He has to be nuts to think I would go meet a perfect stranger for lunch. You don't think he's going to follow through with his weak threat, do you?"

"Beats the hell out of me. Let me take this to the lab for fingerprints. Too bad it's typed. I tell you with the availability of computers, no one writes ransom notes by hand any more. What's this world coming to?" chuckled Bill, trying to be humorous.

Maggi failed to see any humor in the situation.

"You will see to it that Glen gets a chance to look at this, won't you?"

"Of course I will. Why wouldn't I?"

"I don't know. I'm just double-checking."

She was anxious for him to leave. Cop or no cop, he still gave her the creeps. Having him alone with her in her house magnified the feeling.

"I'd love to stay and chat Maggi, but I've got work to do. Maybe I'll take a rain check."

She thought, I'm not offering one.

She followed him to the door, locking it behind him.

Maggi was unaware that the case Glen was working on involved Teddi. He was in her neighborhood when Teddi called him that morning to discuss the Toyota. He stopped by to get the details. There was not much he could do to help her. He told her to continue doing what she had been; keeping the doors and windows locked and to call if she needed help.

Shortly after dark, Maggi's doorbell rang again. It was another delivery boy, a different one this time. They repeated the process from earlier that day. This time, Maggi examined the boy more closely. He looked as if he was around twenty-one, no uniform, and no advertisement on his car. She looked at the clipboard sheet he had her sign, hers was the only name on it and there was no company name at the top.

This time when he drove away, she stepped out onto her driveway and was able to get a license plate number.

She called it in to Glen.

"Don't open that envelope, let Bill or me do it."

"Please don't send Bill back over here; he gives me the creeps."

Glen looked at his watch.

"I'm supposed to meet Debbie in an hour for supper. I guess I can call her and tell her I'm gonna be a little late. That won't come as any big surprise. I'll swing by and grab it from you on my way."

"Thanks, Glen."

He must have been pretty close by, because it did not take him long to get there. Her house sits on top of a hill at the end of a circle drive. She and Jean share the drive. Glen met a car leaving the circle as he drove up to Maggi's.

"Who was your company?" he asked

"What company?"

"Oh, I just saw a car leave, I thought it was coming from here."

"Nope, not from here. Was it a little green car?"

"Yeah, a teal green Ford Escort."

"That's the guy that visits with Jean about dog show stuff. I haven't seen his car there for some time."

"So let's get this letter open and check out the trouble you've gotten yourself into with this admirer."

Glen slit the end of the envelope in the same manner that Bill had done earlier.

"Do they teach you guys that stuff in detective school?" teased Maggi.

"As a matter of fact, they do."

255

He slid the contents out onto the coffee table. There was a letter and what appeared to be the backside of two photographs.

Glen flipped the letter over first with the end of his knife. They read it together.

Maggi,

You don't follow instructions very well, do you? Not only did you not meet me for lunch but I saw that cop at your house. Chances are your other detective friend, Karst, is in on this as well. So I thought it would be fun to bring him into our little adventure.

It's obvious you won't meet with me on my terms. I have so many stories to tell you. I think you could easily fill a book or two with my games. I'm no different than your other fans. I've been reading the papers and watching the talk shows. I think it is quite interesting how you are using suggestions from others for your stories.

I'll have to admit, until the recent publicity, I had no idea who you were nor had I read any of your books. Now I can say I'm one of your greatest fans. Together we can write some great stuff. That is, of course, if you are willing to stray from your traditional way of writing. You see, you never really capture the essence of the pain and suffering of your victims. You don't describe in enough detail the blood and the dying. I can help you with that.

I can help you get inside the mind of the killer. I can help you know the power a man feels when he takes a woman against her will. Just to make sure you plan to take me seriously, I've enclosed a couple of photos. One of these lovelies will be my next victim unless you agree to work with me.

I'll expect an answer from you this time. Just put an ad in the personals section saying, I understand. M.M. Then I know we will be happy working together. If I don't see that in forty-eight hours, one of your friends will have a new message for you from me.

BIC

"What in the hell is BIC?"

Maggi thought for a moment, "Brother in crime," she said.

Glen flipped over the first photo. It was a candid shot of Teddi going into Maggi's office.

"Oh my God, not Teddi."

Glen flipped the second picture over. His eyes met the soft blue eyes of his wife, Debbie.

Maggi watched as the veins began to bulge on Glen's neck and his face turned crimson.

Chapter 12

Bill knocked at the apartment door while two uniformed policemen stood off to one side. A blond young man dressed in a sweatshirt and blue jeans answered the door.

Bill showed him his badge.

"Are you the owner of the dark blue Chevy parked outside with the license number XY..." Bill read the number from his notebook.

"Yes, that's my car. Is something wrong?" he asked, noticing the two policemen in the hall.

Bill asked, "Do you mind if we come in to ask you a few questions?"

"No. Come on in."

There were three other boys in the apartment that quickly came to attention when the police officers entered.

"What's this all about?" asked the boy.

"Do you work for a messenger service?"

"No."

"Did you loan your car to someone else earlier today?" he asked, looking at the other boys.

"No."

"So you did not deliver an envelope to a Ms. Morgan at 55..."

Before Bill could finish the address, the boy answered, "Yes, I delivered an envelope to her."

"I thought you didn't work for a messenger service."

"I don't. Some guy came up to me on campus and said he needed an envelope delivered in a hurry. He had another appointment across town and was looking for a student who wanted to make a few bucks. He took my name and phone number and said if I did a good job he'd look me up for future deliveries. He paid me fifty bucks. I made sure I did a good job. That's easy money."

"Do you know the guy's name?"

"No. He said he'd call me if he needed me."

"Can you give me a description of him?"

"Tall, well built, an older guy, with gray hair."

"How old?"

"I don't know, pretty old, around forty I'd guess. He made me think of my dad."

"Can you tell me anything else about him? Did he wear glasses or have any facial hair?"

"No."

"I'd like you to come downtown with us to do a photo line-up," said Glen.

260

"Why? What did the guy do?"

"We're not sure he did anything, he may be involved in part of an investigation we're working on. It would be a big help if you would work with us on this one."

"Okay, I can go with you right now."

At the police station, Glen and Bill showed the boy photos of six men. One of them was Peter.

"That's him right there!"

The boy made a positive I.D. of Peter.

Glen and Bill looked at each other, pleased with the results.

"No, wait. I think it could be this other guy here. Or maybe ... no, it's definitely one of those two."

"Can you narrow it down any more? Does one look more like the man in question than the other?" asked Bill.

"Not really, but it could be either one of them. Ya know, I really don't remember. He was in a hurry and it was cold outside. It all happened so fast. Do you want me to tell him you're looking for him if he calls me again?"

"No. If he calls you again, you notify us immediately. Don't tell him a thing."

As Glen and Bill watched him leave the building, Bill said, "Damn, I thought we had him."

Glen just shook his head.

Glen met Debbie at the restaurant. He told her what happened at Maggi's.

261

"I think maybe I should take some time off and not let you out of my sight for awhile," he suggested.

"I'd feel safer if I knew you were out there catching him. Who do you think he is?"

"How the hell would I know?"

"You know what I mean. How would you profile him?"

"Debbie, at this point I can't tell you anything, except he's dangerous and pretty damn sly. I'll bet he's been stalking Maggi and you and Teddi for a while now. He seems to know too much."

"Has anyone told Teddi yet?"

"I tried to call her but she wasn't home."

"Oh Glen, let's skip supper. Let's go to her house and see if she's okay."

"I can send a car over, that would be faster."

"Do it then and let's follow up ourselves."

Glen flagged the waiter down. He explained something came up and they had to leave. He apologized and left a nice tip.

When Glen and Debbie arrived at Teddi's house, a cruiser was parked in her driveway but Teddi did not appear to be home. Glen sent the car away while he and Debbie waited for her to return.

"You know, Glen, she's a bit of a sissy when it comes to going out at night. I'm worried."

Glen got out and walked around the house to look for anything out of place. Nothing caught his attention.

262

"Let's go home, Biscuit. We'll call her from there until we find her. Do you have her cell number?"

"No, but we can get that from Maggi."

"Oh shit!"

"What?"

"I was so worried about you, I forgot about the guy that was tailing Teddi."

"What guy?"

"She called because some guy was following her and he made her nervous. She thought she lost him when, shortly after she arrived home, he drove by. She was pretty shaken up by it. Damn, I hope he wasn't this weirdo."

Once Debbie got Teddi's cell phone number they kept trying to reach her but there was no answer.

Maggi was worried too. She agreed with Debbie that Teddi did not like to go out alone at night.

The phone rang in the middle of the night at Maggi's. She answered hoping it would be news about Teddi.

"Maggi, you're not playing by the rules. I saw the cops at your friend Teddi's house tonight. I also saw Detective Karst guarding his pretty little wife. You didn't waste any time sharing with him. If you don't want to play by the rules, I'm gonna change them too."

He slammed the phone down.

263

Maggi immediately dialed Glen to tell him about the call. Now they were really worried about Teddi. It appeared the forty-eight hours was not an option.

Glen had three women to protect and had no idea which one of them the weirdo was after first. He could not be in three places at once plus he knew he could not bring in the typical backup. He needed unmarked cars and plain clothes officers on this one.

He called it in, but his sergeant told him no reserves could be sent to the scene. Glen did not have enough hard evidence to warrant a team of officers be sent to Maggi's. He had no choice but to handle this on his own.

Right after he called it in, his phone rang. It was Teddi. She was home. She went to a movie and just returned.

"Teddi, lock your doors and stay put. Debbie and I will be right there."

As they were about to leave the house, Glen caught a glimpse of a man in his peripheral vision. He hesitated. He turned towards him but he was gone. He quickly remembered his conversation with Jennifer Parker, his psychic friend. Could the image that appeared then disappeared, in his living room, be the same man that might have a message for him?

"Debbie, go ahead I've got something to take care of before I can leave."

He waited until he was sure Debbie was outdoors. He felt foolish, but following Jennifer's instructions, he spoke out to the figure that was no longer standing there.

"What do you want? Do you have a message for me?"

When there was no response, Glen felt ridiculous for trying to talk to someone that was not there. As he walked back to the door to join Debbie, he heard a voice behind him.

"Protect," there was a pause, "Debbie."

Glen spun around to look in the direction of the voice. He was not sure whether he really heard a voice or if he heard his own thoughts. There was no one there. He tried to speak to him again, but there was no response. He knew he needed to do something to make Debbie safe. He went into his closet. He pulled opened a drawer and took out Debbie's gun. He loaded it and slipped it into his coat pocket. They drove swiftly to Teddi's house.

On the way he phoned her and told her to be ready to leave with them. He told her to turn some lights on and make it appear she was home. Maybe leave the television on, too.

When Glen and Debbie arrived in Debbie's car, Teddi obeyed, she rushed out and jumped in. They sped away.

Glen could only hope the admirer was not watching at that particular moment. He hoped he and Debbie made a clean break with Teddi.

"Where are we going?" asked Teddi.

"I'm taking the two of you to Maggi's house. If I can't be in three places at once to watch, I'm going to group you together. We just have to do it in such a way that he has no idea the three of you are together.

"I'd prefer to have the all of you hidden someplace else, someplace safer. My idea to use disguised officers in your place was vetoed by my sarge."

Teddi was glad Glen was forcing her to see Maggi. She really did miss her but was not ready to make the first move. She only wished it could be under a different set of circumstances.

Glen called Maggi.

"Maggi, I'm dropping Debbie and Teddi off at your house. Is there a way they can come in the back door in case your house is being watched?"

"There's no way you can drive to the back. You can let them out on the block behind me and have them walk through the yards to get here. Don't forget mine is fenced in."

"That's okay. I'll go with them and help them over the fence. I'll call you when we get closer. Draw your drapes to make sure he can't see inside your house. He needs to think all three of you are alone in your own homes."

Debbie was a little upset by Glen's statement.

"What do you mean, you'll help us over her fence. I think we can handle that without you. We're not

266

helpless. You just drop us and take off as planned. We'll call you when we're inside."

Glen pulled into the driveway of the house behind Maggi's. He shut off the lights and the engine. Just as Debbie and Teddi were about to leap from the car, Glen grabbed Debbie's arm. He slipped her gun into her hand. She felt the cold metal as the gun slid into position. How she loved that gun. She had not shot it much since her days in training at the police academy. She and Glen had made the decision that one cop in the family was enough; she never joined the force.

She slipped the gun into her jacket pocket and kissed Glen. He hurried her out of the car then he walked to the door of the house behind Maggi's. He flashed his badge to the residents. He told them he needed to use their home for a surveillance point. They stepped aside to let him in.

Teddi waited in the shadows for Debbie to join her. She followed Debbie's lead through the yards to the fence. Debbie chose a section of fence that was most sheltered from view. She helped Teddi climb to the top. Teddi dropped to the ground on the other side in the cold, wet snow. Debbie quickly joined her.

They paused to look and listen. There was nothing that told Debbie to wait; they proceeded across the huge lawn to the back door.

Glen called Maggi to tell her he made the drop. The two girls slid into the unlocked backdoor, bolting it behind them. Maggi went onto the mudporch to join them. She caught the look in Teddi's eyes. She knew Teddi missed her as much as she missed Teddi.

"I'm surprised you two aren't dressed in black with stocking caps," teased Maggi, trying to lighten the mood.

Teddi's adrenaline was running high.

"That was thrilling. I'm just glad we're safe inside."

"What do we do next?" asked Maggi.

"Follow your normal routine. Remember, he has to think you're alone," explained Debbie.

He watched carefully from the window of the house to be sure no one else was in the yard while the girls made their way to the door. Now that he knew they were safely inside, he wanted to be in the house with them.

He told the girls his plan and they were relieved he was going to be there soon.

Teddi and Debbie stayed in the dark kitchen while Maggi went about her evening rituals. She drew a bath and followed all of her normal routines. Her phone rang.

"Eenie, meenie, miney, mo, which one of you three will enjoy the show?"

He hung up.

Maggi ran down the stairs to the kitchen.

"Girls," she whispered. "That was him. He's playing games with us. He's going after one of us. I think Glen's plan is working. I think he believes each of us is home alone."

"My guess is his target will be Teddi. No dogs and no chance of Glen coming home. Go back to your routine. We'll let Glen in when he arrives."

Debbie was nervous but in control. Teddi was trembling.

"I can't wait until Glen gets here. I'd feel better knowing he was here with his gun."

Debbie tried to put Teddi at ease. She slipped her hand into her pocket and brought out her 45-caliber, Colt Defender, with custom wooden grips that Glen had made for her.

Teddi gasped.

Just then the dogs barked at Glen in the backyard. Teddi ran to the door to let him in while Debbie held the dogs back in the kitchen. She waited with them for Teddi and Glen to come in. She heard the lock on the door click. She knew they locked it again. Bailey broke free from Teddi's grip and ran snarling out to the mudporch.

Immediately, Debbie knew he would not growl at Glen or Teddi. She raised her gun and watched the doorway from the darkness of the kitchen. Bailey stopped snarling and all was quiet. Debbie sighed with relief. Bridgette's lip turned up as she began to snarl while at Debbie's side. The hair stood up on the back of Debbie's neck. Bridgette kept snarling but would not leave her side.

Suddenly, a figure appeared in the doorway. It was not Glen or Teddi and he had a gun. Debbie yelled, "Freeze!"

The armed man turned to her, raised his gun. The sound of the shot was deafening. Maggi ran down the stairs. She turned on the kitchen light. Debbie was standing over the body of a man bleeding on her kitchen floor.

"Call 911!" yelled Debbie.

The back door was rattling violently. Maggi ran to the door with her phone in hand. It was Glen. He heard the shot and feared the worst. When he stepped inside, he found Debbie trembling with her gun still in her hand.

He checked the man for a pulse. There was none. He called it in. He went to Debbie. Slowly, he peeled the gun from her fingers.

Maggi looked around the room.

"Where's Teddi? Oh my God! Where's Teddi?"

Glen and Debbie both looked at Maggi then each other. Glen turned on the rest of the lights in the kitchen then the mudporch. In the corner of the room lay Teddi's body, crumpled and limp.

Maggi began to cry. Glen stopped her from running to Teddi.

He went to her side. He felt for a pulse. It was strong. So was the odor from the cloth on the floor next to her.

"She's okay, I think. I'm pretty sure she's drugged."

Backup was at the door. Glen called out to them to get an ambulance on the scene. He scooped Teddi up and carried her to the sofa.

Soon the house was swarming with police. Glen was pleased when Bill arrived. He was slightly overwhelmed with a hysterical Maggi, his wife the shooter, a dead man on the floor and Teddi passed out on the sofa.

The EMTs took care of Teddi. Glen looked after Debbie and Maggi while Bill headed the team to ID the body.

Bill walked into the living room where Glen sat with the three women. He carried a small plastic bag with chloroform and cloths in it. He held it up for Glen to see.

"No shit! You don't think this is our rapist, do you?"

"We'll know more when we search his place. He came complete with ID and an address. I'm gonna meet a crew over there."

Debbie knew Glen well enough to know he would stay by her side if she needed him. She also knew he wanted desperately to be in on the end of the rapist case, if this was it.

"Glen, you go with Bill. We'll be fine here. I think there's more than enough cops to keep us company," she smiled.

271

He kissed her hard on the lips. He kissed Maggi on top of her head as she sat on the floor next to Teddi lying on the sofa. Then he rushed out the door with Bill. On his way, he asked one of the guys at the scene to stay with the women until he could get back.

Glen and Bill met the crew at the intruder's house. They called for an immediate search warrant and the crime scene guys had it with them when they arrived. Bill had lifted the keys from the body.

Inside, it looked like anyone else's house; neat, tidy and well furnished. They walked from room to room. Nothing seemed out of the ordinary. They heard a yell from the basement. Glen and Bill ran from the second story down the stairs. In an office, in the corner of the basement, on his desk, he had Maggi's books, pictures of Debbie, Teddi, and Maggi. On the bulletin board behind the desk, he had it set up like they would downtown. Pictures of the vics, news stories, and a map of the area with stick pins marking his hits. In the desk, they found more bottles of chloroform and a nice tidy stack of clean, white cloths.

"Looks like we got him," said Bill.

Glen should have been overcome with excitement about finally nabbing this creep but instead he had a look of sadness on his face.

"What's the matter with you? I thought you'd be dancing in the streets about this being over."

Glen pulled the drawer he was looking into out of the desk and handed it to Bill. In the drawer, on top of a photo of a graduating class from the police academy, was the guy's badge. Bill was right when, early on, he thought this could be a cop gone bad.

Jean showed up, but the officers at the scene refused to allow her inside. She returned home and called instead. One of the officers took the call and handed it to Maggi. She refused to take the call so Debbie took it.

"What happened?" Jean asked.

Debbie said, "It's a long story and tonight's not the night to talk about it."

Debbie looked over at Teddi; she was waking up, thanks to the help of the EMTs.

"Everything's fine, Jean. Now, we really need to finish things up here. Tonight's not a good night."

Glen called Debbie, he said, "It's over and it looks like he could be the rapist."

"What's wrong Glen? I thought you'd be more excited than this."

"I am, Biscuit, but he was one of us. A cop."

Teddi was coming around slowly; she refused to go to the hospital.

"What happened?" she asked, looking around the room, seeing police everywhere. "Where's Glen?"

"Teddi, that wasn't Glen you let in the door. He was the rapist. He drugged you then came into the kitchen. He had a gun. I shot him. We're just lucky he

273

didn't use it on you. We'll never know if he intended to kill Maggi with it. But if I had to make a guess, I'd say that was his plan."

Maggi looked up at Debbie. That thought had not crossed her mind. She was so concerned about Teddi nothing else mattered.

The rest of the evening was filled with answering questions and dealing with the crime scene investigators in the house.

Maggi needed to take the dogs for a walk so one of the officers went with her, just as a precaution.

While Maggi was away, Teddi motioned for Debbie to sit next to her.

"Debbie, I lied. I wasn't at a movie alone. Peter is in town. We just had to see each other. I promised him I wouldn't let anyone know he's here. But now that the rapist has been caught, that should clear him, shouldn't it?"

"Yes, Teddi, he can come out of hiding. It's over. You should call him and tell him. Maybe you'd like to have him come over to be with you while we finish up all the loose ends."

Debbie joined Maggi in the yard with the dogs and the officer. She told her about Peter and Teddi.

Maggi was relieved that everything worked out. Now Teddi and Peter could once again be together.

While they were standing in the yard talking Maggi saw headlights driving up the street. She expected them to keep coming to her yard when she noticed they turned into Jean's.

"That's peculiar," she said.

"What?"

"Why would Jean be getting company so late at night?"

"That is odd, isn't it?"

Following her instincts, Debbie reported it to one of the officers in the yard. He went over to investigate. No cars would go unnoticed while the investigation was still ongoing. He walked over to Jean's to visit with her guest. He wrote down the man's I.D. and Jean could vouch for him. He saw nothing that would raise any suspicions. He called it in and the man had no record. He returned to Maggi's house.

It seemed like the night would never end. No one on the outside could begin to understand the amount of time and work involved at a crime scene; this one was an easy one. Nothing was left to the imagination. Debbie was able to explain every step of the way. Still the paperwork needed to be done.

Finally, Glen arrived to retrieve his wife and end the investigation at Maggi's. He was followed into the driveway by a rental car. Peter stepped out.

Glen walked up to him. He put his hand out to shake.

"Peter, where in the hell have you been hiding?"

"That's exactly what I've been doing. I'm sure by now you found out about my past arrest. I knew with my record and no alibi, my story looked pretty damned weak. I panicked. I didn't want to go to jail again for something I didn't do, especially with murder connected to it."

"You were beginning to turn into a number one suspect. You really should've worked with us on this, you know."

"I know."

"What are you doing here? How'd you find out it was over so fast?"

"I was in town. Teddi and I went to a movie tonight. I couldn't stay away from her any longer. I came back and told her the whole story about the girl from before. She said she already knew about it from you. We hid out in a dark movie theatre. I had no idea this thing would blow over tonight and I would be cleared."

"So Teddi called you then?"

"Yeah, I'm gonna take her home."

Peter and Glen walked in the door. Bill had followed Glen in his car. He walked in about the same time. Debbie ran to Glen. He kissed her then slipped his arm around her waist while he visited with the men on the scene.

Peter went to Teddi on the sofa. He held her and kissed her. Maggi stood up to walk away and give them room.

Bill walked up to Maggi and slipped his arm around her waist.

"I'm here for you, baby," he whispered.

Maggi wriggled out of his hold and called for her dogs. They jumped up on her.

"These are all the comfort I need. Thank you," she said.

Chapter 13

It took an entire week before the girls could begin
to relax. It is not commonplace to be targeted for murder.
The whole episode gave Maggi a new point of view for her
writing. She could draw from her own emotional
experience. She knew what it felt like to be a target. She
could remember the uneasiness she felt in New York when
Morrison questioned her. She thought of her meetings
with her criminal attorney, asking for his help to defend
her. Thank goodness her attorney did not feel the D.A.
had enough evidence to build a case against her. She
would be a more solid writer as a result of it.

She remembered the letter from the rapist, offering
to help make her a better writer. In a round about way,
he will accomplish his goal. He reminded her of her
vulnerability. First Linda, then the rapist found her easily
when they put their minds to it. She always laughed and
told Glen her dogs would protect her. She was so
fortunate that chloroform was used to stop Bailey, instead
of the gun. There is no telling how Bridgette would have
reacted. It was obvious the dog would have stood her
ground to protect Debbie from the intruder.

As Maggi sat on her sofa, sipping tea and watching the fire, she relived the entire episode. She recalled the first days of the rape investigation. She remembered the lectures from Glen to be more careful. The letters, the phone calls, the close encounters played across her mind like a movie.

She reached for a pad and pencil, jotting down a few notes. She thought this whole ordeal could turn into her best novel. She wrote feverishly, not wanting to leave anything out, while it was fresh in her mind. She paused to sip her tea. Smiling, she set the pencil and pad down. Notes were not necessary, once she realized this would be imbedded in her mind forever. It would be impossible for her to forget what happened or her feelings at the time. Instead, she allowed her thoughts to wander toward a title and cover design.

Her chain of thoughts came to an abrupt end when she remembered the three unwritten books in her contract for the email murders. She wondered if she should work the rapist and his desire to tell his story into one of her books. That idea was vetoed almost as soon as it entered her mind. This story would be a good stand-alone story. She was not planning to tell anyone about it until it was written.

Her tea was too cold to sip; she went back into the kitchen for another cup. Glancing at the clock, she thought she had better dress and be on her way with the dogs. She was off to write book two.

Teddi and Peter were gone to Hawaii for a couple of weeks. Glen was back at work; relieved the rapist was out of the picture. Debbie was considering teaching a class on self-defense for women. Maggi was about to return to the quiet life of a mystery writer.

With the dogs loaded, the journey began. Maggi turned off the radio; she was not in the mood to listen to it. She considered the emails that would make up this new book. Her outline, as always, was meticulous, every chapter well planned. Her time estimate was about three weeks to write the first draft in preparation for editing.

The warm sun was shining in her window. The traffic was calm. Maggi knew spring was approaching and with it always came the promise of something new in her life. She looked forward to the excitement of it each year. Thinking back over the last few months, she contemplated the deaths she was linked to.

It crossed her mind that the rapist might also have been the killer that had attempted to blackmail her. It was obvious he was sly. He knew his way around police procedure. He could have been stalking her; planning this all along. The rapes could have been some sort of release for his tension while he plotted to play games with Maggi and her life. He did, after all, have all of her books. He had photos of her and Debbie and Teddi. After a more thorough search of his house, photos of Jean and Maggi's dogs also turned up.

Evidence, she thought, he left nothing they could use at the rape scenes. The same was true with the email murders. Nothing could be traced to anyone, nothing except that one book of hers. It is possible it was the same guy. Suddenly she had an overwhelming urge to call Glen to discuss it.

She dialed the phone then promptly hung up. This trip was a writing trip. She needed to block her life out of her mind and concentrate on her new characters. Talking to Glen or anyone else was taboo during writing time. She tried the radio again to occupy her mind. It was not working; she decided to stop for a bite to eat. The sign ahead read Leinad, Colorado.

"Sounds like a good place to stop."

The dogs just wagged their tails.

The small café in Leinad was filled with the lunch crowd. She ordered a tuna salad sandwich and a cup of tea. As she glanced around the room, she paid particular attention to facial features. Memorizing faces she thought she could give to her characters. Soon she and the dogs were back on the road. A few more hours and they will be at their destination in the mountains. Maggi was about to turn the radio off, when she heard the report of a storm moving in.

"Great," she said. "Now what should we do? Maybe the booming mountain town of Leinad would have a nice hotel for us. Or maybe not."

The dogs in the back began to beat their tails in rhythm, thinking she was talking to them. Pulling over to the side of the road, she took out her map to consider changing her course.

"Oh, hell."

Checking for oncoming traffic, she quickly made a U-turn in the road heading back in the direction of Fort Collins. That night, after taking the dogs for their evening walk, she kept her promise to Teddi to call her. She reported that she and the dogs reached their destination.

"Hi Teddi. We didn't make it to the lodge; the roads were going to be closed because of an approaching storm. We will be staying in Fort Collins for a while. I'll contact you in three days according to plan."

Maggi was glad Teddi was not answering her phone. She was hoping she and Peter were having a wonderful time in the warm weather.

Morrison saw the file on Harmon sitting on his desk. He decided to give Glen a call to see if anything new had developed on his Denver cases that might be connected.

"Karst, this is Morrison. I'd like to toss this Harmon case aside for now, unless you have anything new we can add."

"Not a thing. The only connection we have is that someone contacted Maggi about killing these people before they were killed but we can't link anyone. It's been unusually quiet here lately."

"So you're telling me the D.A.'s not going to bring your friend to trial?"

"That's right. You know we've been tossing around the idea here at the office that maybe the real suspect is dead."

"Why?"

"A serial rapist who was killing his victims also stalked Maggi. He wanted Maggi to write about him in her books. Hell, the bastard even threatened my wife. To make a long story short we got the son of a bitch when he tried to break into Maggi's house. Don't know if he's connected but all is calm; so we can hope."

"Any way we can connect him to our homicide here?"

"I don't think so. Harmon probably had other enemies or did something really stupid because he was drunk. I can send you the lab results from the rapist to see if there's a match with Harmon's death."

"Okay Glen, thanks for your help."

Bill popped his head in the office.

"Let's go. We have a homicide. I'll explain on the way."

When they pulled up in front of the apartment building, neighbors were lining the sidewalks leaning over the yellow tape. They were trying to get a better view. On the stairs to the building lay a woman's sprawled out body. The groceries she had been carrying were scattered from the impact of her body dropping to the ground.

Blood stained the concrete, from a wound on her face, caused by the force of her fall on the sharp edge of the step.

"What do ya have?" asked Glen.

"We've got a female, Caucasian, in her mid twenties, multiple stab wounds to the back. No witnesses," said one of the officers.

Glen took a closer look at the woman. She was beautiful, well groomed and nicely dressed.

He rose to scan the crowd. He noticed one woman in the crowd that had just arrived. She was crying. He walked over to her.

"Excuse me miss, do you know this woman?"

"Yes, she used to be my roommate until she got married. She lives in this building and I live across the parking lot," she said, as she pointed north of where they were standing.

Glen looked in that direction. The area was immaculate. The vehicles parked in the lot were newer cars. This was a prominent, high-class apartment complex. A crime like this in broad daylight was quite out of the ordinary.

Glen ducked under the tape to speak to the ex-roommate.

"Can you give me more information about her?"

Through her tears, the woman was able to give Glen everything he wanted to know, except who killed her.

He learned she had been married for almost two years and according to her friend it was a happy marriage. She just learned she was expecting a baby. She and her husband had been trying for the last year. They were both ecstatic. She was a receptionist at a dentist office; her husband was the dentist. That was how they met. He was away at a convention. They closed the office while he was gone. She had a doctor's appointment today. Her friend was coming by to have lunch with her. They made plans last week. According to the woman, she was a very likeable person, with no apparent enemies.

Once Glen had the necessary information, he told her she was free to leave. He knew the family had to be notified next. He searched for Bill in the crowd to compare notes.

With every new homicide in the Denver area, Glen would become uneasy, fearing Maggi would be connected. He questioned how long before the thought would stop entering his mind.

Before he left the scene with Bill, he walked off by himself to call Debbie.

"Hey Biscuit, I'm at a crime scene, a homicide. Maggi wasn't working on a story where a good-looking pregnant woman gets stabbed at the entrance to her apartment building was she? The husband's a dentist and the wife works for him."

"Doesn't sound familiar but I'll check the files. Glen, are you going to worry about Maggi every time there's a new homicide? The last few you've worked on were in no way connected to her. I'm sure in a city as large as Denver, people are going to kill people without any connection to Maggi Morgan. I think the whole email murder episode has died down."

"I know, I worry too much. I just want to cover all my bases before I start the investigation."

"I'll call you if I find anything."

"Ready to go visit with her parents?" asked Bill, as he approached Glen.

"Can anyone ever be ready for that?"

That night, when Glen came home, he was depressed. Talking to family members always hit him hard. He remained soft hearted, even though he had spent several years as a cop. It still bothered him to watch the pain caused when he had to break the news. Some guys get over it but chances are Glen would not be one of them.

Teddi and Peter returned from their trip to Hawaii with a new depth to their relationship. Peter proposed while there. Teddi could not wait to show Maggi the diamond he placed on her finger. They planned to return to Hawaii for their honeymoon in six months.

Teddi, loyal to Maggi until the end, wanted to make sure the new book was finished and the touring behind them before she married Peter.

Maggi called Teddi and Debbie to tell them she finished and would be home in a few more days. She suggested they come by her house for lunch or supper when she returned, to celebrate.

Teddi planned to announce her engagement at that time.

When Glen made his daily mid-afternoon call to Debbie, she told him about Maggi's plan for a party. She hoped his schedule, in a couple of days, would allow him to join them at Maggi's for the small celebration.

"You know, if you would've asked about ten minutes ago I'd say without a doubt I'd be there. We're heading out on another call. Sounds like a suicide, some rich lady in Cherry Creek. I'll tell you about it tonight when I get home. If we find out it's really a suicide then barring any other surprises, I still should be able to make it."

"I can't believe he didn't tell me to check Maggi's email folder," she chuckled.

Madison, her dachshund, tilted her head as Debbie spoke.

The dog kept Debbie company while she folded laundry. Carrying a basket of folded clothes to the bedroom, Debbie stopped just shy of the doorway.

"Cherry Creek, suicide. No. It can't be," she muttered.

She set the basket down on the spot then turned almost trance-like to go to the office. She thumbed through the folders, searching for the stack of dead women. From that group she looked up suicide. She

287

removed the sets of pages that were stapled together, each set representing one victim.

At the top, on the right side of the sheets, they penciled in where the deaths were to take place, in case Maggi wanted to group them to an entire neighborhood or school district or other location. As she thumbed through them, coming up empty, she smiled to herself.

"Now Glen has *me* paranoid."

There it was, the second to last one in the group, Cherry Creek.

Debbie could feel her heart rate increase as her eyes scanned the email. It was from a husband who wanted to kill his wife, making it look at first like a suicide, then a homicide. That way he could still collect the insurance money. As she read more, she learned this woman was a gold-digger. She married a man who came from a wealthy family. He had enough inheritance to live comfortably for the rest of his life and still be able to take care of his kids long after his death. She blew through his money in no time. He had to return to work just to keep the house. She drove his kids and all of their friends away. He did not have the nerve to do it himself but hoped Maggi would arrange it for him.

He explained she used sleeping pills to fall asleep each night. He suggested an apparent overdose, which turned out to be murder. He needed it to happen while he was away so he could not be connected to it.

Debbie set the folders down.

"I'm sure it's just a coincidence," she muttered. "Lots of women choose sleeping pills for suicide. Debbie, get a grip. This is not related."

She put away her papers and returned to the laundry.

With the laundry finished, she got out her notes for the self-defense class she was planning. She wanted to keep busy until Glen came in for the night.

Glen was late as usual.

"Hi, honey. How'd the case go?"

"Not as smooth as it looked. Turns out this woman was suffocated by someone using the pillows on her bed. Another damn homicide with the husband out of town on business. He's on his way back. We'll know more when he gets here. Considering what happened, I can kiss my weekend off good-bye."

"Did you find anything at the scene that would help with the investigation?"

"I don't know. I didn't work the scene; I went with the body. I had a funny feeling about it. I stayed while they did the autopsy. The strangest thing, she had traces of a sleeping pill in her stomach contents. After she should have been asleep, additional pills were swallowed that were not digested. Anyway, the exam showed she died of suffocation, not from an overdose of sleeping pills. It looks like the pills were forced down her throat after she was dead. Whoever did it was pretty sloppy. He had to

289

know this would be discovered and considered a homicide."

Debbie poured Glen a glass of his Buffalo Trace bourbon. He sipped it while he stared off into space. She knew he was thinking about the case. She also knew the similarities were too close with Maggi's email to keep it to herself.

While Glen was deep in thought, she retreated to the office to find the email. With the paper in hand she stood directly in front of Glen, waiting for him to look up at her.

"What's that?"

"I thought you might like to read this."

He took the pages from her. He rolled his head onto the back of the sofa.

"No, not again. Where is she? Can we find her?"

"She called and said she'll be home soon. She wanted us to get together, remember?"

"I remember, but where is she now?"

Debbie shrugged her shoulders.

Glen tried all of her phone numbers. She did not answer any of them. He left messages for her to call him immediately.

"Glen, she was away when this happened. She couldn't be connected. She planned to go the lodge to write. You scolded her about using Fort Collins since it was too close to use as an alibi."

"You're right Deb. I think we're just trying too hard to make connections where there aren't any. At least, I want to cling to that thought for a little while longer."

The next morning, Maggi was packing to head home with the dogs.

Glen was at the office going over the reports from the woman's death while he waited to speak with her husband. At the scene, the CSI crew found a couple of long black hairs, not belonging to the woman, on the sheets. They also learned she had company that night while her husband was away. There were two wine glasses on the coffee table in the living room. They were able to get two distinct sets of prints from the glasses. They also found a wad of chewing gum wrapped in a tissue in an ashtray.

This case should be pretty cut and dried. The killer, obviously, was not a pro. Maybe they were lovers that had a quarrel that escalated. Not only did Glen have to deal with a distraught husband, but also he had to tell him his wife might have been having an affair.

Glen looked up as the husband and a woman with dark hair were escorted to his office.

"Hello, Mr. Moline. I'm Glen Karst. Thanks for coming in. Can I get you two a cup of coffee?"

"No thank you, Detective Karst. This is my daughter, Karen."

Glen shook hands with Karen.

He asked Karen to wait in the posh victim witness area while he interviewed her father. He would visit with her when he was finished.

He interviewed Mr. Moline for nearly one-half hour before asking him any questions that pertained to the death of his wife. He intentionally asked him background questions such as his phone number, address, school education, other residences and how long he lived in the area. He asked him about his business and travel. He used this line of questioning to study the face of his subject while being asked questions he would have no reason to lie about. Then he would compare those reactions to the responses he would get when he asked questions that could be answered with lies.

"Mr. Moline, I have to be certain of your location the night your wife died."

"I was in Chicago at a meeting. I shared a room with two other men. Actually, we had a suite."

"Can they vouch for your whereabouts the entire night?"

"Yes."

"Great. I'll need their names and phone numbers for my records. If their stories match yours, we can quickly eliminate that part of our investigation."

"Do you have any idea what happened? I was told it was a suicide. Now you think it might be a homicide?"

"That's right. We look at all deaths as homicides until we prove otherwise. Do you know if she had plans to see anyone that night?"

"I don't know. She led a well ... she never told me anything."

Glen raised an eyebrow to that comment.

"Did you and your wife not get along?"

"Not really."

Glen continued his line of questioning about his marriage until he felt he had a good picture of the situation then sent him to wait while he interviewed Karen.

After spending some time asking background questions he began with the more direct line of questioning.

"What was your relationship with your mother?"

"She was a witch," blurted Karen.

Glen studied her more carefully. That was when he noticed her long black hair.

"You and your mother didn't get along very well, I take it?"

"She's not my mother. She was his wife. I get along fine with my mother," she snapped.

Glen gave her a sharp look.

"I'm sorry, Mr. Karst...er ..."I'm sorry, *Detective* Karst, but no, we did *not* get along at all."

"When was the last time you saw her?"

"I don't remember. A couple of years ago."

"Do you live here in Denver?"

"Yes."

"Would you voluntarily give us a DNA sample? Seems we have some evidence from the scene and it would be the fastest way to rule you out so we can narrow down our search."

"Are we suspects?" asked Karen.

"It's just procedure to identify the innocent. Like I said, the DNA samples would quickly rule you out."

"It's fine with me," she said.

Mr. Moline had agreed to the testing earlier.

Glen escorted them down the hall to have their cheeks swabbed for the DNA samples. He was pleased that they also agreed to be fingerprinted.

They left Glen with a long list of people to contact. There was the maid, the gardener, her trainer and then, of course, a long list of friends from the country club.

While thumbing through the pages of notes and names to contact, Glen wished he was not such a thorough cop. This was going to take days to complete.

Before he dove head first into the interviews with the people on the list, he wanted to wait for the DNA matches to be sure it was not the daughter. He thought she was a strong suspect.

Maggi and the dogs arrived home before nightfall. She called Debbie and Teddi to make arrangements for the celebration the next day.

"I don't think Glen will be able to make it; he's working on another case. But you can count me in."

Teddi asked, "Do you mind if Peter comes along?"

"That would be just fine, Teddi. I'll see you two at lunch tomorrow."

After nearly losing Teddi once before, Maggi decided to bite her tongue where Peter was concerned. Besides, she thought, maybe she was wrong about him. Maybe his feelings for Teddi were genuine.

Bill and Glen waited as patiently as they could for the results from the lab. First, they read the husband's results. He was not a match for prints, saliva or the hair sample. Next, they read the results from his daughter. She was cleared on the prints, no match on the saliva and finally, she was cleared for the hair sample.

"Damn, when I saw that black hair I really thought we'd have a match," said Glen.

Bill read through more of the report. "Well, it says here that the hair sample is definitely a woman's. Guess we'd better run those prints and DNA against what we've got in the computer and start wading through your list of people to question."

"How long has it been since we've had an open-and-shut homicide to work on?" complained Glen.

"Seems to me when your wife nailed the rapist, that was pretty open-and-shut. Knowing she's that good with a gun should make you want to tow the line a little more."

295

Glen grinned and fired back, "I didn't teach her *everything* I know." He looked at his watch; it was nearly lunchtime. He wondered if he dared to slip away for a few minutes to have lunch at Maggi's. He decided against it, not wanting Bill to invite himself along.

Glen dropped off the papers to begin the computer database search for the prints and DNA then offered to buy Bill lunch.

"Where do you want to begin with Mrs. Moline? Shall we divide and conquer or do you want to double-team everyone?" asked Bill.

"Let's divide and conquer. Maybe we'll be able to salvage part of the weekend."

"Okay. You take all the men on the list and I'll take the rich female friends."

"That's fine with me. I'm a happily married man."

"Yeah, you'd better say that, buddy, living with Annie Oakley."

Glen ordered a slice of cheesecake so his lunch with Bill would not be a total disaster.

After lunch they dropped back by the office on the off chance that there was a computer match for their search. They could pray the match belonged to someone on their list.

"Do you have my stuff for me?" Glen asked Susan, from the computer lab.

She smiled wide, bouncing her red hair in a nod.

"I've got a match for you. I believe you owe me lunch."

"Bill will take you. Don't want to upset Debbie," teased Glen.

Susan's smile melted from her face. She would love to go to lunch with the handsome Detective Karst. She had no desire to be seen in public with Bill, not to mention having to listen to him for the entire meal.

Glen winked at Susan as he picked up his papers to leave.

Bill grabbed the papers from Glen.

"Hey, I saw you flirting with Susan. I thought you were the happily married man."

"Holy shit!"

"What?" asked Glen.

He watched Bill with the report. He tried to snatch it from his hands but Bill resisted.

"What?" repeated Glen.

"This can't be right."

"Damn it Bill, give me the damn papers!"

Glen read the name that came up as a perfect match for the saliva from the DNA and the prints.

Maggi Morgan.

Chapter 14

Maggi was disappointed when Glen could not make the celebration. Debbie picked up on her uneasiness. When she had a moment to get Maggi alone in the kitchen, she asked, "What's wrong? Are you having trouble being cordial to Peter?"

"Nah, that's pretty easy once I actually saw how happy he's making Teddi."

"Then what's wrong?"

"I really hoped Glen would be here."

Debbie felt a twinge in her stomach hearing Maggi express her disappointment.

"Why?"

Maggi went to the door of her kitchen to see where Teddi and Peter were. They were in the living room where they could not hear the conversation.

"I'm not sure, but I think someone was in my house while I was gone."

"Are you sure?"

"I just said I wasn't sure and I hate to go to the police about it. But then, on the other hand, I hate to just ignore it. I wanted to run it past Glen."

"Is something missing?"

"No, not that I can tell anyway."

"Well then, what makes you think someone was here?"

"It's just a feeling I had while I unpacked. I sensed things were touched and moved in my drawers. I went through the house, looking for other things that might be out of place but nothing really stood out."

"Was it just in your bedroom?"

"No, that's what makes me feel uncomfortable and paranoid at the same time. I feel like my entire house was under exploration. I'm pretty picky about the way I put my papers in folders in my files. When I opened my file cabinet to look through the folders there were some papers sticking out of a few of them. I know that sounds dumb, but I'm careful that way."

"Maybe you should call it in."

"And say what, that some corners of my papers in my files were bent? All of my jewelry, crystal and china are intact but someone maliciously abused my sheets of paper."

At first Debbie felt Maggi was being too sharp-tongued with her but quickly realized she was truly concerned about a break-in.

"Show me the files you're talking about."

Maggi led Debbie into her office. She opened the four-drawer file cabinet. The top drawer had nothing out of place, the same with the second. The third drawer containing Maggi's personal papers, such as her divorce papers, health records, insurance papers and other documents, were the ones that Maggi felt had been gone through.

"How long ago do you think that happened?"

"I have no idea. I haven't been in this drawer for some time. There's been no need to look at any of those papers."

"Who has a key to your house?"

"Just you, Teddi, and Jean. I changed the locks after I stopped using my cleaning lady."

"Have you asked Teddi if she came by to look for something? Do you remember sending her on an errand here a while back and just forgot about it?"

"Not in that drawer. Usually I'm sending her after something book related or to check messages or grab some clothes I might've forgotten."

Teddi entered the office, looking for Maggi and Debbie.

"Hey, are we going to eat or what? I'm starved."

Debbie turned to Teddi, "Can you remember the last time Maggi sent you on a search for something in her files?"

"Why? Is something missing?"

"No, it just looks like someone searched for something in my files a little hastily."

Teddi looked at the drawer Maggi had pulled open.

"All of your book stuff is in the first two drawers. I've never had a need to look further."

Maggi slammed the drawer. "Let's get lunch going. I think I'm imagining things."

Bill and Glen were trying to figure out how and why Maggi's DNA and prints showed up at the crime scene.

"You really don't think she was there, do you?" asked Bill.

"Hell no, she wasn't there. She was in the mountains writing when this woman was killed. Someone is setting Maggi up, but who and why?"

"Does she have any witnesses to verify she was away writing?"

"After what she went through a couple of months ago, I'm sure she learned her lesson about alibis."

"You know, Glen, we have to use this evidence, we can't ignore it. We do have procedure to follow."

"I know that," snapped Glen. "I plan to treat this case as any other, even if Maggi's involved."

"You're too close to the case. I think you should remove yourself from it. It might be too hard for you to be objective. Think about it. If this were any other suspect, you'd already have an arrest warrant. You'd have been to the D.A. with probable cause. Instead, you're trying to figure out who's setting her up."

Glen rubbed his hand over his face. He knew Bill was right; he needed to remove himself from the case. He really wanted to remain objective, but also knew how hard it would be.

"Okay, I'm going to voluntarily step down, but you'd better keep me posted on what's happening because I plan to work this on my own time."

"Glen, you sound like you can't trust me to do the right thing here. I agree with you, it probably wasn't Maggi, but we have to do what we have to do. I'll get Alex to work on this one with me."

Glen took the rest of the day off. He wanted to plan his strategy for his private investigation. He knew that in less than seventy-two hours there would be a warrant out for Maggi's arrest. He felt so helpless. He had to sit back with his mouth shut while the evidence mounted against her.

Alex and Bill took their information to the D.A. to examine. Maggi was linked by emails to the golfer, the attorney and now the woman from Cherry Creek. They did not bring up the New York death. With the evidence obtained at the crime scene, the D.A. felt he had probable cause to issue an arrest warrant.

Monday morning Bill called Maggi's attorney to ask him to bring her downtown. He explained they had a warrant for her arrest but thought since she would be more than willing to cooperate, it might be less embarrassing to have her come to them rather than being cuffed and arrested.

Maggi and her attorney, Ronald Curtis, arrived promptly at two o'clock for their meeting with Bill and Alex. After Alex closed the door behind him, Maggi's eyes stayed focused on the door.

"Where's Glen?" she asked.

Bill answered, "He took himself off of the case due to a conflict of interest."

Maggi felt ill.

Bill began the questioning.

"Maggi, where were you last Thursday night?"

"I was away writing."

"Where were you writing?"

Maggi remembered Glen's warning about going further away to write and to always be sure she had witnesses to her whereabouts. Since things had quieted down after the death of the rapist, she let her guard down. How she wished she could tell Bill she was at the lodge in Steamboat Springs instead of in Fort Collins.

"I had a room at the Quality Inn Suites in Fort Collins."

"When did you leave to return home?"

"Friday afternoon."

"While you were there on Thursday, did you talk to anyone or go to dinner with…"

Before he could finish his question, she said, "No, Bill. I didn't have any witnesses and I have no alibi. I was in my room writing. I came and went by the back stairs because often I had the dogs with me on my way out."

Ronald Curtis, trying to stop her from incriminating herself, said, "Just stick to the questions he's asking."

"Do you know Lisa Holcomb?"

"Who?"

"Lisa Holcomb. Have you ever been in her home?"

"I'm sorry but I don't know a Lisa Holcomb."

"Would there be any chance you had an errand to run in Cherry Creek on Thursday evening?"

"No, I was at the motel."

"So you're telling us you don't know Lisa Holcomb and you've never been to her home?"

"That's correct. Why?"

"Ms. Holcomb was found dead in her home on Friday by her personal trainer."

"I don't understand the connection," said her attorney.

"At the scene, our crew found a pair of wine glasses on the coffee table. The prints were a match to your client."

"That's impossible," complained Maggi.

"Have you fingerprinted my client already?"

"No need to, she was in our system."

Ronald turned to Maggi with a surprised look on his face. He wondered if his high profile client, whom he worked on books with, could be lying to him.

"Look, when I started writing my books I went to the police station to interview some cops. I had lots of

304

questions about procedures. I asked them to fingerprint me and run a DNA test. I wanted to see how it was done and how the results ended up in the database. That's why I'm in the system.

"How could my fingerprints end up on a wine glass at this woman's house last Thursday night? I don't know her and I was in Fort Collins."

Alex added, "There's more Ms. Morgan. We have DNA from the scene to match yours."

Ronald asked, "How did you obtain her DNA at the scene?"

"A piece of chewing gum was found wrapped in a tissue in an ashtray. It contained Ms. Morgan's DNA. We also found two long black hairs on the bed of the victim."

Maggi quickly pulled a hair from her head, handing it to Alex.

"Here, run this. You won't find a match."

He left the room to take it to the lab.

With Alex out of the room Maggi felt more free to talk to Bill.

"Bill, what in the hell's going on? I want Glen here. He knows I'm not guilty. You really don't think I'm connected to this, do you?"

"Maggi, how I feel about you or what I think doesn't matter. I have to go with the evidence at hand. I need to tell you this matched another one of your email murders."

Maggi sat back in her chair, feeling weak. Tipping her head forward, looking onto the table, she recalled the book she just finished writing. She closed her eyes then began to speak as if she were reading from her book.

"This woman was from Cherry Creek, married to a rich guy. She was breaking him and she died from suffocation with sleeping pills in her system, making it look like a suicide."

Her attorney stared at her in amazement.

"Yep, that's the story," said Bill.

The door opened as Alex returned with the results from Maggi's hair.

"It's a match."

Somehow, Maggi was not surprised.

"May I have a word alone with my client, please," asked Ronald.

Bill and Alex left the room.

"Maggi, I think you'd better tell me what's going on."

"Oh, come on Ron, you know the story. I told you when I hired you a few months ago about the emails and the deaths. You told me not to worry because the D.A. couldn't come up with probable cause to arrest me. This is just more of the same."

"Maggi, this is not just more of the same. This time they have physical evidence linking you to the scene. This is no longer circumstantial. This is real."

"I wasn't there. I don't even know this woman."

"You didn't know any of the other people that ended up dead either but you knew about them. I'm just not sure how this is going to look to a jury."

"Jury? What do you mean jury? Surely it's not going to go that far. That's impossible."

"Maggi, it's not looking good for you. I just wished you had someone that could say they were with you on Thursday night. You've conveniently not had an alibi for any of the homicides. Unless we find out who's setting you up, we might not be able to build a very strong defensive case. You had knowledge of the victims, you wrote their method of death in great detail in your books, and now they can place you at the scene with no alibis to the contrary."

"What about witnesses in her neighborhood? Did anyone talk to the neighbors to see if she had company? Could anyone tell the police if there was a suspicious car? What about her husband?"

Alex and Bill returned. Ronald repeated Maggi's questions to them.

"No witnesses, no company and no suspicious cars. We talked with her husband but he was away at a convention where he shared a room with two other men. They can vouch for his whereabouts.

"He didn't try to hide the fact that he and his wife didn't get along. His daughter hated her. When Glen saw her long black hair she was his number one suspect but the hairs didn't match. Now we know you're connected," Bill pointed out.

"Maybe he hired a hitman," suggested Maggi.

"That's possible but the hitman would have had to have your prints and DNA."

"Don't you see it's obvious I was set up?"

"We don't know that for sure."

Alex added, "Even if Holcomb arranged for someone else to kill his wife, his plan had to include the email request for you to kill his wife. He had to plan it while he knew you were away writing and then he'd have to somehow get your prints and DNA at the crime scene. Don't you see, Ms. Morgan? There are just too many coincidences."

"That's right, Maggi. How can you explain his knowledge about you and his access to the physical evidence, if you say you don't know him or his wife and you've never been to their home?"

Ronald realized they were getting nowhere with this conversation. If anything, Maggi's cooperation and answers to the questions were damaging to her case. He feared her openness may have already caused problems with her defense.

"Gentlemen, I believe it's in the best interest of my client to end this conversation."

"I guess, if your client is ready to post bond she can leave with you, Counselor."

Maggi looked up from her position with her head in her hands. She had been staring at the tabletop, running her fingers through her hair, as if that would somehow help her remember something that would set her free.

"What do you mean post bond? Are you serious? You really do think I did this, don't you?"

Reality was hitting hard. Although she was there being interrogated about the murders, she never really thought anyone would take it seriously enough to consider her a prime suspect. Now she found out she was the *only* suspect.

Ronald took the arrest warrant from Bill to see what the bail had been set at. He handed the paper to Maggi, pointing at a figure of five hundred thousand dollars.

"Can you make ten percent of that?" he asked.

"I suppose, with a few phone calls. I don't just have that kind of money sitting around my house," she said sarcastically, angry for being put in this situation.

He handed her a slip of paper. "Tell me who I should call."

She wrote down the name of her investment broker then handed it back to Ronald. He excused himself to make the call.

Alex walked out with him.

"Maggi, Glen's here. He's waiting outside. He'd like to have a word with you," said Bill.

"Oh my God, yes. Please, yes, let him in."

309

When Glen stepped into the room Maggi ran to him, falling into his arms, crying. He paused, waiting for her to regain her composure.

"Maggi, listen to me," he said, separating himself from her so he could look at her.

She took the handkerchief he offered.

"Getting to be a habit," she said, as she wiped away her tears.

Glen smiled a weak smile at her. He knew she was in trouble and he was not quite sure how to get her out of it.

"Maggi, maybe you shouldn't make bail."

"What? I can't go to jail. Not even for one night. How could you even suggest such a thing?"

"Come on, listen. You might be safer here. What if the killer strikes again while you're here. That would surely make you look innocent, especially if he set up the scene with physical evidence again."

"Glen, no. Please don't ask me to do that. Can't you put me under house arrest or send a cop to stay with me to prove I'm not responsible if he hits again?"

"It could be dangerous for you if you leave here. Whoever he is, desperately wants to make your life miserable. If he thinks you're getting away with these crimes that he's setting you up for, he may decide to kill you."

"You don't really think my life is in danger, do you?"

310

"Yes."

"But why? Who wants to see me dead or in jail?"

"If I knew that, he would be sitting here right now, not you."

"I'll just hire a bodyguard. I can afford one. That way I'll have an alibi if something happens."

"I can't force you to take my advice. I just think you'd be safer here. What do you think?"

"I don't want to stay here. Let me talk to my attorney."

Glen gave her a long hug. He left the room to send her attorney in.

"Well?" asked Maggi.

"Done. Bail's been posted and you're free to leave."

"I'll arrange for you to appear before the judge in the morning so you can give your not guilty plea. Then a trial date will be set. We need to discuss if you want a speedy trial or want to stretch this out."

"Will it be a trial by jury?"

"That's up to you."

"What do you recommend?"

" I think you'd be better off with a jury."

"You think a judge might really believe I did this, don't you?"

"I'm not saying that. I just think your chances of creating a reasonable doubt are greater with a jury."

"Glen thinks I should wave the bond and stay here until I go to trial. He thinks I'd be safer or maybe the real

311

killer would strike again, proving I couldn't commit the murder and be in jail at the same time."

"What do you want to do? If you decide to stay put then we'll need to set a date for a speedy trial to get you out of here and put all of this behind you as soon as possible."

"Is there a chance I'd be found guilty?"

"Of course, there's always that chance. We don't have much right now to prove your innocence, except for character witnesses and the absurdity of you leaving such incriminating physical evidence at the scene."

"I want out of here as soon as possible. I want to go before the judge in the morning and plead not guilty. Then I'm going to grab the first plane to South America and be gone."

"Hey, don't even kid around about that or you'll be considered a flight risk and you won't be going anywhere."

"Okay, what's the plan?"

"Let's drag this out a little. Give me some time to work on your defense. The best thing that could happen to you would be if they catch this guy before you have to go to trial. So I guess I'll see you in the morning."

Glen was waiting in the parking lot for Maggi. She walked up to his pickup.

"Go straight home. I'll be right behind you."

Maggi let the dogs out while Glen let himself in.

She poured two glasses of bourbon then joined him in the living room.

"I need to know everything. Don't leave anything out. I'm not working the case anymore so if there's something you need to tell me, I'm not obligated to tell Bill. Although, ethically, I feel I should. I guess it depends upon what you tell me."

Maggi looked at Glen with shock on her face.

"Maybe you should leave if you don't believe me. There's the door."

"Shit, Maggi, knock it off. We have work to do. Don't pull that temper tantrum crap with me. Now tell me everything."

"Glen, you already know everything. There's nothing more to tell. I guess the only thing you don't know is I never made it to Steamboat; I stayed in Fort Collins. And to answer your next question, no, I did not plan alibis."

"You know what, you've already been through enough this morning so I'm going to spare you another lecture. Obviously, I'm just wasting my breath with them anyway. Did you write this woman's death into your book you just finished?"

"Yes, almost word for word."

"What I'm going to do next is talk to her husband again. I'm going to ask him about the email. If he sent it to you asking you to kill his wife, complete with her name and address, we have to find a way to pull him into this as a suspect."

313

"Do you really think he could be a suspect? That's stupid; of course, he has to be a suspect. He sent the email, didn't he?"

"That's it Maggi, put your detective hat on. Pretend you're working on a plot for one of your books. You seem to think best when you're playing both parts in your books, the criminal and the police. Who knew you were gone writing?"

"You, Debbie, Teddi and probably Jean since she's so nosey. She's always watching my yard."

"What about your agent?"

"Warren? Yeah, I guess so. You know what? We've been over this before. All the same people that had access to the emails know when I'm gone to write."

"There has to be a connection. I'm going to start with Jean."

"What are you going to do?"

"I'm going to ask her where she was on the days in question and see if she has alibis for those dates."

"When are you going to do that?"

"There's no time like the present. I'll be right back."

Glen finished his drink then walked across the expansive front lawn through the tree row to Jean's property. That same green Ford Escort was parked in her driveway.

He rang the bell.

"Glen, what are you doing here? Is something wrong with Maggi?"

"No, I just need to ask you a few questions about those emails you girls were working on."

"Is it true what I read in the papers that people are dying just like in Maggi's books?"

"It would appear so. Am I interrupting anything? I see you have company."

"Oh him, no. He's just here to work with my dogs. I'm training him to be a judge. I think he's ready to leave. Just sit here a minute and I'll tell him I'm finished."

Jean returned to the room. Glen watched out the window as the car pulled away. Something seemed familiar about him but Glen didn't get a very good look at his face.

"Now, what can I help you with?" she asked.

"Were you aware that Maggi was gone writing recently?"

"Yes, I was pretty sure when I didn't see her or the dogs for a number of days."

"Did you see anyone unusual around her house while she was gone?"

"No, can't say that I did."

"Maybe you weren't here the whole time. Where were you on last Thursday?"

"I was in Chicago at a dog show."

Glen wanted to ask her straight out if she had any witnesses but he had to be more tactful.

315

"Were you judging?"

"Yes, as a matter of fact I was. There was a last minute cancellation."

"What's it like being a judge? I'll bet it's pretty tough."

Jean was pleased that Glen was taking an interest in her work.

"The days are long and you spend a lot of time on your feet."

She showed him photos of herself with some of the winning dogs at the show. Glen quickly noticed the date on the pictures did put her in Chicago during the time Mrs. Holcomb was killed.

"It was probably a good thing for Maggi that she had her dogs with her. Who would she have gotten to take care of them with you gone?"

"There've been other times when I've had to leave at the same time as Maggi but I have my judge friend stay here at the house to take care of the dogs."

"Maggi's, too?"

"Yes, he loves Bridgette and Bailey."

Glen took his time with Jean. He stroked her ego as he extracted answers from her. It took much longer than he expected. Fortunately for him, she kept a diary of events. As he asked her about different dog shows and events, he was able to read over her shoulder as she thumbed through her book at the dining room table. He did not feel comfortable writing notes on his pad. At this point, he really did not want her to know she was being questioned. He memorized the places and names she had in her book to check with the dates of the previous murders. He knew if they panned out, she would be cleared of any suspicion.

Glen returned to Maggi's house armed with dates and names in his head. He quickly jotted them down for future reference.

"Well? Did you learn anything?"

"Yes, if her diary is accurate, she, unlike you, has an alibi for nearly all of the deaths. I didn't check the one in New York. I assumed she doesn't travel that often."

"Oh, she might surprise you. Even though she's retired from the dog world she still manages to go to many of the shows. I think that's the only place she feels comfortable with people and she gets recognized occasionally for her many years as a judge."

"Speaking of judges. Her judge in training was there but he left before I had a chance to meet him. Funny thing too, he seemed familiar in some way."

"I really doubt if you and Jean travel in the same circles."

"You're probably right. But I'm gonna give it more thought. Maybe it'll come to me who he reminds me of."

"While you're here, I need to tell you about someone possibly breaking into my house while I was gone."

"Maggi, that's great. Tell me what happened."

317

"What's so great about having someone in my house?'

"Whoever came into your house is probably the same person that took some of your hair. What about your chewing gum?"

Maggi was excited now. She felt silly for not having thought it through herself.

"Yes, that's it. I always wrap my gum in a tissue before tossing it in the trash. I hate to pry gum out of the trash can."

Glen shared in her excitement. "Okay, he or she could easily have gotten your hair from your brush and your gum from your trash but what about the wine glasses? How did your prints get onto the glasses in Holcomb's house?"

Maggi checked the glasses at her bar. She carefully counted them twice. They were all there.

"Wait," she said.

She pulled a chair up to the cabinet in her kitchen. On the very top shelf she kept her good wine glasses that she rarely used. She counted them. That's not right, she counted again. A huge smile crossed her face.

"What?" said Glen.

Elated with her find, she said, "Catch."

She jumped from the top of the counter to Glen's arms.

"That was stupid. I could've dropped you," he said, as he stood her on her feet.

"I knew you wouldn't."

He was glad to see that devilish sparkle in her eye.

"I had a set of twelve glasses and now there are only ten. Someone took two of my glasses and, of course, they'd have my prints. I'm the one who put them away."

Chapter 15

Early the next morning, Glen was waiting for Bill to come to the office.

"Took you long enough," he said, when he finally arrived.

"I always get here at this time. What's up with you?"

"I have something that I think might be of interest to you on Maggi's case."

"Wait a minute."

Bill called Alex into the room.

"I went home with Maggi yesterday. She told me she thought someone had been in her house and had gone through her things. We put our heads together and figured if someone, namely our killer, entered her house, that's where he could have gotten her hair and her chewing gum. We were stumped about the prints on the wine glasses. Maggi checked her glasses and discovered two of them were missing."

Glen reached into his jacket pocket and took out one of the remaining wine glasses from Maggi's kitchen.

"Can you check this one against the two you have in evidence?"

Alex took the glass from Glen to compare it with the others.

"What else do you have for me? I have a hunch you're going to make my job easy on this one."

"Talked with Jean, her neighbor. She had access to all of the emails while she was working in the office with Maggi, Teddi and Debbie. They chose the deaths for Maggi to write about."

"Did you learn anything important from her?"

"Not really, but I think she's going to check out with alibis for almost all of the dates in question. Here's a list of the places and the people she was with. Sorry, I don't have phone numbers and addresses. I thought you could get those from her if you think you need to follow up."

"What's next?"

"You should ask the husband about the email he sent Maggi. We really can't rule him out as a suspect."

"Are we sure who sent those other emails? The golfer's wife denied it and the *good old boys club,* could have been anyone. Hell, Maggi could have sent them to herself as a cover," Bill pointed out.

"Or our killer could have sent them to Maggi as a cover."

"Okay, you have a point there."

Alex returned with a smile on his face, "We have a match."

Glen punched his fist on the desk.

"I knew it!"

Bill took over the lead, "Alex, go interview the husband again about this email."

"Glen, don't you think if we're closing in that Maggi could be in trouble?"

"Are we closing in? Is there something you're not telling me?"

"You know everything I know but I have a feeling that something's going to break. This guy obviously didn't think Maggi was getting into enough trouble from her connection with the other deaths, so he placed evidence at the scene to frame her. If this doesn't work, he may get violent. We know murder is easy for whoever he is."

Alex met with Mr. Holcomb at his office. His daughter, Karen, was present.

"Mr. Holcomb, what can you tell me about this email?"

Holcomb read the email.

"I don't understand. Is this some type of a joke? I didn't send this."

"Is this your email address?"

"Yes, that's my office email, but I didn't send this."

"May I look at your computer?"

"Feel free."

Alex brought up the email screen. He checked the sent messages folder. He scrolled down to the corresponding date. There was a copy of the email that was sent to Maggi.

Alex turned the screen so Holcomb could read it.

"I didn't send that email."

"I did," admitted Karen.

"What? Why?" asked her dad.

"I saw Maggi Morgan on the Oprah Show. I thought it sounded like fun. I really didn't think she'd kill her. I'm glad she did, but I didn't think she would."

"Who in the hell is Maggi Morgan?" her father asked.

Alex explained, "Maggi Morgan is a famous mystery writer. She had readers send in the names and stories of someone they would like to see her kill in one of her books. She's writing books using the email stories."

"I don't get it. Did she kill my wife?"

"We're not sure."

"Did her prints match the ones at my house?"

"Yes, sir, they did."

"Have you arrested her?"

"Yes, sir."

"Then she's guilty?"

"Not exactly, she's just a suspect."

"Do you have other suspects?"

323

"Not at this point, but we'll keep you posted as we learn more. I really need to get back to the office. Thank you for your time."

Teddi phoned Maggi to ask if they were going to work.

"I'm not sure I'm up to it today."

"Are you ill?"

"No, Teddi. You're not going to believe what happened. I was arrested yesterday for the murder of some woman in Cherry Creek."

"What! No way. Maggi, what are you talking about?"

Peter was sitting across the room from Teddi, engrossed in her conversation with Maggi.

"Yesterday Ronald called and told me to meet him at the police station. There was a warrant for my arrest. Seems someone killed that poor woman according to one of the stories I just wrote in book two."

"So, why were *you* arrested?"

"Because I'm the prime suspect. I was gone again, with no alibi."

"Maggi, I thought Glen told you never to let that happen again."

"He did but you know me."

"Go on, what happened?"

"I met Ronald at the police station. They questioned me about all the email murders."

"Yeah, but they tried that before. There was no evidence to link you to those other murders, so what makes this one different?"

"This time, they found my prints, DNA and a couple of my hairs at the scene."

"That's impossible...Isn't it?"

"What? Are you doubting me, too?"

"No, but I just wondered how you explained that to the police."

"Glen's helping me with that. Remember, I thought someone had been in my house?"

"Yeah?"

"He thinks whoever it was took those things to plant at the scene."

"Maggi, I don't think you should be alone. Peter and I are coming right over."

Before Maggi had an opportunity to say no, she heard a dial tone.

"Peter, let's go to Maggi's."

"Why? What's going on?"

"Maggi was arrested for murder yesterday. She's out on bond."

"Do you think she'll be convicted?"

"What do you mean convicted? You didn't even ask about it. What makes you think she's even connected to the case?"

"I was listening to your conversation. You made it sound serious. I thought maybe she stood a good chance of being convicted."

"I'm sure Glen's gonna get her off. They're working on it right now. I really don't think she could possibly be found guilty. They think someone's setting her up."

"I suppose someone in the public eye, like Maggi, won't go to prison. Her kind usually gets off with a slap on the wrist."

"Peter! You make her sound guilty."

"I'm sorry. I'm back in reporter mode, remembering other stories I've written where celebrities were involved in crimes. They got off when the average Joe never did."

"Okay, if you say so. Are you ready to go?"

"You go ahead without me. I've got a few errands to run."

Teddi went into her room to pack a bag. She thought, under the circumstances, Maggi should never be left alone without an alibi.

Peter walked Teddi to her car. He kissed her good-bye.

"I'll catch up to you later. Make sure you leave your phone on, so I can reach you."

Peter went to Barnes and Noble. He bought a cup of coffee then waited. Shortly after he arrived, Warren appeared at the coffee counter. He joined Peter.

"How's the book coming?" asked Warren.

326

"It's nearly finished."

"Good, I think you stand to make a bundle off of this one."

"It's not really the money I'm after, it's more the recognition as a writer."

"How much longer are you going to wait before you let me read the rest of it?"

"Soon. It shouldn't be much longer," answered Peter.

"When are you going to tell Maggi that you're writing a story about her and her email murders?"

"I don't know. It's just fiction, you know. I might have gotten the idea from what she's been going through but it's not a true story, by any means. I'm not even using her real name in the book."

"I thought you were."

"No, I'm going to change the main character's name after it's finished. That was just a writing aid for me to use as I developed her character."

"Brad's pretty excited about it. His publishing company hopes to release it close to the same time that Maggi goes to trial," announced Warren.

"How did you know that Maggi might be going to trial?"

"Haven't you read today's paper?"

He handed the paper to Peter. The headlines read:

Mystery Writer Maggi Morgan Arrested for Real Life Murders.

Peter read the story. It was exactly as Teddi had told him earlier.

"Now, do you see how important it is that you finish your book?"

"I promise you, it'll all be finished soon."

Peter's cell phone rang. He answered it then asked Warren. "Are we finished here, Warren? I need to take this call."

He waited for Warren to leave.

"Okay, now what were you saying? Yes, I just read it."

"We need to talk in person. Where can I meet you?"

Peter hesitated for minute, "Let's meet at a truck stop outside of the city."

"How about the Tomahawk?"

"That'll be fine. Say in two hours?"

Peter kept his word. At the Tomahawk Truckstop, outside of Denver, he sat at a booth near the window where he had an unobstructed view of the parking lot. Finally, a small teal green Ford Escort pulled in. The driver got out and met Peter inside.

"Did Teddi tell you anything more than what's in the paper?"

Peter answered, "I heard her talking to Maggi about Glen getting her off."

"I wouldn't think he'd be on the case since he knows her personally."

328

"Me either but apparently he is," agreed Peter.

"I don't like that one bit. I'd feel better if Glen were out of the picture."

"You're not planning to ..." Peter looked around the room.

"Are you nuts? I'm not gonna kill a cop."

"I'm glad, because if you were planning to; I don't want any part of this."

"It's too bad about what you want. You're already involved and don't you think for one minute, I'm gonna let you out of it."

"Hey, I didn't kill anyone. You can't accuse me of that."

"What about poor Mr. Harmon from New York?"

"I can't believe I told you about him. That was an accident. I went to talk to him about his wife. I was afraid if he found out somehow that she was staying in my house that he'd be gunning for me. I just didn't want him to think I took his wife away. I had no idea he'd be so drunk he'd try to attack me."

"Well, if it happened like you said, if you were just talking to him, how'd he end up dead?"

Peter looked around to be sure no one was listening.

"I told you, he came to the door in a towel. He'd just gotten out of the tub to answer the door. When I tried to explain to him about his wife, he went crazy. He was drunk remember? He grabbed me by the throat. We

329

struggled. I tried to get away from him. I ran to lock myself in the bathroom but he was too fast for me. He forced his way in. He lunged for me, I moved and he fell into the tub. He reached out to grab something for balance then pulled the hair dryer into the tub with him. I didn't kill him."

"Why didn't you call the police? Why did you set Maggi up?"

"I panicked. I paced around the apartment when I noticed her book on the kitchen table. I remembered the scene about the guy in the tub so I went with it. I figured she'd get off; no one would believe she was really connected just because a passage of her book was highlighted. Thinking about it on the way home was when the idea hit to write this book about Maggi and the killings."

The waitress came by to see if Peter's companion needed anything.

"I'd like some pie but I can't; I'm a diabetic. I'll just take a cup of coffee."

"I still find it hard to believe that you didn't plan it according to her book. I think it's too big of a coincidence that a copy of her book just happened to be there and this guy just happened to kill himself that way. There's no way you're ever gonna get me to believe it. I wonder what the police would think of your story?"

"It's the truth. I didn't call them because I didn't want to explain what I was doing there. I wanted to tell him about Maggi and his wife, hoping he would go after Maggi, not me."

"I guess you never got over loving her, did you?"

"She dumped me then just disappeared. The next thing I knew, she was some famous mystery writer. Let's just say, I'm a jealous person that needs revenge. Not unlike you," said Peter.

"Just so you keep your mouth shut about our little deal here. Is that understood? I don't want any revenge or jealousy messing up what we've planned."

Peter, angry, stood to leave, "Once this is over, I don't ever want to see you again. I can't believe I ever trusted you. I should have seen our friendship was a fraud, based on your need to share the pain of having Maggi dump us both."

Debbie was on the phone with Maggi when Teddi arrived. Maggi let her in then locked the door behind her.

"Thanks, Debbie, but I really think I'll be fine, now that Teddi's here."

"Maggi, we still think you should call us tonight before you go to bed. I'm afraid my husband's going to insist that you check in multiple times a day."

"Really, Debbie, we'll be okay. Try to convince him of that. Of course, if you'd like to come over and bring your gun, we won't object."

"I will if you want me to."

"No, I was just kidding. I promise I'll call at bedtime, no matter how late that might be."

"What was that all about?" asked Teddi.

"Debbie says Glen's over-reacting. I think he's still feeling badly that he wasn't in the house with us the night the rapist showed up."

"He shouldn't feel bad. He masterminded the whole plan and armed Debbie before he joined us. It all worked out."

"I know, but you know how protective he can be."

Teddi and Maggi had an uneventful evening playing Scrabble. Teddi checked her watch frequently.

"Where's Peter?"

"I'm not sure. He's not answering his phone."

"I wouldn't worry about him. You know how he has a way of just showing up. He'll probably be along soon."

"I know but I really thought I'd hear from him by now."

Teddi got up to look out the window.

"This must be him. I see headlights coming up the street."

Maggi looked over her shoulder.

"Nope, looks like Jean's boyfriend."

"Jean has a boyfriend?"

"Oh, I don't know. Some guy shows up once in a while. She says she's teaching him about dog shows but they train at some pretty strange hours."

"What's he look like?"

"I don't know. I've never seen him up close. Glen almost saw him yesterday but he left before Jean could introduce them."

"Aren't you curious?"

"Of course I'm curious."

"Let's go take a peek."

"Teddi! I'm surprised at you. I can't believe you'd say something like that. I'm the one who would usually come up with a great idea like that," she laughed.

"Do you think it's safe, out there in the dark?" asked Teddi, losing her nerve.

"What are the chances of someone lurking outside again? I think we should be fine. It's just next-door, we'll take a flashlight and ..." she looked around the room, "these."

Maggi, giggling, handed a fireplace poker to Teddi then went to look for a flashlight.

"What'll we say if we get caught?"

"We won't get caught."

"Oh, Maggi, I'm not too sure about this."

"Come on, Teddi. Remember when you and Debbie sneaked around in the dark the night the rapist came? It made your adrenaline rush. It made you feel alive. Let's go for it. If we get caught, I'll do all of the talking."

Maggi grabbed Teddi's hand and headed for her bedroom. She found black turtleneck sweaters and sweatpants.

Teddi giggled as they changed into their cat burglar clothes.

"I can't believe you talked me into this," whispered Teddi, as they left the trees dividing the two properties.

Maggi turned off the flashlight as they neared the house. Through the window ahead of them they saw Jean pacing the room, agitated, as she spoke to her guest.

Jean walked to the window. Maggi and Teddi dropped to the ground on their bellies, trying not to laugh. Teddi could not look, so Maggi did.

"The coast is clear. Let's get to those bushes up against the house. We'll be hidden there."

They ran quickly. Breathlessly, they leaned their backs against the house. Maggi glanced at the window. She did not see anyone standing near it; she moved cautiously to get a better view.

Maggi could see Jean sitting on the sofa. A man now paced the room. He turned toward the window. Maggi gasped then dropped to her knees.

"What?" asked Teddi.

"It's Daniel."

"Daniel who?"

"My Daniel, Daniel Morgan. What's that bastard doing with Jean?"

"Your ex is with Jean? I wonder what they're up to?"

"My thoughts exactly. There has to be some way we can hear what they're talking about."

"Not without getting inside and, Maggi, I draw the line there."

"Maybe, I should just knock at the door, you know, do the neighborly thing and borrow a cup of sugar," said Maggi, disgustedly.

"I think we should go back to your house, before we get caught."

"You go ahead. If I'm not back in fifteen minutes, call Glen."

"Maggi, come on. You can't break into Jean's house. Don't be foolish."

Maggi hesitated. Seeing the two of them together was such a mystery to her. She wanted to know why but agreed with Teddi; they should return to the safety of her home.

"You're right, let's go back."

Before they could leave, Daniel and Jean were at the door, arguing.

"I'm tired of waiting," he said.

"Just a little while longer. How can they possibly let her off with the evidence they found? They're gonna have to convict her," said Jean.

"If she doesn't get the death penalty then all of this is for nothing. I say we end it now."

"Oh Daniel, can't you just wait a few more months?"

"No. Are you with me or not?"

"What's your plan exactly?"

"She's out on bond now and I want to make sure she's dead before her court date."

"I don't think that's such a good idea."

"Don't forget, Jean, you were the mastermind behind all of this. It was you that snooped around her house and found out I was still in her will. It was you that picked the victims from her emails. Hell, you even drove for me when I shot that golfer."

"What does Peter say about all of this?"

"That pansy's getting cold feet, too. I should never have told him what we were up to. He got what he wanted out of the deal, a storyline for his novel. All he had to do was keep us informed about where she was at all times. His little girlfriend made that easy. His connection to Teddi is the only reason I let him in. Thank God he was stupid enough to tell me about Harmon's death so I could use it as insurance."

Jean was not listening to him. Her thoughts were on his comment about killing Maggi.

"How do you plan to get away with it?" asked Jean.

"I've been out of the picture for so long, no one would suspect me."

"They will when you come forward to claim her estate."

"That's where you come in. You'll get her dogs, that's what started all of this, remember? You should have access to the house so you can pull those papers from her file and show them to Glen. Then he can find me. I'll pretend to be totally shocked that after all of these years she forgot to rewrite her will. There's no way I'll be connected."

"I suggest you get rid of that car. Glen already saw it here at the house. If he finds you and sees you driving it, he'll figure it out pretty quickly."

"Does this mean you're going to help me one last time?"

"Do I have a choice?"

Jean's Jack Russell Terrier dogs ran out of the house while she stood at the door, talking to Daniel. They sniffed around the front yard then found Maggi and Teddi in the bushes.

Maggi tried to shoo them away but that only excited them more.

"What's wrong with your dogs?" asked Daniel.

Jean called them back. Their obedience training was obvious when they returned to her. They would have preferred to explore when they found the women hidden in the bushes.

Maggi and Teddi inched their way in the dark along the house to the backyard. They stayed in the shadows until they reached the trees on Maggi's property.

"Give me your phone," said Maggi.

"I left it in your room when we changed."

"Damn, I don't have mine, either. Let's get back to the house without being seen."

Daniel got into his car and pulled forward to make the turn around the circle drive when he spotted the two figures running across the lawn toward the house. He shut off his lights and ran after them.

The women were unaware they were being followed. They ran into the house to call Glen. Neither of them locked the door. Daniel let himself in. He had already made friends with Maggi's dogs, thanks to Jean, so they were not concerned as he searched the rooms looking for Teddi and Maggi.

He stepped into the doorway of Maggi's bedroom as she was hanging up the phone.

"Damn, Glen's not answering. He must have another call. I'll try Debbie's phone."

"I don't think so," said Daniel, with his gun aimed at Maggi.

Teddi froze.

"Daniel, what in the hell do you think you're doing?"

"Securing my future babe. You left me high and dry. I want what you've got and I'm about to get it."

"How do you know I haven't written a new will?"

"So, you did hear our little conversation. I guess that's just a chance I'm willing to take."

"Daniel, don't be crazy. You can't get away with this."

"Watch me."

"Teddi, get something to tie her up with."

Teddi stood still.

"I said, do it!"

Maggi nodded her head at Teddi to follow his orders. Daniel reached down for Maggi's phone being careful to keep his gloves on; he called for Jean to join them.

When Jean arrived in the bedroom Teddi had already tied Maggi.

"Check to be sure she can't get loose; then tie up Teddi."

"Daniel, are you sure you want to do this?" asked Jean, regretting her involvement with him.

"Daniel, please, please don't shoot us," begged Teddi, through her tears.

His nervousness was apparent as he walked back and forth across the bedroom.

"Daniel, really. There has to be another way," said Jean. "I can't bear to watch you shoot them."

"You didn't seem to have a problem watching me shoot that guy in the back, while you waited in the car."

"I know, but this is different."

"Okay, I have another idea."

He reached into his pocket removing a syringe and a small bottle. He checked the amount of fluid in the bottle. It was less than half full. He was concerned there was not enough. He checked his other pocket and found a second bottle that had even less in it. He drew 1cc while the three women watched.

First, he went to Maggi, who squirmed and fought him. Jean held her steady so he could inject her. He repeated the process three times until he felt he had injected a lethal dose.

Next, he injected Teddi.

They waited and watched as the minutes ticked away, until they began to have seizures then lapsed into a comatose state.

"Untie them. Let's make those cops have to think when they find them," said Daniel. "Let's get out of here. By the time someone finds them in the morning, it'll be too late. They'll just assume whoever set Maggi up has killed her."

Jean returned to her home. Daniel sped away in his car.

Maggi's phone rang. There was no answer. Glen tried Teddi's cell but still no answer.

"Something's not right, Debbie. Let's get over there."

They rang the bell and pounded on the door. No answer. Debbie used her key to unlock the door. They ran through the house calling for them.

"They must not be here," said Debbie.

"Oh, shit!" yelled Glen. "Call 911!"

When Debbie entered the bedroom after calling 911, Glen was frantically trying CPR on Maggi. Debbie went to work on Teddi. They were non-responsive.

When the ambulance crew arrived they were barely breathing. One of the EMTs worked on Maggi, bagging her, while the other inserted an IV of glucose. The same procedures were being done on Teddi in the other ambulance.

At the hospital, Debbie and Glen paced outside the emergency room door. Glen knew the emergency doctor having worked with him on some of his cases.

It seemed like an eternity before the doctor came out to talk with them.

"Glen, it doesn't look good. Their blood tests showed high doses of insulin in their bloodstream. Their pulse rates and oximeter readings are dangerously low. They're going into renal failure. In a nutshell, all of their organs are shutting down. We've done all that we can do. I'm sorry.

Now it's time to test "*your*" ability as a detective. Can you find the "Elusive Clue"?

It's a word puzzle hidden within the story.

The answer to the puzzle will spell out the name of the killer.

To solve the puzzle:

A. You must locate the page or pages containing the puzzle.

B. Locate the letters you will need to unscramble the name of the killer.

I hope you enjoyed the book. If you haven't already read them, try "Tryst with Dolphins", the sequel "Dolphins' Echo", and Death Foreshadowed for more exciting mysteries and once again the challenge of finding that "elusive clue".

Patricia A. Bremmer